THE TORRENT OF THE BLACK HORSEMAN

TALES OF THE FOUR HORSEMEN

BOOK THREE

JESS K. CHAVEZ

For the seekers,
May the rainbows remind you what awaits you on the other
side of the storm.

Winter Safehouse
N
W
S
E
THE RANGE
The World
of the
Four Horsemen
Ashram
The Refuge
Dugal's
Glennlyle
Beach
Safehouse
THE WASTES
Swamp Safehouse
Gloria Byrd

CONTENTS

GLOSSARY/PRONUNCIATION

ix

Elohim {*El-oh-heem*} - God the Creator
**Elohim Shomri* {*El-oh-heem Shaw-om-ree*} - God my Protector
Malkhut Shamayim {*Mahl-KOOT Shah-MY-eem*} - Kingdom of Heaven
Ruach {*Roo-ahhk*} - Breath or Spirit of God, the source of life
Lavo Veshuv {*La-Voh Ve-Shoe-ve*} - Come forth
Baim Lyy {*Bay-Mm Lie*} - Return to me

**not referenced in this book, but in past books*

PROPHECY OF THE FOUR CORES

When the tipping point has been reached and darkness is unrestrained, four riders will be drawn forth out of necessity to lay waste to the world. Their destruction will be absolute. The only hope for mankind is in the gift of four living personifications of Elohim's heart, the essential Cores of His Pure Love. Each Core is created to bond with her Horseman, forever breaking the hold of darkness on them with the power of Elohim's love. The Horseman will then ride for Malkhut Shamayim, bringing about the destruction of all evil in the world. But if the heart of the Core is rejected or fails, the Riders will be leashed by hell, and all will be lost to darkness.

When a Core connects with her Horseman,

an unbreakable bond will form. The Light to his Dark, Woman to Man, the Cores will bring balance in every way to the Horsemen. The seal of each Horseman will be forever altered in outward appearance, as will the depth of their inner being. For once you are made weak, only then can you truly be made strong.

The Cores have been marked by Heaven, but the gift of Heaven will be unknown to them until activated. But just as they are touched by Heaven, they will also be pursued by evil. Evil must be overcome, dreams will guide, and love covers in multitude.

The only signs of the Cores' coming are this . . . born orphaned, alone, and unnamed, they will be brought to the world on a day made holy by its twin of seven. You will find them with three of sevens; a unique mark of Heaven they will bear.

PROLOGUE

Again I looked and saw all the oppression that
was taking place under the sun:
I saw the tears of the oppressed—and they have
no comforter; power was on the side of their
oppressors—and they have no comforter.
And I declared that the dead, who had already
died, are happier than the living, who are still
alive.
But better than both is he who has not yet been,
who has not seen the evil that is done under
the sun.

Ecclesiastes 4:1-3

"Vale! Rain!"

Ash had once again been recruited to play babysitter for his rebellious younger siblings. He was naive and stupid enough to think that as *almost* adults at sixteen, they would put off childish things and start pulling their weight, which was why he had entrusted them with the task of gathering more firewood.

Giggling and the sound of splashing pulled him from his inner ranting.

He should have known.

Anytime they could, they tried to escape to the lake. He supposed he couldn't really blame them. There was little in the way of joy and pleasure in their lives, and the lake, with its steep banks, rope swing, and deep, cool waters, provided an escape they all craved. Not to mention, relief from the sweltering summer heat that felt suffocating at times.

Ash finally broke through the trees in time to see Vale make a running leap for the rope and swing out over the water, only to let go into a perfect backflip, complete with a shout of joy.

An involuntary smile graced Ash's face. He couldn't help it with Vale; she had that effect on people. Ever since his mother had found her as a baby, abandoned and nameless. It didn't even matter that Mama already had two children, and one a baby; she'd happily taken Vale into their family, raising her and Rain like twins. And once Vale's effervescent personality had begun to show, she'd captivated anyone who met her. Even down to the wild female albino hawk she saved and named Roy, who now followed her everywhere and showed zero interest in anyone but Vale.

She'd always seemed wrong for this world. Too soft and bright for this somber, harsh existence that left people ruined and broken. On top of her vivacious personality, Vale was uniquely beautiful. With her white-blonde hair and crystal-blue eyes, she couldn't help but draw attention. Unfortunately, she lived in a world where it was far better to slip into the background than draw the wrong kind of attention.

Years ago, as Vale started to outgrow childhood, Ash

and his family had taken to hiding away at their cabin more. They avoided town and any gatherings unless absolutely necessary, and even then, they were always ready with an excuse for why Vale wasn't with them. And now that Vale was sixteen, it was of paramount importance to keep her hidden. Mama had insisted that something in her gut urged her—nothing good could come from anyone in town seeing Vale now, especially Lyle, the self-proclaimed town leader, and his cronies.

Lyle had started out as a pest—a mere annoyance Ash and the other townspeople had tolerated. But in recent years, his nature had grown darker and more power-hungry, even a bit demented, if the rumors were to be believed. Stories circulated of cruelties he had inflicted on others who had wronged him in some way.

But Ash had convinced himself it was probably Lyle circulating these stories, maybe hoping that the fear those tales inspired would garner him more respect and power. The alternative wasn't something he could wrap his mind around. Lyle was only a few years older than Ash himself and, at one time, he had just been a gangly teen with no family, wandering around town wreaking annoying yet relatively harmless havoc. Lyle was a snake in the grass for sure, but Ash couldn't believe he was a poisonous one. And he definitely wasn't capable of the rumored atrocities being gossiped about in town.

Still, Mama had always erred on the side of caution with their family, so keeping away from town seemed like the easiest way to avoid Lyle. And if Ash were being honest, it worked out best for him anyways, because he needed his siblings' help to keep things running smoothly with the farm.

"Ash, join us! Please! For old times' sake?" Vale's sweet

singsong voice brought him back to the present. It was almost enough to sway him.

"Yeah, get in here, you old curmudgeon!" And then Rain's voice was enough to remind him why he was out here in the woods in the first place, instead of getting all the chores done.

"You two had a job to do, remember? Do I have to do everything? I can't keep this place up by myself. And if you don't want to help me, then do it for Mama. She's running herself ragged."

"Sorry, Ash, it's just so blasted hot, and we did chop half of the pile. We'll finish, we promise," Rain insisted.

"Yeah, and then we'll help with whatever else you need," Vale blurted, her cheeks flushed from her jump. They both had the decency to look ashamed, and Ash couldn't help but take pity on them.

"One jump, and then back at it, okay?" Ash said as sternly as he was able. He was only four years older than them, but being the oldest in a broken family, his dad having inexplicably disappeared right after Rain was born, he'd had to grow up quicker, so he felt light-years ahead of them on the inside. "Now, move out of the way before I drown you both . . . Geronimo!" He swung out on the rope.

As Ash hit the cold water, he felt cleansed of every worry and expectation that seemed to constantly plague his mind, and he remembered why they cherished this place. There were rare moments of peace and joy like this, and they became fewer the older he got. He often missed the naivety and ignorance of youth.

After way more jumps than the one he'd promised, Ash sat beside Rain on the grassy edge of the embankment overlooking the lake while Vale floated on her back—she was always the last out of the water. Only the sound of Rain chiseling away at a piece of wood filled the peaceful silence —a hobby he had taken up a few years ago. He'd gotten really good at creating little animal figurines. Ash puzzled over the one he currently worked on.

"What are you making?"

"I'm attempting a bird." Rain's brow furrowed and his mouth pinched as he chipped away at it. "Watching Roy has gotten me thinking about how incredible it would be to have wings and fly. I definitely wouldn't stay here, following Vale around all day. I would see the world, find somewhere incredible to take our family." He paused his carving to blow away the wood chips and dust, inspecting his creation. "It's tricky, and it might not be perfect, but what is in life?" Rain looked up at Ash with a smirk teasing his lips.

This was a familiar line of discussion Ash was not eager to get into again with his younger brother. Rain thought Ash placed too much pressure on himself to hold everything together for their family. What Rain couldn't understand was that Ash gladly took on that responsibility to keep it from falling to him and Vale. They were blessed to have the home they did when so many had far less. And even more blessed that it was far from town—giving them the isolation they craved.

But it required work and serious devotion to maintain. He wasn't seeking perfection, as Rain might think, just the security that Ash knew was achievable.

"Don't start, little brother," Ash said. "Be glad I'm wired to hold things together, otherwise this would fall on you and V."

Rain sighed and patted Ash on the shoulder. "I know, and we appreciate everything you do, Ash. But you can't control everything—you're not super human. Sometimes, no matter how hard you work, the harvest doesn't come in, or the bugs get to it first, or lightning strikes and burns down the barn." A wry smile lit his face at the disastrous memory. "I just don't want to see you work yourself to death."

"I appreciate your concern," Ash said, staring out across the shimmering deep blue of the lake. Despite the pressures and concerns of this life, Ash couldn't see himself ever leaving the farm. He loved his home and he loved working the land—caring for the animals, maintaining the property, and creating a space that was their own. Their own haven away from the world.

"Here," Rain said, handing him the bird carving after a few final touches. "For you—wings to take you far away, since I know you'll never leave this place." Rain smiled at Ash as he took the beautiful carving.

"You're getting really good at these, little brother. Maybe your carvings will give you the wings you crave and take you far from here one day."

Rain smiled. They both stood as Vale headed up the embankment toward them. The three gathered their clothes and shoes and hurried back home. Vale whistled a soft, bright tune that caused tendrils of joy to cling to Ash while Roy glided above their heads. As they broke through the trees to their little homestead, Ash noticed that Mama was no longer in the garden and the gate swung open.

Ash's brow furrowed as he walked up to close it. Mama was always concerned about animals getting in there; closing the gate was one of the few rules she was particularly firm about. Vale and Rain chased each other behind him, whipping each other with their semi-wet garments, oblivious to his unsettledness. He walked up the steps to the house to see a note nailed to the doorframe.

Hart Family,

Your presence is required in the town square.

ALL of you are expected.

No excuses will be accepted. Your mother is waiting with us. The manner of her return to you will depend on the swiftness of your response.

Your leader,

Lyle

Ash stood on the porch, staring at the paper's sharp, almost frenzied handwriting as the wind rustled the torn edges. Lyle had taken Ash's mother. The gravity of this situation sucked the oxygen from his lungs. What would she want him to do in this scenario? Since their father had abandoned them, his mother relied on Ash as her support, her confidante, and the protector of their little family.

It was not that long ago that she had shared her idea of uprooting their family and finding somewhere else to live. She'd overheard a traveler at the market in town speak of a group called the Prophets of The Way—good people intent on living in the light of Elohim and who took in people in need. People who sought to live a life apart from the darkness as they did. Ash had been quick to discourage the idea. Best case, they packed everything up and traveled all that way for a fairytale that didn't exist, and they were left with nothing. Worst case, it seemed like just the type of story someone would use to lure unsuspecting innocents to their doom. And the devil you knew was far better than the devil you didn't.

But now, with Lyle having taken his mother, Ash wondered if he'd been too hasty in rejecting her suggestion. And doubt had begun to worm its way into his mind regarding the stories of Lyle's depravity. Should he have given them more credence?

"Why do you look as though you've seen a ghost, Ash?" Rain came bounding up the steps and slapped Ash's back. But when he saw the note and stilled long enough to read the words, Rain froze right alongside him.

"What do we do? He must want Vale. Arlo said he's been asking around town about her."

Ash didn't respond right away, since his mind was running through scenarios like a flip-book. Arlo was Rain's friend who lived in town. Being the son of the general store owner, he seemed to have a good bead on the happenings, but he was also a bit of a gossip, which was why Ash had always taken everything he said with a grain of salt.

"Boys?" Vale said from the bottom of the steps. "What's wrong?"

"Lyle has Mom, and he wants us all to go into town," Rain said from beside Ash.

"Well, let's get this over with," Vale said with a casual air.

Maybe Ash had done too good a job shielding Vale from hard things. She always seemed to take an apathetic approach to problems.

"This is serious, Vale. We can't just stroll in there. Lyle is unpredictable."

"Lyle. Seriously. He's creepy and annoying, but hardly dangerous," Vale responded flippantly.

"Really, and you have so much experience with the man, do you?" Ash demanded a bit too harshly.

Vale's cheeks reddened in fury or embarrassment. Either way, it was no secret she hated being sequestered away. It was a low blow for Ash to remind her of her limited experience with the world, but he was agitated and nervous about how to proceed.

"Look, let's grab Dad's old binoculars, and we can sneak in through the forest along the south road," Rain suggested. "If we stay low, we can get close enough to the town to get a good view from the higher vantage point."

Ash nodded. It was a decent plan. At least it would give them an idea of what they were heading into. He said a prayer to whomever would listen that he wasn't making a grave mistake.

The vantage point along the south road was perfect for seeing the center of town, as it was slightly elevated by the hill it sat on and offered a great covering for them with its abundance of trees and bushes. Lyle stood with their mother, his hand grasping the back of her neck, which made Ash's blood boil. Like she was some sort of stockyard animal he needed to control. Ash's mother was the most kind and gentle soul he'd ever known, incapable of causing harm. And even more subdued since his father had abandoned them. Like some of the life in her had fled with him.

A sizable crowd of townspeople lingered around the outskirts of the square. Clearly required to be in attendance, but many attempting to distance themselves from Lyle's sickening display. No one stepped in to say anything against Lyle's treatment of Ash's mother. Cowards, the lot of them.

As Ash zeroed in on Lyle, he was taken aback at the man's appearance. It had been a long while since he'd last laid eyes on the man, but Lyle appeared jittery and jumpy, and an air of darkness seemed to blanket him. Not just from his greasy, unkempt dark hair and the grey pallor of his skin, complete with dark circles under his eyes. It was something unseen but noticeably felt—unnatural.

One of his lackeys approached him and handed him a megaphone.

"This woman is accused of not paying her town tax. She's also hiding away a daughter who is now of age to participate in the annual tribute. And as such, she's withholding payment and what is due to me for the care and protection of this town and its people . . ."

Lyle rambled on, but Ash was stuck on this *tribute* business. He had overheard Arlo mention that, going forward, a tribute would be required of families with daughters of age sixteen and higher. The specifics were kept secret, but it was said they gave something to Lyle and he bestowed a personal gift in return. However, Arlo had discovered that one of the girls to offer tribute had hung herself from a tree a week later. Of course, Ash had only overheard the conversation between Rain and Arlo while working on the barn, so he had little time to spend stewing over the gossip shared by his teen brother's friend. Now, he wished he'd listened more.

". . . and as punishment for these serious infractions, and as a lesson for other citizens, she will be sentenced to death, unless someone from her family presents themselves in her place."

Ash's stomach dropped out. And the gasps of his siblings beside him told him he was not alone in his shock. This could not be happening. Had it been so long since he'd been to town that he hadn't known the depth of the darkness that now resided here? Or of the demon that Lyle had become?

Rain yanked the binoculars out of Ash's hand to see for himself. Ash couldn't think. This couldn't be real. He had to be dreaming. But as he looked to the town center, Lyle shoved his mother to her knees. Rain stood abruptly from their hiding place and dropped the binoculars.

"NO!" he yelled, and before Ash could do anything, Rain ran for their mother.

"Ash, what's he doing?" Vale asked in a raw voice, her eyes filled with tears. "We need to go after him!"

Ash grabbed Vale's arm, holding her in place as he watched Rain run recklessly forward. As if in slow motion, Lyle raised his arm at him. The sudden, deafening echo of a gun being fired made Ash jolt, and he watched in horror as his brother's body dropped to the ground—lifeless.

Vale's free hand came to her mouth as she tried in vain to stifle her guttural scream. Ash stared, frozen, unable to come to terms with what he had just witnessed. And too cowardly to bring the binoculars to his eyes, confirming this nightmare was real.

His mother, who was still on her knees, wailed uncontrollably, stretching and reaching for her youngest son, who had only made it halfway to her. Lyle raised the same gun that he'd fired at Ash's brother to the back of his mother's head.

"NO!" Ash stood and yelled. His mother's eyes connected with his, and she shook her head no, right before a gunshot rang out again, and she slumped forward. Ash desperately scanned the gathered crowds for anyone that would help, but there was none to be found. He was met with either the dejected faces of the surrendered or the eager, bloodthirsty gazes of sycophants.

Lyle looked at Ash, smoke curling from the barrel of his gun. Even from a distance, Ash could see the demented, saccharine smile on his face and the covetous look in his eyes when his gaze fell on Vale as she stood from their hiding place. Lyle's cronies headed toward them. Ash grabbed Vale's arm and ran, dragging her with him.

She stumbled behind him, sobbing and tripping. He finally stopped, grabbed her shoulders, and shook her firmly.

"Vale!" he barked. "There will be time for that later, but right now, you need to run. If you want to live and you don't want their deaths to be in vain, then you need to run."

Her expression sobered. She nodded, and they took off. They raced through the forest, around trees, over felled logs and bushes. Ash was grateful they'd had a childhood filled with similar activity. But the crashing behind him suggested they hadn't lost their tail yet.

Another shot rang out, and Ash fell to the ground, his thigh burning.

"ASH!" Vale yelled and came to his side, trying to drag him onward. But it was useless, he had at least eighty pounds on her.

"No, V, just go," Ash tried to persuade her.

"I am not leaving you—you are the only family I have left." Her voice wavered, and he finally noticed her pallid features. No longer would she be a carefree, naive girl. Even if they lived through this, any remnant of their youth had been well and truly destroyed. She threw her arms around him as Lyle's lackeys surrounded them. They ripped her from his arms, screaming, right before a blow to his skull turned all his lights out.

As Ash blinked open his eyes, the light of a lantern blazed by his bedside. It was night, and he was back in his own bed. He would've thought it all a nightmare he'd dreamed up if not for the pounding of his head and the burning pain of a bullet wound in his thigh. How had Lyle gotten his hands on a gun and ammunition anyway?

A groan escaped Ash's mouth as he tried to sit up.

"Go slowly," a voice spoke from beside his bed. "Here, I have a glass of water for you." Ash recognized Arlo, but his voice's usual exuberance was deadened as he handed Ash the glass.

"My mother was able to get the bullet out of your thigh while you were out, so you should heal okay—physically, that is . . ." His voice trailed off.

"Vale?" Ash's voice croaked out the question.

It was met with silence, the uncomfortable kind that hid truths capable of destroying a person. Finally, when Ash was just about to ask again, Arlo spoke.

"She's here, in the other room."

But there was something Arlo wasn't saying. And in that silence, despair spread through the room like mist and settled—unmovable.

"What is it Arlo? There's something you're not telling me."

At Ash's words, Arlo dropped his head to his hands and cried. He'd never seen the boy cry. Even as a child, he was always lighthearted and easygoing. But his shoulders shook with the force of his grief. And the dread coating Ash's bones began to spread like frost, chilling him further. He stood, biting back the pain of walking on his leg, and hobbled to the door. He rounded the corner into the room that held Vale.

On first glance, nothing seemed off, other than Roy lying on the pillow beside Vale's head, which was unusual since the bird hated being indoors. Vale slept, a blanket covering her from the waist down. Ash went to her bedside, and Vale whimpered as her brows furrowed. He went to pull the blanket up to her chest so she'd be warmer, then he noticed something amiss under the blankets.

Slowly and carefully, he pulled the blankets back to reveal what had unmistakably caused Arlo to go to pieces. The lower half of Vale's right leg below the knee was missing. She whimpered again—clearly the pain of the injury couldn't even be dulled by whatever sedation she was under. His gaze moved up to her face, and he could see bruises on her arms, neck, and face.

She'd fought them. She'd tried to get away. And she'd done it all alone. The horror of the destruction that had been wrought upon his family seared through his veins. A scream lodged in his throat, and Ash backed out of the room and ran to the front door. He fell to his knees on the porch, heedless of his own injury, and emptied the meager contents of his stomach over the side. Ash finally let himself fall apart.

After a time, Arlo came to the door.

"He wants you to help her recover so that he can keep her as his wife. He removed her leg so that she would not be able to flee from him ever again. The only reason he didn't do the same to you was because of the gunshot wound. My mother convinced him that it severely damaged your leg and you would be a cripple for life, so you'll need to lay it on thick whenever you are around him."

"Vale will never willingly be his wife, Arlo," Ash replied sharply.

"Why do you think you are still alive, Ash?" he countered, grief over the situation in his tone.

The breath seized in Ash's lungs. Of course, Lyle meant him to be leverage. Ash looked at Arlo, really looked at him. The boy who had been his brother's best friend seemed light-years older than he remembered. Maybe they had both aged years overnight.

"I don't understand this," Ash stammered, his tone rough. "How can someone do this to another human being? And what kind of man forces a woman to be his property and then takes her leg so she can never run from him? I mean, he was never a prize citizen, always a lost, bullish type—a product of growing up alone and without a family, I suppose. But this? This is completely deranged!"

Arlo swallowed and came to sit next to Ash on the porch. "Frankly, he's a sadist who takes pleasure in breaking things, the same way he is broken. I am not convinced there's much humanity left in him. A few months ago, he came back from a trip and he was different—darker. Ever since then, he's been single-minded in his hunt for power, like he's possessed or something.

"For some reason, he seems to see Vale as his crown jewel. Maybe because she's been so sequestered, so off-limits? Who knows why, but it's almost like distancing your-selves from town made him want her even more. And once he did glimpse her, he became like a dog with a bone. All I know is, it is futile to try and make sense of the vain imagin-ings of a twisted mind."

"I'm surprised he's not here looking after her himself, then."

"Well, he's dealing with a bit of rebellion in town. Some of the farmers rose up after witnessing what was done to your family, and then hearing about Vale, of course. But don't get your hopes up. With the number of followers he has and the gun he's so fond of using, I don't imagine it will last long. He's got too many people under his thumb for them to go against him now."

Arlo's words soaked in like blood absorbing into the dirt,

and Ash became resolute. He may have failed his family, but he would kill himself before he would be used against Vale. He would do whatever it took, make whatever sacrifice necessary, to ensure Vale's survival far from Lyle's clutches. Ash didn't believe in anything anymore, not after yesterday, but still he prayed—more like begged—for divine help to spare Vale this fate. And for a miracle to take her far away from this hellhole.

CHAPTER 1

VALE

There's a stillness in the air around us, and despite the silence, anticipation hangs heavy on the crisp breeze in the muted daylight of the forest. The beast of a horse we sit atop pounds its hooves restlessly into the dirt. Almost eager, but for what, I don't know. Zion took us out of The Refuge, home to the Prophets of The Way—otherwise known as the good guys—so quickly, there was no time for planning, let alone goodbyes. Just hurry up and wait.

Story of my life.

Wait to be found. Wait to fight. Wait for pain. Wait for hope. Maybe even wait to die. And I am sick of waiting. It's all my life has been. When I was young, I waited to grow up so I'd have more freedom. After The Ruination, I waited for death. When Sida and I were constantly being hunted, I waited to be captured. And while stuck in The Wastes, I waited for hope. Now, I no longer know what I am waiting for.

I try to shift my body so I am not fully pressed up against Zion, or Z as he's more commonly known, desperately needing space from this infuriating man. But all he does is glance at me over his shoulder and then pull my arms tightly around him. Almost as if he knows how uneasy I am atop a horse. His new mission of being my official babysitter is more than suffocating, and quite frankly, I am sick of his overbearing manhandling.

Out of habit, I search the skies for Roy. I haven't seen her since I was abruptly snatched by Z outside The Wastes, with not even a moment to think about what was happening. And after that, I was shut up in a stone room in the recesses of The Refuge—a prisoner of Z's paranoia over the enemies hunting me. Maybe I can convince him to distance jump—a handy ability the Four Horsemen are all equipped with that allows them to travel across great distances in a mere moment—to that field outside The Wastes so I can try and find her. Or more like so she can find me.

Z's muscles tense against me. He must sense things I can't see, being the Black Horseman of Justice or something like that. Honestly, I wouldn't have believed any of this if I hadn't seen Cai's giant red horse appear out of nowhere. Sida, an ally of the Prophets of The Way dedicated to finding the Cores, had been going on for years about my purpose and who I really was, sometimes discussing the details of some supposed prophecy with me. She was always so passionate about it, it was hard not to get sucked in.

It's been so long since I've felt passionate about anything, especially since losing everything I cared about. An event I have coined The Ruination—an apt description.

And now Sida lies in a bed back at The Refuge, fighting for her life, and I can't even be there for her the way she was for me. I swallow past the lump forming in my throat. This world just doesn't have the same pull and wonder for me that it used to.

I honestly thought the prophecy was a just an exciting bedtime story—my true purpose was to be a Core, created out of Elohim's pure love as a sort of redemption for a Horseman and the answer to the destruction of the world. Who wouldn't dream of a higher calling than being a damaged, aimless girl with nothing to her name? Then I met Ansel, and it was like the first pieces of the puzzle coming together. She felt like a sister to me almost immediately. And when I saw her and Cai together, I allowed myself to hope.

However, it wasn't until Z showed up that Sida's words felt real to me. Something in me that I thought had long since died stirred to life. But then he saw my leg, and everything changed.

He thinks I am broken. And maybe I am. But I am not broken in a purely physical way. It's something inside that is irreparably damaged.

Before, I was carefree and joyous—exuberant, even. I was naive and had hope for the future. Now, it's like all those things were surgically cut away, leaving giant, gaping, bloody holes in their place. That's all I am now, a shadow of what used to be. My leg has nothing to do with it.

If only my wounds could be just physical.

Z's voice pulls me from my downward spiral.

"Hold tight," he says calmly, his face always a stoic mask of cool focus and intensity. "They are close, and we need them to give chase."

I begrudgingly squeeze him tight for fear of falling off

this behemoth. I had almost no up close experience with horses before Z, and now I've been thrust into an uneasy relationship with an intimidating and gigantic animal that seems far too similar to the man connected to him. Fierce, focused, and, if I am being honest, a bit scary. The animal's name is Fury, which seems fitting. I trust the man more than the animal right now. At least I know Z would never hurt me. He seems hell-bent on my protection, however infuriating it might be at times. The horse, I am not so sure about.

Fury takes off, and I glance over my shoulder in time to see unnaturally huge, man-like monsters chasing us. These must be the Silent that Cai and Ansel were talking about. Monsters recently bred by the Amilign, a twisted sect of monks intent on getting to the Cores before the Horsemen. I suppose I should be grateful this is my first real encounter with them. Surprisingly, they are able to maintain pace with Fury, which is disturbing on so many levels. They are at least far enough behind us to not be an immediate danger, so I try to breathe easy, but it seems over the past few weeks I've been thrust into a world that is more than meets the eye. The reality I've known has shifted, and it's unsettling.

It makes me think that all the conversations with Sida about Elohim and my purpose are more than just bedtime stories. But I struggle to reconcile it all with my experiences. If Elohim's purpose in creating me is to be some key element of His love, designed to save a Horseman from being leashed to hell forever and thus bringing about the end of the world, then why would He allow me to be broken like this? That's the opposite of love. Not to mention, if the hope of this world rests on me saving Z through our bond, then we are well and truly lost. I am merely a mission to Z—nothing more.

Fury somehow picks up the pace, and I feel as if my

teeth will rattle loose in my head. I don't know how much longer I can last at this speed. I am completely ill-experienced with riding a horse, let alone at this pace for such a long time. Who knew it would take such strength and stamina? From a distance, people always made it seem so easy. One more thing I misjudged in the naivety of my youth.

The pulling feeling comes over me—the sign that Z is distance jumping us. All goes dark, and we reappear in a different and denser part of the forest, with barely any room for Fury to make his way through the foliage. Ahead of us lies a dilapidated old cabin that looks like it hasn't seen a visitor since the dawn of time.

"This thing looks as old as you," I comment wryly from behind Z, reminded of when he first told me his older-than-a-century age.

"Close, but not quite," he says coolly. I swear the man is a vault, his emotions tightly locked away. Seemingly more machine than man. I have made it my unspoken goal to get some kind of reaction from him.

He jumps from Fury's back, and the way his muscles move beneath his shirt and his pants glove his thick, muscular legs has all rational thought fleeing from my head. Ugh, I hate that he has that effect on me. I purposely tear my eyes away from him to the treetops. How can someone be so annoying and so distracting at the same time? Frankly, it's obnoxious and only makes him more maddening.

Fury walks me right up to the door of the little wood shanty and waits. Z goes into the place, and I hear him rattling around, probably scaring away any animal inhabitants that consider this dump their domain. Well, this can't be worse than The Wastes. But in the thick cluster of trees, and with the sun bidding us goodnight and giving way to the rising moon, the darkness makes it feel more ominous than quaint.

Z appears in the doorway. "It's dusty, but it'll do for one night. I pulled the sleeping bags out of the locked case, so at least you'll have somewhere clean to sleep." He must see the question on my face because he goes on, "We have a few locations like this one, set up with essentials for quick and unplanned trips. Though this place is a little worse for wear."

I glance around, unsettled by the darkness, the silence, and the thought of being closed in like this, vulnerable to whatever will stumble upon us here. Z must see my trepidation, because all of a sudden he is at my knee, his hand on my leg.

"I won't let anything happen to you, you have my word. I will not sleep tonight, but I will keep watch with Fury while you rest. I jumped us about four hundred miles from our last location. It'll be a while before they find us."

I nod, embarrassed by my nervousness. I am clearly no warrior. But I never claimed to be. I was always more of a daydreamer. And even that has been broken in me. It's hard to dream when you only bring death and destruction everywhere you go.

Z's hands reach up to grab my waist to help me from Fury's back. His hands graze the bare skin under my shirt, and I gasp at the contact. His touch is hot and sends a shiver through me that I have no desire to explore right now. He gently sets me down, and I glance up into warm, honey-brown eyes that resemble a storm brewing. The intensity in them surprises me, and his jaw clenches.

He hands me the crutch that was given to me on my arrival at The Refuge, a handy little thing that can fold up for easy transport. It's allowed me some semblance of freedom and independence that I haven't felt since before The Ruination.

At least Z has learned.

Initially, he felt the need to do everything for me and treated me like I was inept. Now, he understands that not only am I capable of being independent, I need it. I crave it. If only he could see I am more capable than he believes. But as I take a step forward, I put the crutch on uneven ground, which gives way, causing me to stumble. Before I can hit the ground, an arm snakes around my waist and I am hauled back to slam into a hard, warm chest that smells of cedarwood and the fresh, earthy breeze that blew around the lake of my childhood. I freeze at the recollection as memories flood my mind unbidden. I tremble as the pain and grief appears at once, even after all these years.

Z misinterprets my reaction. He steps back from me, holding my shoulders for stability.

"Uh, sorry, I . . . uh . . . didn't want you to fall." For the first time since I've known him, I see uncertainty and a hint of despair in his eyes. "I would never hurt you."

But I can't speak. I can't say anything to counter his assumption. To let him know my reaction was not about him. And he turns on his heel to head into the dark forest, leaving me to stare after him.

I slowly make my way into the cabin, a bit more cautious with where I place the crutch as I walk. I collapse on the sleeping bag atop the small bed in the corner, thoroughly exhausted by the unexpected emotional onslaught I just experienced. And more than a little curious and dismayed that I am just now noticing that Z smells like the best memories of my childhood.

He smells like home.

CHAPTER 2

VALE

Thirty days of running.

That's what today marks. And Z has been persistent in his guarded detachment. Maybe that should give me peace; I mean, it's probably for the best. But it has the opposite effect. Sida's stories seem to occupy my thoughts too frequently, filling me with what-ifs.

He's all business as he mounts Fury, pulling me up behind him with one arm. He takes my crutch, folding it up and locking it onto the harness around Fury. He says not one word as he pulls my arms around him and leads us out of yet another dense forest into a clearing.

I can't keep track of the number of rural locations we've jumped to, never staying long enough to feel settled or even get to know a place. I honestly don't know how much more I can take. The thought causes me to scoff at myself, which earns a quick glance over the shoulder from Z. He probably thinks my sanity is slipping. But in reality, it's not lost on me that I spent the majority of my life in one spot, craving the freedom to go where I wished. And now that we're constantly on the move, I crave the familiarity and comfort of consistency.

There's been little in the way of news regarding the tracker in my blood. Apparently, the Prophets are devotedly working on a solution. Yet every time I ask Z, he simply says that Elias will reach out when he's got something. The only nugget of information I have been able to get from him is that Sida survived and will make a full recovery. I am grateful for that knowledge, at least. I can breathe a little easier knowing she's okay—maybe even safer now that she's far from me.

Another unique gifting the Horsemen have is the ability to speak to each other through a mental link. Even with Elias, though he is not a Horseman, but clearly something otherworldly too. If I had that ability, you can bet I would've been talking to my brothers constantly. And yet I don't get the sense that Z does. The few times I've seen a Horseman use their mind link, they seem to get a far-off look in their eyes. But that doesn't seem to happen with Z. Something tells me it's not just me that Z holds himself back from, but maybe his brothers and Elias as well.

So, in the meantime, we continue with our hideout-hopping—never staying anywhere longer than a day and a half. Other than my stint in The Wastes, I haven't lingered very long anywhere since The Ruination. Fury takes off, and the telltale pulling of a jump pours over my body. At least I've gotten used to that by now.

The unfamiliar scent of salty air and the loud crash of waves assault my senses. I open my eyes to my first-ever glimpse of the ocean. Wonder fills me, and I am as shocked that I am still capable of mustering that feeling as I am that I am finally staring at the beauty and vast magnitude of the ocean. A dream I've had since childhood. One that first took root when I fell in love with our lake back home.

Z begins to head further inland, taking us away from the ocean. But I am not ready to say goodbye to the feeling that I thought had long since abandoned me. I place my hand on his shoulder.

"Please, can we stay a few more moments?"

He nods and leads Fury closer to the water. I am fascinated by the push and pull of the waves, and the shifting of the sands from dry to wet. It's absolutely mesmerizing. I want to run through the waves and feel the sand squish between my toes. The thought sobers me and threatens to steal the small taste of joy.

I'll never run again.

But I quickly push away the realization and close my eyes as I let the warm, salty sea air blow across my face and through my hair. It almost feels like a hug.

"Hang on," Z says over his shoulder, pulling me from my reverie.

He spurs Fury into a gentle run across the shore. I'm grateful I changed into a knee-high, yellow sundress I found amongst the supplies at the cabin this morning—an easy staple to stock since they don't have to fit perfectly to work, homemade sundresses are frequently among the safe house wardrobes. Fury's hooves send sea spray up onto my legs and small droplets onto my face and in my hair. It's amazing and makes me feel free. It's better than running. And a sentiment I thought was lost to me—joy—begins rising in my chest, a gentle warmth that radiates outward. A smile lights my face.

Z takes us a bit deeper into the water so that my foot is splashed by the waves. The cool liquid is a refreshing distraction. A large wave comes at us, and Z guides Fury closer to shore, but not before it breaks and soaks us from the waist down.

An unexpected laugh bursts from my chest, and a surge of true joy flows through me. Z's muscles tense under my hands, and he turns to glance at me over his shoulder. He's probably as shocked as I am by the laughter, because I haven't laughed since before I met him, since before The Ruination. But I am too enraptured to really care. And then, all of a sudden, he jumps off Fury's back.

"Scoot up and place your hands here, at the base of his mane." He shows me where to place my hands. "This area is called the withers, and it will give you something to hold. And squeeze his body with your thighs as best you can."

I do as he says, looking at him questioningly. He's about to be sorely disappointed. I have no idea how to make a horse do what I want. But the minute that thought enters my head, Fury turns and starts a gentle, smooth run down the beach. I realize just how unique this horse is. The sun on my face, the wind in my hair, and sea spray on my skin— I have never felt anything so freeing. It's as if all the stuff that usually hangs off me—the limitations, grief, burden of guilt, expectations, and hopelessness—cannot keep its grip on me.

It falls off, and I am set free.

I don't know how much time passes, but Fury does all the work. Weaving in and out of the water, switching between slowly meandering and galloping, which takes my breath away and makes me feel alive again. It's almost as if he knows what I want and accommodates me. I carefully move my hand from his mane and reach forward to rub his soft neck. He gives a gentle whinny in response, and somehow I warm to him.

Maybe he's not so scary after all.

"How about one more speedy chase back to Z?" I am curious to see how much he can understand. Surprisingly, he throws his big head in a gesture similar to a nod and takes off. A laugh erupts from my throat. Thoroughly caught up in the joy of this moment, I forget to pay attention to Fury's change of direction. He makes a slight turn from the water that I don't anticipate, and I slip from his back, hitting the waves with a splash as the water swallows me whole.

But I am not scared. I feel only wonder at the sensation that reminds me of swimming in the lake back home. Not that I need to worry about swimming here, since it's shallow. Right as I think that, a wave hits me from behind and sends me tumbling.

Suddenly, Z is there, pulling me from the water. I hop up onto my leg, but stumble in the sand, knocking him over and landing on top of him. He wraps a hand around my waist and uses his other hand to drag us backward to dry sand. My hands are on his chest, and I gaze at him through sopping wet strands of my hair. I must look an absolute mess, but he only stares at me with eyes that are deep pools of mystery. A hint of amusement plays across his features. But it's so brief, it's gone before I can analyze it further.

"Thank you for that." I smile. "This is the best day I've had since The Ruination." His hand comes up to my face, and his fingers graze my skin as he guides the wet strands behind my ear. Something stirs to life inside me. He seems to suddenly realize our predicament, and that he just touched me, because his hand drops.

I am suddenly aware of the heat of his body coming through the cool, wet clothes, warming me. It's a glaring contrast, and something crackles along my skin at each place we touch. I look at him, his eyes locked on mine. He trembles beneath me, his jaw and fists clenched, as if it is taking everything in him to stay still. I realize this is violating his unspoken *keep your distance* rule, and he won't be able to move until I do. I shift my weight off him and he immediately hops up. He's playing it cool, but avoiding my eyes.

Fury trots over happily, and it's funny how he seems more like a playful pup than some scary harbinger of doom now.

Z gives me a hand up. I place a hand on Fury for stability while Z vaults up onto his back with practiced ease and pulls me up behind him.

I am so confused by this man. So withdrawn and guarded in one moment, but then going out of his way to do something so incredibly kind as giving me Fury and letting me splash and play to my heart's content. And just when I think he might soften and open up, he clams up again and looks like he's ready to run in the opposite direction.

I heave a sigh behind his back. Annoying. As usual with him.

But I suppose it doesn't really matter. I have bigger problems than Z's confusing nature. I need to figure out a way to get this tracker in me neutralized so I can go about living my life. Specifically, so I can try and find out if my brother Ash is still alive.

My last memory of him is hazy because I was in and out of consciousness from the pain and shock of losing my leg. I vaguely remember being loaded into a wagon of some kind and Ash talking with a woman with distinct curly white hair. When I came to, he was gone. And that's my last memory of him. Why did he let me leave with a stranger, and why didn't he come with us?

I woke later and met Sida, who tended to me and helped me recover. She explained how she felt Elohim guide her to our house and how my brother begged Sida to take me far away. She's also the one who ran with me every time we were found. Little did I know upon first meeting her that this sweet-natured, snowy-maned lady was also a fierce warrior.

I smile at the memory. The first time we were discovered, she pulled out a bow and arrows and started picking off the guys that were after us. A mix of bounty hunters, hired thugs, and, later, even a few Amilign monks—it didn't matter, they were no match for her. I knew then that I was in good company. It was also then that I began to realize that Lyle must have been in league with the Amilign this whole time—that's the only way I could have ended up with this tracker in my blood.

Tall grasses sway in the breeze as Z leads Fury deeper inland. We begin to head up a dirt path to a little house. I guess this is our next stay before Z drags us somewhere new.

Z tenses and goes impossibly still while Fury snorts in agitation. The small picket gate sways back and forth, occasionally slamming against the fence. The creak of the hinges and the broken latch that hangs limply add an eerie stillness to the atmosphere. Z jumps off Fury's back and rushes up the path to the house.

"Closer, Fury," I say, but this time he tosses his head in agitation.

Is this horse telling me no? It's almost comical.

"Look, buddy, I will go with or without you. Your choice."

He lowers his head, as if in reluctant acquiescence, and slowly meanders up the path—which is when I notice a change in the air. A tangy, coppery smell that turns my stomach further. The scent I associate with The Ruination.

I ungracefully slide off Fury's back, keeping my hands

on him for stability as I grab my crutch and open it up. I head up the stairs of the little house, and the minute I push the door open, the scent smacks me in the face and threatens to empty my stomach.

There is blood everywhere.

The body of a man lies in a pool of sticky blood in the kitchen. A woman's body sits slumped over on the small couch. Z stands with his back to me at the entrance to one of the bedrooms.

I can't move. I want to go to him. To see if he's okay, but also because I desperately need an anchor. But it's too late. I am not here anymore. All I can see are the bodies of my mother and my brother, lying in the dirt in their spilled blood—lifeless. I can't wake from the nightmare of those images. My heart is pounding in my rib cage. My eyes burn, and even oxygen struggles to make its way through the tightness of my chest. The pungent scent of blood drowns out my other senses.

The years disappear, and I am sixteen again.

I know what happens next. My leg is taken. I am shaking, and I faintly hear the crazed whinny of a horse.

Arms come around me and lift me from the ground, carrying me away from the horror. I curl into a warm chest as sobs wrack my body. My hand fists in Z's shirt, and I breathe in the calming scent of cedarwood and a crisp, cool breeze.

"That's it, deep breaths," his voice says, but it's not soft or calming. It's firm and unyielding. It's promising. And not the promise of something good, but something dark and devastating.

It sounds like the promise of retribution.

I collect myself enough to look up at Z. His eyes are

completely black. I get the sense that this is not a good thing, and Fury stomps about in the yard.

"Are you okay?" I manage to ask.

"Yes," he says robotically as he reaches Fury.

I don't buy it. But I am not okay either. So I guess we will be *not okay* together. I desperately need his arms around me to keep me grounded in the here and now. I fear the loss of them will send me back into memories I need to lock back up for the sake of my sanity.

"Please don't put me down," I say softly, cursing the need and vulnerability in my voice.

He says nothing, but his arms seem to hold me tighter as he continues down the path with Fury trailing us. I let the rhythm of his pace calm the erratic beating of my heart.

And as he walks, I focus on the distant crashing of waves, trying to keep my mind from wondering if I have ever felt as safe as I do when I am in the Horseman of Justice's arms.

CHAPTER 3

ZION

I carry her for miles. Down the beach, near the water's edge, so the ocean breeze can attempt to cleanse away the scent of blood that feels like it's coating us. I focus on the feel of her in my arms, desperate for that to be enough to cage the beast inside me that I fear is stronger than I am.

It will have to be enough, because I won't add any more burdens to her shoulders. She has been through so much already. But I need to last long enough to see her made whole again and to see justice delivered.

Her earlier plea broke something in me. I wanted to tell her I would never put her down, but the words lodged in my throat as my desire to comfort her warred with the need to keep my distance.

She dozed off in my arms a few miles back, and I'm grateful. She needs a reset after what we just discovered, which must have had her reliving her traumatic past. How is it I do nothing but screw up with this girl? I should have turned Fury around right when I recognized the smell. But I knew that family, and I was ruled by my emotions. I had hoped, by some miracle, that I would find them alive. Yet not even their son, still in his bed, had been left untouched. I suppose I should be grateful she didn't see him, too. My heart fissures further under my grief.

I stumbled across this family a couple of years ago during my travels. They gave me a place to stay and we discussed life, Elohim, and our hopes for the future. Despite me being the Horseman of Justice, they weren't wary of me the way so many seem to be. Most people are either fearful of my judgment or suspicious because of a situation in their own life that lacked the justice they desperately needed or wanted.

In contrast, this family was curious but welcoming. I've visited a few times over the years, making sure they are well and catching up. I've been trying to get them to move to The Refuge for a few months now, but they were convinced their home was sufficiently isolated. It was their oasis, so maybe it's fitting that now it will be their burial grounds, too.

The need to bring them justice aches inside me, but it will have to wait. As so many of the others have had to over the years.

A soft sigh escapes Vale's lips, and it has an unusual calming effect on me. It's getting harder and harder to keep her at a distance like I need to. But getting closer will only lead to more heartache when I finally have to let her go.

I am like a moth to a flame with her, and I am beginning to see how she could quickly become the air in my lungs if I am not careful. But I could never do that to her. I won't be so selfish as to tie her to the man who failed her. It will be the one selfless thing I do for her before it's over. Because I know without a doubt that letting her go will be the final straw that leashes me. I'll just have to trust my brothers to handle things once that happens.

The air is starting to cool as the sun dips below the horizon, and I know I need to set us up for the night before we jump to the artisan metallurgist shop tomorrow morning. Hopefully, the order will be ready, and I can make amends for the horror of today.

Fury finds a spot out of the wind and lies down, knowing what I am thinking without me saying it. Despite her hesitancy with him, he wants her as safe and cared for as I do. I place Vale in the soft sand, still slightly warm from soaking up the sun all day, and rest her head on Fury's soft neck. He slowly brings his head closer to his front legs, making a sort of cocoon for her. Thankfully, she doesn't wake. Today must have really taken it out of her.

After scrounging around the area for some wood for a fire, I quickly get it blazing and finally lie down on the opposite side of the fire from Fury and Vale. In the light of the flames, she looks ethereal and delicate. Though I know her to have a resilient strength and fierceness—she's a force of nature.

From her white-blonde hair and sky-blue eyes to her fair skin, she looks as though she has never been touched by the sun. Fury's black coat is in stark contrast. It's as if her skin reflects light itself, creating a luminosity that is almost hard to look at.

As I gaze at her, the yearning to go to her, be near her, touch her again, crashes through my blood, causing a hot sweat to break out across my skin—making a mockery of my perfectly constructed control. I roll over so my back is to the fire and everything I want but can't have lying next to it. I stare out at the moonlit waves, hoping they will calm the raging storm inside me, but after an hour, it becomes clear that I am in for a long and restless night.

Well before dawn, I tire of tossing and turning and get up, dusting the sand off my clothes, to catch some fish for breakfast. There's a rocky point where I should have no problem spearing a few with the spearhead I carry with me, secured to one of the sticks lying around. I've always had a fondness for the water, and fishing has been a favorite pastime of mine. I took to it quickly upon our arrival to this world, and, during my travels, began carrying a spearhead among my supplies for such a reason. It's an activity of solitude and introspection that helps me feel connected to Elohim—His peace is a bolster as the darkness battles for control inside me. But it's a peace I feel slipping between my fingers, like trying to hold water.

My traitorous eyes stray to Vale, sleeping soundly curled up against Fury's neck, and a ridiculous surge of jealousy rushes through me. Fury opens an eye, and if a horse could glare, he would be. Then he lets out a huff and closes his eye again. I swear, for a horse, he has far more attitude than should be allowed.

It doesn't take long to catch a few fish. I head back to find Vale awake and stoking the fire. The chill of the early morning ocean air is biting at times. Fury is grazing in the grass near the beach, so the two of us have a quiet, awkward breakfast of avoidance and unease.

When it appears we both have had enough, we speak at the same time.

"I'm sorry . . ."

"Sorry for . . ."

We stare at each other, and I clear my throat. "I'm sorry I exposed you to that yesterday. I wasn't thinking. I should've left immediately. Please forgive me."

She stares at me as a mixture of grief, pity, and exasperation flits across her face. "You can't control everything, Z. I could've stayed with Fury, but I didn't. I was going to tell you that I am sorry for your loss, because I get the feeling you knew them."

I nod.

"Are we just going to leave them there?"

"No, I'll reach out to Elias and let him know. He'll have someone come to give them a proper burial."

She nods.

I make no mention of her response to the grim discovery and my carrying her, which, based on her body language and reticent gaze, tells me is a mutual choice. In an effort to distract us from the awkwardness and soothe her unease, I opt for small talk, which I am notoriously bad at.

"So . . . you seemed to love the water. Was that your first time in water? I mean, seeing the ocean . . . being in the ocean?" Ugh, utterly hopeless.

She smiles. That sunny, subtle grin that would captivate and melt even the coldest heart. It lights up her whole face, and I have to focus extra hard to hear the words she's speaking and not be swept away by her natural luminescence.

"It was my first time seeing *and* being in the ocean," she says with bright eyes, as if she's reliving the memory right before me. "It was incredible. But I've always had a special love of water. There was this lake not far from our house, outside of the town I grew up near, and my brothers and I would spend much of our time there together." And suddenly, the sunny expression is gone, and in its place is a grey thundercloud of memories.

"What was the name of the town?"

Her eyes leave mine as her hands fiddle with the sand—

seemingly seeking distraction. Just when I think she's not going to answer, she clears her throat.

"It had another name before . . . earlier. But in recent years, it was changed to Glennlyle, named after the monster who rules there."

I give her a solemn nod. The door effectively shuts on any conversation after that. But I tuck that nugget of information away, breathing deep to calm the rage in me that begs for release. I am a beast stalking prey, and the only thing that keeps me from losing myself is the knowledge that very soon, justice will be coming to those who dared leave scars on Vale.

We silently put out the fire, mount Fury, and jump to the next destination, eager to leave this place behind.

We are greeted by dank air that smells of oil and burning rubber. Loud grinding and banging assaults our ears. Fury stands in thick mud facing a giant brick factory surrounded by dense trees, a muddy road cutting the only path through the forest.

"Uh, not your best pick," Vale says from behind me.

A smirk lights my face, but I don't show her. "I just need to run into this shop real quick. Stay with Fury. I'll be right back."

I am grateful I thought of placing this order right after meeting Vale and getting her safely back to The Refuge. It's finally finished and it's incredible. These guys are the best at what they do, hidden away from major cities for a reason —their skills are too valuable an asset for evil if they were discovered by the wrong people.

We stumbled across them at their lowest point, when their community had been decimated. They had all lost something—family members, friends, or even limbs, like old Joe's leg—and now, they dedicated their talents to helping fight the darkness. We offered them a place at The Refuge, but with no adequate facility for them to use their skills, they were content to stay in the abandoned and isolated factory we discovered and made into a haven for their creative outlet. Plus, with most of them being skilled metal workers, machinists, or engineers, they are well suited to defend themselves.

I collect the order and say my goodbyes, leaving the artisans to their forgery and flames. I can't wrap it, but I hold it behind my back as I return to where Vale waits with Fury.

"I have a surprise for you," I say as I approach.

She looks at me with her brows raised and eyes wide, but I don't blame her. This is unusual behavior for me, yet it's one step in a long journey of giving her back her life.

I pull the prosthetic leg from behind my arms and hold it up for her to see.

"It's a prosthetic leg I had made for you. I got your exact measurements and casting from the healers when you first arrived at The Refuge, and then I came here to have it made to those specifications. One of the guys, Old Joe, has had years to perfect his designs, seeing as he is an amputee as well. This is his most recent revolutionary design. It will allow you full mobility, including the ability to run and fight, with maximum comfort and the flexibility to adapt as necessary. And we can always come back if it needs any changes or tweaks to the design for your specific needs."

She stares at me, expressionless, and I begin to wonder if I have made a grave mistake assuming she would want this. But just as I prepare to backtrack and apologize, her hands come up to her face, covering her eyes, and sobs begin to shake her shoulders. I know little about women, so I have no idea if these are sad or happy tears.

"I'm sorry, Vale, I shouldn't have assumed. I never meant to imply—"

"No, I'm not upset," she says between sniffles. "Just overwhelmed. I had accepted I would never run again, never have that kind of independence. This is just . . . so unexpected. I thought you saw me as a burden, since it seems you want as little to do with me as possible. It's so incredibly thoughtful, it just caught me off guard."

I guess I was doing a better job than I thought at keeping her at a distance. I stare at the prosthesis in my hand, afraid of what will happen to me when I connect with her deep, perceptive gaze.

"Nothing about you is a burden. It's not that at all. It's just better this way. I can't risk you being hurt again, and I am doing my best to protect you."

She huffs an aggravated sigh. "I don't understand your logic, or lack thereof. But I won't push right now. Thank you for this gift, Z. It means more than you know."

I nod and begin the process of attaching it to her leg. I decide it's probably best to jump us to the next location before she tries it out, since this place is covered in mud.

"Let's get outta here, and then you can try it out, okay?"

"Okay, but can you take me back to the place where you first met me?"

"Sure, but why?"

"I have a friend, a hawk I raised from a hatchling. She's been my companion since I was a child, and when you snatched me, she got left behind. I was hoping that if we show up again, she'll find us."

I am skeptical, but I would give her anything that's within my power.

"Of course."

With our destination decided, we jump.

CHAPTER 4

It's been two full days, and though Z says nothing, I know he itches to head to a new spot. But I won't leave without Roy. I know she'll find us. And I am so sick of not staying in one place for longer than a day. I mean, it took the Silent, the monstrous humanoid men or creatures created by the Amilign monks, well over a week to find us at The Refuge. Z's being overly cautious with this. It makes me want to dig my heels in like the stubborn, ornery mule that used to break into Mama's garden when I was a child.

But I suppress the urge in an effort to keep the peace. After all, he's doing his best to protect me and even went out of his way to give me an incredible gift. It was so kind and completely unexpected from this Horseman whose personality I thought I had nailed down. It just adds to the confusion that surrounds his hot and cold behavior.

There's been a bit of a learning curve with the new limb. I've fallen more than a few times. But I am eager for it to feel like it's a part of me. So I continue to push myself, determined to adjust quickly.

"Don't kill yourself, they said it would take at least a month to fully adjust," Z says from his spot in the grass, just outside the sands of The Wastes. Being this close to the place where I hid with Sida gives me the creeps, but I don't say that to him. I am just determined to avoid going anywhere near the sand.

"Yeah, I will not be waiting that long." I slowly pick up the pace into a swift, steady walk, but my prosthesis catches a rock and I go down hard. Suddenly, Z is at my side.

"Are you okay?"

I nod.

"You need to take it easy."

I roll over and grimace at the stinging sensation.

"Here, let me take a look."

My cotton dress is bunched around my thighs as Z's hands gently grasp my skinned knee, immediately distracting me from any pain. Now, all I can think about is the rough skin of his warrior hands and the trail of heat he leaves behind everywhere his caramel-colored skin touches mine. He pulls out a salve from his pocket and begins gently applying it to the scrapes on my knee.

I am desperate to distract myself from the sensation of his touch, so I open my mouth and start blurting.

"It's been three years since my leg was taken. I try not think about The Ruination much, but when the anniversary approaches, it's hard not to, ya know? Thankfully, they knocked me out before they took it, so all I really remember is fighting them to get free. So many hands were grabbing at me, even choking and hitting me. Then they strapped me to a table and I just remember thinking something bad was about to happen, but then the lights went out. I was in and out of consciousness for a while after. And I craved the blessed unconsciousness—the agony of being awake was so overwhelming.

"When I finally did wake up, it was to grief. Not just for the loss of my leg, but my whole family was gone—either killed or just missing, like my oldest brother, Ash. I still don't know why he didn't come with me. Sida said he wanted to keep me safe, but I think the real reason is that he blames me. I mean, how could he not? Because of me, our brother and Mama are dead. And all Ash ever did was try to take care of us." I finally notice that Z's hands are still, gently holding my leg but unmoving. Even the atmosphere seems to be holding its breath. My face flushes at the unsolicited info dump I just delivered to him.

"Sorry, I . . ."

"Vale, I . . ."

Our eyes connect, and the intensity of emotion brewing in his eyes takes my breath away. I swallow and lower my gaze from his soul-penetrating one. A finger under my chin lifts my eyes to his once again.

"Vale, I am so sorry I wasn't there to fight for you. You should have never gone through something like that. It will always be the biggest regret of my life that I didn't protect you."

His words spark a thousand different questions in my mind as he goes back to applying the salve. He feels guilty? But why? He didn't know me then. He couldn't possibly blame himself. And yet, his words suggest he does. The confusion should hold my focus, but instead my attention is on the gentle way he holds the underside of my thigh. The press of his fingers sends crackling tremors through me. His warm, honey eyes are solely focused on his task as his breath grazes across my skin. A flush heats my face, and I gasp at the shiver his touch evokes.

He freezes, and his gaze lifts to my eyes. I bite my bottom lip as my pulse picks up, and a muscle in his jaw tics. I feel like there is a wild bird locked up in my chest. A small crack in his composure, and all of a sudden, he puts my leg down as if it's a hot iron. Then he's up, walking away from me.

Little by little, the heat gives way to cold until there is nothing left, not even smoldering embers. Just the biting cold of a January ice storm.

A familiar, high-pitched screech has me scanning the sky for the white feathers I long to glimpse. And then I spot her, making a beeline across the sky, only she's not headed for me. With horror, I realize she's got her wings tucked in as she shoots across the sky like an arrow straight for an unsuspecting Z. When she reaches her target, her claws come out and she scratches and pecks at his head while he tries in vain to shield himself from the onslaught.

It shouldn't amuse me. I should be horrified. But with the constant mood swings he puts me through, I won't say it doesn't feel like a bit of sweet revenge.

I issue a sharp whistle, and Roy flies over to me, resting on my shoulder. She rubs her soft little head into my cheek while my finger strokes her chest feathers.

"I missed you, too. I didn't leave you willingly, you know."

"Charming bird you have there," Z says as he tends to some of the scratches on his head.

"At least you don't have much hair for her to pull out," I say with a smirk, glancing at his almost shaved head, with the exception of a very short, mohawk-like growth down the center of his scalp. "Like I mentioned, she's smart. She must recognize you as the one who snatched me in the first place."

"Well, now that you have her, we should get moving again."

I huff out an irritated breath as I put the prosthesis on again and stand. By the time I am done, I realize my huff was louder than I intended because Z is staring at me.

"Is there a problem, Raindrop?" he asks wryly.

For someone who has always been so stoic, I am as surprised by his brazenness as I am by the glimpse of this other side to him. I suppose it was only a matter of time until we pushed one another to the breaking point. But *Raindrop?* Now I get obnoxious nicknames from him like I am a child. Because I rain on his parade, I guess.

I know I should remain calm, but I am annoyed, and the nickname doesn't help. For too many reasons to list, but the most glaring one right now is that I must be dragged all over the world by this brooding meat sack of contradictions. And it's a volcano erupting—so much for keeping the peace.

"You know what, yes. There are many problems. The least of which is that I am sick of being dragged all over the place by you, staying a day at most before moving again. I am tired of it. It took the hunters a week to find me at The Refuge, so at the very least we should be able to stay somewhere for a few days.

"But you know what my biggest problem is in all this? You! You're hot and then cold, kind and then indifferent. I was told for years by Sida about this prophecy that gave purpose to my life. Made me feel as though despite my circumstances and experiences, despite the fact that destruction seems to follow me everywhere I go, that I was made for more. Only to meet you and find out you have zero interest in anything to do with me, other than some twisted obligation to keep me safe. Based on what? Duty? Guilt?

"But safe for what, Z? Sida told me that being a Core was a great honor. We were created with the heart of Elohim, a physical representation of His love, destined to bond with a Horseman and save him from some darkness within that would one day seek to control him. But you'd rather cozy up to the darkness than be bonded to a broken Core, is that it? If you don't want this connection, then why are you working so hard to protect me? I never asked you to! In fact, I am beginning to wonder if I would be better off not knowing you at all." The words spew from my mouth.

Z looks like the pressure in his jaw could crack his teeth. His fists are clenched at his sides. His face is a mixture of pain, fury, and surprise. "I am trying to keep you safe! After everything . . . I need . . . it's important that you are safe. Once Elias has a solution that will remove the tracker, I will stop bothering you and leave you in peace."

"So that's it? Why couldn't I just stay with Ansel and Cai? I am sure they'd be willing to keep me safe. I bet even the other two, Nic and Lucia, would be willing to keep me safe. Other than the fact that you're supposed to be my Horseman, why did it have to be you? You clearly don't want this, so were you forced?"

"No," Z says, his frustration visibly mounting.

But I don't care. I am a pressure valve finally releasing.

"Lose a bet? Or were you paying Elias back for something? You owed him, so he picked you to babysit the gimp."

At my words, his eyes flash solid black.

"You are MINE!" he bellows, causing Roy to take flight. "You have always been mine. Mine to protect. And I failed. But I will not fail again. I will deliver justice and give you your life back before my end. I will succeed in this one thing, if nothing else." He's seething and shaking.

But my heart seems to trip over itself as the truth of his words slams into me. "What do you mean, before your end?"

My question sobers him, and his barriers come up again. "It's of no concern to you."

"Stop shutting me out, Z! How can you say that I am yours and then push me away and lock me out? You do not get to make all the decisions! If we are partners in this, then you have to give me all the facts. Or I am not going anywhere with you again."

The muscles of his jaw tighten as he clings to his mask of indifference. He opens his mouth to speak and then closes it. Fury comes up to stand by me as Z turns on his heel and walks away. Not giving even a glance back.

"I guess you get babysitting duty for a while, huh, big guy?" Fury's soft, velvety nose presses against my head; his breath stirs my hair, and it tickles. I bring my hand up under his big head to rub his jaw.

"Never thought I'd see the day where I tolerate you more than him." I watch as Z walks into the small thicket of trees in the distance and disappears from sight completely. I heave a sigh.

"Well, might as well get comfortable."

I sit in the soft grass and lie back, letting the sun's rays do their best to burn away my frustration. But my mind won't stop circling what Z said. What could he have meant by *before my end*? I think back on the conversations with Sida about the prophecy. I was mostly focused on the Core business, but the purpose of each Core was to connect with a Horseman. And based on what I've seen of Cai and Ansel's bond, it's a connection that seems stronger than any love on earth. It will protect them from some kind of darkness, and yet Z holds himself back.

Out of some twisted sense of justice? I wish I could figure it all out, what this darkness intends and why Z seems unconcerned about it, but like a loose thread that slips between your fingers, I just can't seem to grasp it. Hopefully, time will reveal whatever he seems to be hiding.

An unknown amount of time passes, then a figure blocks out the sun, casting a shadow across my skin. I squint my eyes open to Z's imposing figure standing over me. The sun behind him silhouettes his frame, making him appear as a dark specter. Unexpectedly, he sits in the grass next to me.

I lean back on my elbows, watching him. He sits with his knees up so his arms can rest across them as he stares out across the landscape and his fingers play with a blade of grass. It's the most relaxed I've ever seen him.

"I am sorry," he says with what sounds like genuine contrition. "I am not trying to shut you out, only to protect you. You are right about one thing—it is my duty—but it is so much more than that. It is also the greatest honor of my life. I should have never made you feel like it was anything less than that."

I don't know what to do with his unexpected words. I know nothing has really changed; he will still be holding himself back. But maybe we can find a way forward.

"Truce?"

He turns to look at me, his eyes returned to the warm honey brown I've come to crave.

"Can we start over as friends?" There's hesitancy in his face, but I can't continue with this up-and-down emotional distancing from him, and maybe I need to be real with him. "I could use a friend, Z. And if you are duty bound to help me, then why shouldn't it be you?"

I see by his expression that he's going to accept right before he nods. "Okay, friends, Raindrop." He reaches over to shake my hand—our private pact.

"Nicknames, huh?" I say with a glare. "Is it because I bring the rain to your otherwise sunny disposition?"

His only response is a sly smirk. "So, I know you're sick of jumping, but there's no shelter here. I searched the perimeter."

Ah, that's where he went.

"I was thinking," he says, twisting the blade of grass in his fingers, "since we have to keep moving around, why don't you help pick the places? I know you loved the ocean, but maybe there are other climates or places you would like to see, too?"

A thrill shoots through me, followed by a spark of hope.

"I've never seen snow," I say with excitement as I grab Z's arm. "Can we go somewhere with lots and lots of snow?" I know it is technically summer, so that might be hard to come by, but there has to be somewhere in this world that is still wintery.

Z stands and extends a hand out to me. "You ask for a lot this time of year, but I think I know just the place." A glimmer of mischief lights his eyes.

"And we can stay for a few days on one condition," he says with sudden seriousness.

"Okay . . ."

"Do not *ever* refer to yourself as a *gimp* again." He steps closer to me as his eyes bore into mine, and he brings a hand up to smooth the stray strands out of my face. "It's because of extreme pressure that a diamond is made so tough—the strongest and most beautiful rock on earth. Don't you see . . . you are a diamond, Vale. You've only been made stronger and more beautiful by what you have survived."

CHAPTER 5

VALE

I tuck Roy into the jacket Z gave me so she doesn't get left behind again. Careful not to crush her, I cradle her with one hand and use the other to wrap around Z's massive frame as much as I can. I had no response to Z's earth-shattering words—this man is such a mystery. His arm rests over the top of mine as his hand presses my hand against the ridges of his abdomen. My cheeks flush, and it's but a moment before we're transported to a winter wonderland.

Roy pops her head out of the jacket, and despite the cold air that causes my breath to emerge in visible puffs, she squirms the rest of the way out and takes flight. But I don't even notice where she's off to, I am too enraptured by what I am seeing.

A thick blanket of white coats the ground and everything in sight. The branches of the surrounding pines are dusted with snow. Behind Fury sits a quaint log cabin, the roof covered in a shimmering layer of snow. We haven't brought any winter clothes with us, but before the jump, I changed out of the dress and into pants and a T-shirt, and Z gave me a jacket. Yet the chill of the air cuts through the jacket like a blade, slicing into my bones.

But I don't even care that it's cold. It's absolutely invigorating. Having spent so much of my life in a sweltering and oppressive heat that seemed to permeate everything, this is a refreshing change.

At some point, Z must have dismounted because I finally notice him standing next to Fury's head, just staring at me. His gaze is unfaltering, and it has me squirming slightly under the intensity. Despite his walls that mask his emotions, there's a flicker of possessiveness and yearning in his riveted gaze.

When heat starts to spread through my veins, he finally breaks eye contact and clears his throat.

"I am going to open up the cabin and get the fire going. You can come inside or stay out here. Either way, it's going to be cold until the cabin warms up."

"I'm staying," I say with a bit of wonder. "This is amazing!"

Z nods and turns to the cabin. Right before he opens the door, I say, "Thank you for this, Z."

He pauses at the threshold for just a moment, but says nothing before he enters. I watch as Roy flies in behind him. She must have had her fill of the cold air—either that or she's keeping an eye on Z.

But not me. I have to get closer, I need to experience this. And there's a flat, open space near the front of the cabin. I slide off Fury's back and plant both legs into the snow. My prosthesis sinks right through like a blade, but my left foot compresses the snow beneath it with a satisfying crunch. I reach down and take a handful of the chilled fluff. It's cold and wet, and the closer I look, the more I can see it is like an intricate puzzle of unique crystals that cling to each other. They are individual, and yet somehow cohesive when united. They glitter in the sunlight, which captivates me even more.

I keep walking forward, grateful that the cold has numbed some of the ache of the sores from the prosthetic limb. The ground beneath the snow is suddenly very flat, and I can move a little quicker.

Behind me, Fury whinnies. I turn to look back, and he's moving his head up and down. In excitement or agitation, I am not sure.

Curious, I take in my surroundings. Is he seeing something I'm not? Other than the open field in front of the cabin, there's nothing but snow and pines for as far as the eye can see. Maybe he just doesn't like me being so far from him?

"If you're so worried, you're welcome to come with me," I say to him, but he just stands there, snorting and tossing his head. I shrug and keep exploring, eager to soak up every bit of this magical experience.

As I walk, I hear a faint, muffled cracking. I pause, looking around for the source of the unusual noise.

"Vale!" Z yells from the cabin. "Don't move!"

I turn my head to look at him, and the fear on his face creeps into my bones like frost. My eyes connect with his, right before the ground beneath me gives way, and I plunge into freezing, dark water. The icy liquid burns its way through my body, stealing any breath and making it nearly impossible to move. Sharp, needle-like pain stabs my body. My limbs start to feel sluggish and unnatural as I reach for something to save me from this dark, watery tomb.

Then a hand reaches into the depths and grabs hold of my wrist, the warmth like a brand as he pulls me from the water. My head breaks the surface, and the icy air hits my skin. Z lies sprawled out on the ice, seemingly distributing his weight across the surface. He slowly pulls me from the ice, and I take a gasping breath as I cough out the frigid water. Z begins inching back toward a rocky embankment—a closer shoreline than the one I began my exploration from. I mimic his position, and let him pull me along the snowy, frozen surface. Everything is shaking, and I can do nothing to help—my limbs no longer work.

Z must determine we are close enough to shore because he stands and swings me up into his arms before making a beeline for the cabin.

Inside, he sets me on the floor, removing my prosthesis before he tears my jacket from my shoulders, chucking it aside. Then he reaches for the collar of my wet shirt and rips it straight down the center before slinging the pieces to the floor. His hands reach for my waistband.

I somehow have enough mental fortitude to grasp his wrist with a shaky hand.

"Wha . . . wha . . . ttt arrrree yo . . . you do . . . doo . . . ing?"

He looks down into my eyes. "We need to get your wet clothes off immediately. You are at risk of hypothermia. I can already hear your heart rate struggling. I need to get you dry and warm now."

My stomach flips at his words, but I am too frozen to protest. Everything hurts, and I just want the shaking to stop.

"Can you trust me, Raindrop?" he says, and the fear in his eyes is such a rare sight that I immediately acquiesce, shakily nodding.

I lean back onto my trembling arms so he can help me to remove my pants. Then he steps away for only a moment and returns with a big, fluffy towel. He wraps me in it and lifts me into his arms, carrying me to the bearskin rug in front of the fireplace.

"You need to take off everything that's wet. That means your undergarments, too."

I can't look at him, but I nod. I fumble with the clasp on my bra, except my fingers won't work properly. I bite my lip in hesitancy as I look up at him with pleading eyes.

"I ca . . . ca . . . can't."

He nods and visibly swallows as he maneuvers the towel so that the opening is at my back. Then he unhooks my bra and twists the towel back in place so I can hold it closed in front of me. I ungracefully shimmy out of the soaking undergarments. He grabs them and throws them in my pile of sopping wet clothes in the corner. He uses the towel to rub my limbs and back to dry up the water. Then he grabs an additional towel and gets to work on my hair, soaking up as much water as he can.

He gets up to rip the comforter off the bed before coming to sit next to me, wrapping it around me and replacing the now-wet towel with it.

Despite the fire, the cold feels as though it has burrowed deep into my bones and made itself at home—the shaking persists. All of sudden, a wave of exhaustion has my head lolling to and fro until it collapses on Z's shoulder. A warm hand reaches up to my neck, and two fingers press into a spot below my jaw.

"Your pulse is weak. I need to warm you up faster."

He turns me to him as he holds my heavy head in his hands and looks into my eyes. "Body heat is the fastest way to warm you right now. The fire will help, but it'll take a while to get warm enough. Will you trust me to keep you safe?"

"Mmmmhmmm," I mumble. Coherent speech is too much work, and I am past the point of caring. I just want to sleep, and I want the needle-like pain to cease. But then Z rips his shirt off over his head and despite the fact that I am half dead, I can't *not* notice all his golden bronze skin on display. He's a statue of perfection and looks like he was birthed from the rays of the sun.

He slips out of his pants, now wearing only his undershorts, and grabs two pillows from the bed. He places them on the ground before taking his freshly removed, body-heat-warmed T-shirt and popping it over my head. He helps me maneuver it under the blanket so I can get my arms through the holes. I am swimming in it, but it completely covers me. He guides me to lie down directly in front of the fireplace and opens up one side of the blanket so he can slip in with me, deftly wrapping it around both of us to create a cocoon before he pulls me into his arms and presses me to his warm chest. His legs intertwine with mine, and my face is pressed into his neck and chest, my arms between us.

I should be concerned at being bare and vulnerable like this with him, but as the warmth of his skin slowly begins to leach the stinging cold from my limbs, I am lulled to sleep in the cradle of his arms. The last thing I feel before sleep claims me is a kiss on the top of my head and the whispered words, "Elohim, help her."

I blink awake. It's dark outside, and considering we arrived here in the morning, I must have slept the whole day and some of the night. But despite that, I am groggy and bone-tired.

The next thing I notice is Z's hand in my hair, gripping

the back of my head as he holds me to his chest. The warmth of his hand is a soothing balm. Then I become aware of the tangle of our bare legs. It worked—the cold is gone from my bones, and only a delightful, soothing warmth exists in its place. The heat coming from Z's body is like the comforting warmth of the iron stove we lit on brisk winter nights when I was a child.

I am not eager to move from this cocoon. I fit in his arms like he was created to hold me, and like I was made to be held by him alone. The realization sits like a stone in my stomach. We've finally reached a truce together, and this understanding feels like an inconvenient truth intent on stealing this precarious peace between us.

Z's hand spreads out across my back. I am completely exposed under this blanket except for the thin barrier of Z's ill-fitting T-shirt. It should absolutely terrify me, but despite Z's moody and closed-off disposition, I am beginning to realize I've only ever felt safe with him. His intentions were to save my life, even down to the prayer I heard him whisper before I dozed off, and I am only filled with gratitude.

Still, it's a terribly inconvenient predicament to be in, considering we just barely decided to be friends. But I can tell by the looseness of Z's muscles that he is still asleep, so there has to be some way for me to shift away without waking him so I can get dressed.

I try to move my leg that's pinned between his, but it rubs across his upper thighs, and his muscles tense. I know he's awake now because the hand on my back moves to grip my upper thigh, holding me in place.

I tilt my head back and look into hooded eyes. I feel the blush rise to my cheeks as I bite my bottom lip in response to the intensity of his focus. A shiver that has nothing to do with being cold grips me.

"Don't move for a sec," he says in a voice that is husky and uneven. He releases my thigh and brings that hand to my neck, pressing his fingers to the spot on my throat again, all the while never breaking eye contact. My thoughts are oddly slow, and my skin buzzes. His scent is filling my lungs, and I almost feel drunk off him. I could be content to stay here like this with him indefinitely. His eyes never waver from mine.

"Are you okay? Really okay?" The taste of his whispered words against my lips only sends more tremors through me as I struggle to formulate a response.

"Mm-hmm," I manage to breathe out. Almost imperceptibly, his honey eyes darken. All too soon, he rolls away from me and out from under the blanket. He presents his chiseled back to me as he stands and heads directly into the bathroom, shutting the door behind him.

I roll onto my back and take deep breaths to calm the pounding of my heart. Roy takes this opportunity to hop over and nuzzle my cheek.

"Worried about me too, huh?" I say as I pet her chest. And even though I am fine physically, I wonder how long I will be able to endure the heat building between Z and me. Because if what I experienced is just the start, it won't be long before it's liable to burn the world to the ground and take me with it.

CHAPTER 6

It's been three days in this freezing tundra. I had hoped that Vale would want to leave immediately after the lake incident, but she's stubborn and even a near-death experience apparently couldn't steal her sense of wonder. I envy her ability to see the beauty and good when death and darkness are an ever-present threat.

It's just one more thing in an endless list that draws me to her light. It makes this mission of keeping her safe while maintaining my distance feel more impossible with each day that passes. And despite my best efforts, I am constantly presented with my failings when it comes to her. It never occurred to me to tell her to stay put when I went into the cabin to light a fire. I stupidly assumed she would be able to tell that the terrain not far from the cabin was a frozen lake with a fresh coat of snow.

But for someone who's never experienced winter, the newness of the landscape would be an irresistible distraction. If it had been the dead of winter, it wouldn't have even been a problem—the ice would be thick enough to walk on safely.

So once again, I didn't protect her, and watching her plunge into the dark lake was the most terrified I've been in my entire existence. Needless to say, I am eager to leave this place and the new nightmares it's carved on my soul far behind.

"So," I say to Vale as we prepare to leave, "I was thinking somewhere warm this time, if that's good with you?"

"Sure, might do us some good to thaw out a bit more," she says good-naturedly. She extends her hands to Fury, then looks back at me, likely waiting for me to lift her up onto his tall back. I prepare myself for the tremors that grip me every time I touch her and the burn that's like a gunshot straight through my chest. The craving that sets my heart hammering away every time I am close enough that her natural scent of sun-kissed wildflowers fills my head.

How is it possible to crave something and dread it at the same time?

I grip her waist and lift her onto Fury. Then I walk behind him to take a few deep breaths to calm myself. But as I stand out here in the crisp, cold air, my traitorous thoughts drift to the feel of her in my arms, her soft breath against my chest as we lay by the warm firelight, and how it steadied and calmed me in a way I've never experienced. For the first time in this long existence of battling the darkness within, I felt whole. I slept better and deeper than I ever have. Worse, being close to her like that makes me forget why I am keeping my distance to begin with.

But all I have to do is look at her leg and remember why I am undeserving of her. Why it's an injustice to make her look upon the reason for her suffering every day of her life.

And as the Horseman of Justice, that is something I simply cannot allow. I need to help her get rid of this tracker, and then we can find her brother so she can get her life back. Then I will be free to bring justice upon those who did this to her.

If only the prospect of walking away from her one day didn't make my blood boil. I will have to call on my brothers to subdue me when the time comes. Despite distancing myself from them and shutting off communication through our mental link right now, I know they will be there for me —our bond is deeper than one of blood alone. But I need to be focused on keeping Vale safe, not answering their questions and concerns about my state of mind.

Roy flies over to land on my shoulder. Somehow, the albino hawk has warmed to me over these past few days here. And by warmed, I mean she no longer wants to peck and claw me to death. Providing a warm environment for her and saving Vale must have changed her opinion of me.

"Ready to go somewhere warm?"

She screeches a response and flies to Vale.

I hop up behind Vale. Now that Roy is traveling with us, I thought this might be an easier way to keep Vale from accidentally smashing her bird against my back. But now, the scent of her surrounds me as a breeze blows through her silky hair. My arms are wrapped around her to hold onto Fury's withers, her legs press against my thighs, and her back leans into my chest—it's a terrible idea.

It's pure, unadulterated torture.

As we take off for the jump, she curls one arm protectively around Roy, who's now wrapped in her jacket, and the other grips my upper thigh. I almost forget where we are jumping to at the contact. I quickly refocus my mind on the location right as we make the jump, and we appear in a drastically different climate. We're surrounded by tall cypress trees and grasslands, and the hot, sticky air feels suffocating when compared to the crisp mountain breezes we just left behind.

"Wow, you weren't kidding when you said warm," Vale says as she tears her jacket off. Roy takes flight, gliding far above the trees.

"Yeah, probably not the best time of year for this place, but I took a guess that you've never seen a swampland before?"

"Swampland? Like big bugs and alligators that can eat you?" There is a nervousness in her tone.

I chuckle. "Yes, but there's more to it. And, most importantly, it's secluded and safe. I think you'll be surprised by the beauty here, too. It's something special."

I hop off Fury and help Vale dismount, trying and failing to ignore the way she electrifies my blood each time I touch her.

"Baim Lyy," I whisper, and Fury disappears into my seal. I pause at the disappointment in Vale's eyes. "So he finally grew on you, huh?"

She bites her bottom lip in that infernal way that sends a blast of heat through my blood and blushes a little, probably at my ability to read her expressions. "Well, yeah, I suppose he did."

She doesn't say what we are likely both thinking, that he is a good buffer between us. Now that he's gone, it's just the two of us, which adds difficulty to an already challenging situation.

"We need to take a boat deeper into the bayou. There's a little cabin out there with some wooden paths built through the marsh."

The skepticism on her face cuts through the tension

building in me, and I smile. "Don't worry, Raindrop, you'll see."

But now her jaw hangs open as she stares at me.

"Wait, you have dimples," she says, seeming shocked.

I rub my hand over my head under the intense scrutiny.

"Uh, yeah, I guess I do. You didn't notice before?"

"You've never smiled before."

I am slightly embarrassed as the truth of her words sinks in. I guess I never realized what a tight rein I'd been keeping on my emotions, even before Vale came into my life. I think I developed the habit after learning she was out there somewhere, injured. A pathetic attempt at a defense mechanism that just became a part of my personality over the years. It's like the loss of her leg broke something deep in me as well.

I remember when I first felt it, the pain almost felt like my own, and I knew, in that very moment, that it was my Core who'd been injured. The torture of knowing she was hurt out there and I couldn't get to her was more than I could bear. I felt the darkness get a firmer grasp on me that day. And each day since has been harder and harder. I began distancing myself from people, even my brothers. I told myself it was necessary to keep my focus on Elohim, knowing I needed the strength of His connection most, but deep down I think I feared that I would be the first one to lose the battle to the darkness and it would be easier without attachments.

Though being near Vale has slowly been chipping away at my reserve. Healing that part of me.

I help her into the small boat moored nearby and climb in after her. Positioning myself by the oars, I begin rowing. The repetitive work is a welcome distraction. It's not long before my shirt is soaked in sweat from the sweltering climate. As I finally see the dock that leads into a cluster of tall cypress trees, I lift the oars from the water and lean back on my arms, letting us slowly drift the rest of the way.

My eyes connect with Vale's, and she meets my gaze boldly, almost in a daring way. She's not going to make this easy on me. With extreme difficulty, I tear my gaze away from the bright blue of her eyes that reminds me of the hottest part of a flame and tie the boat to the dock.

As we walk down the man-made, wood-planked pathway that meanders through the trees, hovering over the swampy water, the chittering of birds and other creatures creates a cacophony of sound. The sunlight breaks through the canopy of leaves and moss in random beams of light that illuminate the space and somehow add warmth to the murky surroundings.

We finally make it to the cabin that sits high above the water on stilts and I break the silence between us.

"There's a chest of clothes better suited for the climate in there. Once we open up the cabin and get a good cross breeze, it'll be less stifling." I look over my shoulder at Vale, who's peering over the edge of the pathway into the dark water.

"Yeah, don't fall in."

She looks at me with wide eyes as she takes a step closer to me. "I'll do my best."

She follows on my heels into the stuffy cabin that has clearly not been used since the last time I was here. No one else seems to use the place, but I love its isolation.

"Who built all these safe houses?" Vale asks as she walks around the place, taking it all in.

"Most were once home to families who had to abandon them. Some of the families came to join us at The Refuge, while other cases were more tragic. We left many of the dwellings abandoned for years before making them safe houses. I'm sure you've noticed, they are all in extremely isolated locations. A select few, we've built ourselves—mostly the mountain cabins."

"But why do you need them? What with The Refuge being your home and all."

"Well . . ." I pause, considering my words. "As you know, we Horsemen have been around a long time. And our purpose was to familiarize ourselves with this world and prepare for the time of the Cores—the safe houses were an idea we came up with to help. We are only able to jump to areas we've been to before, so the safe houses gave us somewhere to call home during the long stretches of wandering. And at the time, we could only jump alone. We had no idea that would all change once one of us connected with a Core. So we also thought it would beneficial to have somewhere to bring each of you to when we found you."

The gravity of what we did for a hundred years in preparation for them—for her—hangs heavy in the space between us. I clear my throat and turn, seeking a distraction. I begin to open all the windows while Vale heads into the bedroom to change.

She comes out in a strappy, knee-length, light blue sundress the color of her eyes, and I swallow past the thick lump in my throat.

"Is that why there's women's clothing at all the safe houses we've been to? Preparation for the Cores?"

"The prophecy didn't speak to the state we would find you in, but it did hint that you would be pursued by darkness, so we wanted to be prepared. Each safe house has a first aid kit as well."

"But why so many dresses? That seems to be the constant in all these places." She holds her skirt out and smirks at me. "Not that I'm complaining, they are growing on me." She moves her hips so the skirt swishes around her legs.

"Yes, well, other than some stretchy pants and T-shirts, dresses seemed like a great, versatile option. And to be honest, one of the easier options for some of the people at The Refuge to help us with making."

She nods, and as she turns, the back of the dress is low enough to showcase the star in the middle of her back—marking her as a Core. My Core. The simple cotton dress hugs her curves and highlights her porcelain skin, which I know from experience is as soft as silk.

I really need a distraction.

"There's some dried fruit and jerky in the containers on the counter. I'll catch some fish."

I don't wait for a response as I head to the bedroom and close the door behind me. Now that we're out here in this isolated place, I am starting to question my sanity with bringing her here. There's nowhere to go for a walk or get some space, not much in the way of entertainment, and I can't even bring Fury out here as a buffer between us. I have a feeling I just made my life a lot more difficult by choosing this place.

But I've always been drawn to it, probably because something in me resonates with this location. With its hidden monsters, dark waters, and maze-like waterways, it's easy to get lost, but there's also a peace and hidden beauty here if you can look past everything else. I guess some part of me wants, maybe even needs, her to see this side of me.

Digging through the chest of clothes, the options are severely limited. Apparently, I never restocked after the last time I was here. All that's left are some hideous floral-patterned shorts, and a way-too-small tank top. I peel off my sweat-soaked T-shirt, rinse it in the bathroom sink, then hang it over the shower rod and don the obnoxious shorts and mini tank top.

Leaving the bathroom, I see Vale outside the kitchen window on the wraparound patio, standing in a beam of light that illuminates her white-blonde hair. It's fitting how light always seems drawn to her, like she's a mirror that only magnifies the radiance.

As I come out on the deck, she turns to me. Her lips twitch as she tries and fails to suppress her grin.

"What are you wearing, Z?"

"What, you don't like my swamp-island motif, Rain-drop?" I say with a small grin. "Unfortunately, I am the only one that seems to come out here, and I forgot to restock a few things after the last time."

"I will say, it definitely makes you less intimidating."

I wink at her. She lets out a wistful, breathy sigh that I dutifully try to ignore.

"I am going to go catch some fish. I'll be back shortly."

She nods. I don't ask her if she wants to come, and she doesn't offer to tag along. I think we both need space. And I need to figure out if it's even possible to be her friend. Because I am fast realizing that, the more I allow her in, the harder it will be to walk away when it's time.

CHAPTER 7

It feels like it has been hours when I finally hear footsteps on the planks of the walkway. I had almost started wondering if something had happened to him.

Almost.

Being alone allowed me time to explore this place that Z seems so drawn to. Upon first glance, it seemed unimpressive, maybe even a bit depressing with it's unpleasant-looking dark waters, moss hanging like spiderwebs from everything, and the seemingly long-forgotten, aged wooden paths and crude little cabin on stilts. It was easy to see why it had been abandoned.

But it didn't take long for me to see the truth of this place. It is unpretentious—quiet and comfortable. A rustic coziness that conveys a sense of unhurriedness and invites you into the stillness. And the surrounding landscape holds far more than meets the eye. Mysterious and dangerous, it requires a level of caution. Yet as I watch the way the beams of light cut through the canopy, dancing along whatever surface the light touches, there is something mesmerizing about it.

So much like the man who loves it. It was like a weight was lifted from Z the moment we arrived. And he appeared lighter the closer we got to the cabin.

I am especially grateful for the luxury of a bath, another novelty that is completely unexpected out here. Somehow, someone figured out a way to harness the rainwater, store it, and warm it. It's pretty ingenious, and I am curious to know who did this and how, but most of all, I am thrilled with getting to reap the benefits of such brilliance. After I scrub off the grime, I find a warm spot on the deck to soak up the muted rays of the sun trickling down through the tree canopy. I remove my prosthesis, curl up on a chaise lounge, and promptly doze off, Z's earlier reassurance that we are safe and secluded a comforting blanket around me.

I wake to the screen door creaking as Z makes his way into the house with his catch. I should offer to help—I'm fairly good at cleaning fish after years of helping my brothers whenever they would catch them at the lake, but I am loath to move from this cozy spot. I hadn't realized how completely exhausted I am from these past weeks of constantly running for my life and the emotional drain of this thing with Z. It feels dangerous to let my guard down, having lived for so long with my defenses up. But Z is right, there is something special about this place. Something that gives you permission to unwind.

I hear the faucet turn on as Z begins working, and I let the sound of the flowing water lull me back to a dreamy, restful state. The water turns off when he finishes, but a curious sound takes its place.

A distant, repetitive thump of some kind. I sit up, training my ear on the noise. It seems to be getting louder and more defined, cutting through the solitude of this place like a hot knife through cold butter.

Z comes barreling around the side of the deck. He scoops me up into his arms, grabbing my prosthesis in his hand, and runs back the way he came, crashing through the screen door and depositing me on the small sofa.

"They're here." His voice is rough, like building thunder.

"What do you mean? Who's here?" I say, panic rising in my voice.

"The Amilign, and whoever it is they are working with to hunt you."

The memory of what happened to me last time I was caught by evil men comes to the forefront of my mind.

"We need to leave, we have to go, I can't . . . I won't . . . " I can't breathe, the walls of this little sanctuary are closing in on me, threatening to smother me. My chest feels tight, and my heart is a hummingbird caught in a net.

Then Z is on his knees before me. He grabs one of my hands and places it on his chest, over his heart, and I feel the steady thump against my palm. His other hand comes up, cupping my face and forcing my eyes to his warm ones. They are a soothing balm to the panic fluttering around inside me.

"Breathe deep, Raindrop, that's it," he says, his voice somehow calming, like warm milk. "Feel my heart, it's steady and strong. Let it anchor you." His eyes have me pinned with a serious devotion that would make my knees weak if I were standing. "I will not allow any harm to come to you. I will dispose of these fools, and then we will leave here."

I take a deep, shuddering breath and nod slowly. He leans forward and places a gentle kiss on my forehead, and a knot of emotion gets lodged in my chest. He stands too soon, leaving me with the storm of my conflicted emotions while he heads to a closet and begins pulling all manner of weaponry out and slinging it across his body.

As he turns, I can barely see his ridiculous clothes from before, peeking out from beneath thick layers of leather and steel that seem to cover him everywhere except his calves beneath the shorts. He takes off his sandals and slips his feet into boots.

"Are there any weapons you know how to use?"

I can practically feel my eyes bulging out of my head at his question. All I can manage is frantic shake of my head no.

"That's fine. I was just going to offer you a weapon of choice if you wanted additional security. Stay here, and lock the door behind me. I'll knock three times when it's safe to open."

As he heads to the door, panic washes over me. This could be the last time I see him.

"Z!" I shout.

He turns to me, halfway out the door.

"You promised me that you wouldn't let anything hurt me, right?"

He nods solemnly.

"If something happens to you . . . that will hurt me, Z, you hear me? Do not let anything happen to you."

Surprise and a touch of sadness is written all over his face as he gives me another nod and heads through the doorway.

I quickly slip on my prosthesis and lock the door behind him before ducking down near the front window. There's no way I can ignore what he's about to face on his own.

Then the sky begins to darken as the trees tremble in

earnest from whatever it is that hovers above the canopy. Ropes begin to snake down as large figures clad in black slide down to the walkway.

The Silent are here.

There are only three, but they somehow dwarf Z's large frame. He holds two swords in his hands as he steps boldly toward the monstrous figures.

Worries begin to seep into my carefully crafted thoughts, and I curse my inability to use a weapon.

Suddenly, Z erupts. With dizzying speed, he blocks and slashes—advancing, striking, ducking. His movements are fluid, like flowing water. And I am bewitched by his beauty. He's magnificent. He lands strike after strike against these beastly figures, but nothing that seems to slow them down.

One of the monsters takes a running leap, flips unnaturally high over Z's head, and lands behind him. I can barely hear myself think over the rush of blood in my ears, my heart beating so intensely it feels as though it will pound its way through my rib cage. Z is surrounded, and one of these monsters is practically at my doorstep.

I go to the closet filled with weapons, looking for something, anything that appears easy to use. Finally, I pull out a gun-like contraption with wires and huge arrows.

This will do.

I look out the window and see Z is slowing. The walkways limit his ability to move and fight while pinned on both sides. Slashes leak blood all along his arms and legs. The dark water seems to churn, as though whatever lurks beneath can sense the blood being spilled.

Z didn't want me to open this door, but I will be damned if I am going to let another person I care about die. I unlock and open it, keeping the weapon behind my back. Z turns, distracted by the noise, his face a mask of horror at the sight of me. The monster closest to me smiles a grotesque grin that highlights his pointed, razor-sharp teeth.

"How did you find us?" I shout over the sounds of battle. I am genuinely curious, but also need to distract him.

"One of our contacts stumbled on this place not too long ago and saw the Horseman leaving, so we installed a sensor that would let us know when anyone returned. Little did we know we'd hit the jackpot with you. Every time the tracker was about to pinpoint your location, you would move and we would have to let the system reset to pinpoint your new location. Not to mention, strategize how to get to you. Your Horseman was good at choosing distances that required serious planning on our part."

I swallow the fear that sits heavy on my chest as he stalks slowly toward me. I don't respond. I let him get closer, allowing him to think I'm frozen in fear. He starts making his way up the stairs to the cabin door. I'm not confident in my aim, so I need him to get closer.

He's halfway up the stairs.

Z yells something, but I can't be distracted right now. I say a prayer to Elohim and pull the gigantic weapon from behind me.

The brute laughs. "No measly arrow will kill me, girl."

I point the arrow directly at the demon's chest and pull the trigger.

Nothing happens. My stomach hollows out.

"Turn the red safety off!"

I hear Z's voice over the buzz in my ears. I see a red button by the trigger. I click it right as the demon reaches for the weapon, and then I pull the trigger. The massive arrow releases with a snap, going right through the chest of the monster and sending him flying off the stairs and into the murky depths of the water.

Almost immediately, the water begins to churn and thrash with something that's clearly happy about the free meal. Maybe the arrow wouldn't kill him, but let's see him try to survive that.

A second arrow automatically loads into the weapon, and I point it at the next Silent closest to me. I fire the arrow, and he deftly blocks it with his blade, slowly and confidently inching closer to me. Hungry anticipation spills from him.

I raise the weapon to try again. This time, the screech of a hawk sounds like a battle cry, and I watch as Roy dive-bombs the monster's head, clawing and pecking. Enough of a distraction for my third arrow to find its mark—right in his chest. He, too, falls backwards into the dark water.

I lift my eyes to Z in triumph, only to have the breath stolen from my lungs as the blade sticking through his chest is yanked out through his back by the demon standing behind him.

A guttural scream rips loose from my throat. I drop to my knees, helpless. The wind seems to blow violently in response. Almost as if this place that Z loves is crying out for him, too.

His eyes connect with me across the expanse, and what I see there threatens to undo me. Yearning, adoration, and unadulterated love shine out of his gaze. It's like he's saying goodbye, finally letting me see what he's been hiding away in his heart.

That's when I see the shine of a blade in the sun being raised above Z. My eyes widen, and I lurch forward with an outstretched hand, as if I can stop what's about to happen by my sheer will alone.

But somehow, Z stands, swiftly pivoting on his feet as he shoves a deadly-looking knife right up into the heart of this monster. Then he spins around and kicks the beast in the chest, back into the murky water, letting the darkness have him.

He turns, his skin ashen as blood pumps out from between his fingers.

"Z!" I scream as I stumble toward him.

He starts to fall, the last of his energy seemingly spent, and I throw my hands around his waist, putting his arm over my shoulder. He's like a bear, and there's no way I will be able to move him if he goes down.

"Help me!" I cry, tears sliding down my cheeks. "Help me get you inside. I can't do this without you."

He grunts as he painstakingly makes his way up the stairs. I barely get him through the front door before he collapses. His blood is like rivers flowing everywhere. Coating his chest and arms. Coating my hands, neck, chest, and dress in a macabre symbol of my existence—a bringer of death and destruction to everyone I care about.

I shake my head to clear the despair—a wound that will fester. I will save him. I run to the bathroom, grabbing towels and antiseptic, then to the bedroom, where I tear the sheet off the bed. I begin ripping the sheet into strips and drop to my knees next to Z.

His head is rolling around, and he's moaning something unintelligible.

"It's okay, Z, I am here. You're going to be okay."

I tear his leather chest protector off and rip through the already damaged tank top to assess the damage. Blood bubbles up from the wound. The blade missed his heart, but appears to have gone through his lung. Any hope I had of helping him is ground to dust in my chest. I should've known—this connection between us was only ever destined to have one outcome.

Tears flow in earnest as I lean over him, pressing my hands to the wound trying to staunch the flow.

"How do I help you, Z?" I say softly. I don't expect him to answer, so I am surprised when he croaks out his request.

"Stay with me," he says in a voice so low I almost miss it.

"But you'll die if I don't do something," I say through tears that seem to have no off switch. My chest is hollow, and hopelessness threatens to bury me alive.

"I won't, tr . . . trust me." It seems to take what's left of his energy to speak that before he's out.

I stand and rush to the door, locking it and making sure there's no one else waiting for us. But there is an eerie stillness to the trees and water. Apparently, the flying thing left, but who knows know how long it will be until it returns with backup. I pray that Z will be better long before then.

I grab the pillows off the bed and place one underneath his head, laying mine right next to him. I grab the blanket and curl up on my side as close to him as I can get, placing my hand over his heart. I feel the frantic beat against my palm, and I pray to Elohim to save him. Because despite everything I've lost in this life, I know that losing Z will be the thing that breaks me irreparably.

CHAPTER 8

VALE

It feels like not much time has passed when Z suddenly jerks awake underneath me, his hands gripping me tightly like he's ready to jump up and defend me against whatever enemy awaits.

"It's okay, it's just us," I say, placing a hand on his chest to calm him.

He relaxes back into the pillow.

I sit up to inspect him. "Stay still, let me see."

No more bubbles come from the wound. It's a bit raw and slightly open, but shallow. I bring my fingers to his bare skin, wondering if I imagine the responding shiver and his rapid intake of breath. His skin is warm, though not feverishly so, which is a good sign. Somehow, he's healing . . . rapidly. Sida mentioned Horsemen were hard to kill, but I couldn't imagine the extent of that statement.

And yet, all I can see is how this is my fault. He wouldn't have been almost killed, or even in this situation, if he hadn't been with me. Worse yet, maybe next time he won't be so lucky.

I pull my eyes from the wound to look at him. His intense gaze lays me bare—I am still covered in his blood. He sits up suddenly, and his hand grabs my arm, firmly but gently as his other hand cradles my jaw. Concern and fear pour from him.

"Are you hurt?"

He is so close, I can feel the heat from his body. If I lean forward just a bit, my lips will touch his.

"No." The word is ragged—torn from my throat. "It's your blood." An unwanted tear slides down my face, the gravity of the situation finally forcing its release. The air thickens with all the words unsaid. I tremble.

Then his arms are around me, dragging me onto his lap. I throw my arms around him and tuck my head against his neck, listening to the steady thump of his pulse, which pounds out a message of life and strength that finally calms me.

"I'm so sorry," he speaks softly into my hair. The strength of his arms is a ballast in my storm. It has been years since I felt terror and despair like that. I had begun to wonder if I had been too broken to feel such strong emotions. But then Z came into my life.

I cling to him, wishing this moment would never end. Though knowing that all too soon, it will. It's like my life is pieces of a song, created with the hope of being something beautiful, but missing so many notes that it is just this sad bit of nothing now. Z has the power to make it something—a grand finale for a devastated life of disjointed notes. And yet, even if he were willing, I see now that I could never let him. The best thing I can do for someone I love is get far, far away from them. Only harm befalls those that get too close to me.

We sit on the floor like that for a while. Both of us covered in his blood, clinging to each other as though our lives depended on it.

When I finally pull my face from his warm chest, my eyes find his bright gaze. Heat flushes my skin as I sit in his lap, our arms still loosely holding each other. Some kind of current runs in the space between us. A flash of a spark threatens to ignite a flame so hot it would change everything. The trembling returns in earnest for a different reason. Suddenly, Z's hand is on my face, his fingers moving the unruly mess of my hair behind my ears. And in his eyes is a yearning that mirrors my own.

Then the loud tapping of something against glass, paired with the occasional irritated squawk, pulls us from our reverie.

Easing myself from the comfort of Z's lap, I maneuver the old, chipped window frame open to let Roy in. She flies past me to Z, who's still on the floor. She hops all around him, squealing in agitation. As if she could scold him for scaring her, and he would understand. She flies to his shoulder and rubs her head against his cheek.

I stare, equal parts shocked and delighted at this development in their forced partnership. He reaches a finger up and gently strokes her chest. Satisfied, she heads over to me.

Z stands, slowly and stiffly.

"We should clean up quickly and get out of here before they come back," he says. "You take the bathroom, I'll gather some supplies to bring with us. I don't know if any other safe houses are compromised, so we won't be going near another one. But I have an idea of our next stop." He turns his back to me, gathering up clothes and weapons, and I get a glimpse of the seal between his shoulder blades—a horse hoof, surrounded by some ancient script, with a bright blue key in the center.

"Your seal," I blurt out. "I get the horse hoof, but what's with the blue key?"

He stops, seemingly frozen at the question. Something pulls taut between us, and the air feels laced with uncertainty. Just when I think he's not going to answer, he speaks.

"The key represents the Core. It's blue because your eyes are blue."

In any other situation, this would be a good thing—a victory in the ongoing battle within him. But the tension rolling off Z says he is not pleased at the news. Any response dies on the tip of my tongue.

"The words around it say 'I am he whose justice prevails,'" Z states.

And despite the key and its meaning, those last words resound in the silence, a final declaration of his position.

I want to ask about it, point out to him that even his body has accepted what his stubborn pride won't, but I sense his barriers are up again. It's probably for the best.

A wave of weariness rushes through me, and a lump forms in my throat as my eyes begin to burn. Back to his status quo of distance between us I've come to despise, only this time I am grateful for it. Maybe it will make what comes next easier. Once in the bathroom, I let the running water cool the heat in my blood and wash away the tears that follow.

Washed clean, in more ways than one, I put on a pair of fitted stretchy pants and a small T-shirt I found in the chest of clothes. I figure that's pretty versatile attire. As I head out the front door to find Z, my foot snags in the loose fabric around my prosthesis and I trip, barely catching myself on the banister and preventing a tumble down the stairs.

"Whoa, there, you okay?" Z asks as he kneels before me.

"Yes, just a new leg learning curve, I guess." I reach down and fold the fabric of the right leg up so that my shiny, metallic prothesis is on display and I won't be tripping over loose fabric anymore.

We stand, and I notice Z is clean, too, and changed into his now dry shirt and pants—he must've cleaned up when I was getting changed in the bedroom.

"Lavo Veshuv," he says softly, and suddenly Fury stands awkwardly on the wooden patio surrounding the cabin, taking up what little space there is. A surprising burst of joy fills me at seeing him again. He whinnies at me, and I throw my arms around his neck.

"Missed you, big guy." I stroke his neck before laying a kiss on his nose, fighting the lump in my throat. If I go through with my rapidly forming plan, I'll miss Fury more than I thought possible at the start of this journey.

Z attaches some packs to the harness on Fury. He is loaded down with weapons strapped across his back like he's about to head into battle. Z carefully leads Fury down the stairs, and the beast of a horse handles them surprisingly easily. But then I see his large frame on the wooden walkway that now looks tiny and unstable when compared to this otherworldly horse.

Z looks back at me, waiting, but must see the concern on my face.

"It'll be fine. It's been reinforced to handle his weight, and this pathway is just long enough for Fury to get up to speed for a jump."

I nod as I head down the stairs. Fury's back legs practically touch the bottom step, as if he needs every bit of space to make this work.

Z hoists me up onto Fury, and I am irritated by my body's immediate response to his touch. Blood thrumming, heat flushing through my skin, and a shiver down my spine that coils low in my stomach. I have got to get it together.

Z hops up behind me, and I feel his firm thighs gripping mine, his chest pressed up against my back, and his arms around me, resting against my waist. All the sensations overwhelm me, and I don't resist the urge to lean back into him. His muscles tense, as if in surprise, before relaxing.

I give a sharp whistle and Roy flies down to land on my outstretched arm. I bring her in close to my chest and place a hand around her to hold her tight to me.

"Okay, ready?" His deep, rumbly voice in my ear sends more chills through me.

"Yes," I say in a breathy, husky voice that couldn't possibly be mine.

Z clears his throat behind me right before Fury takes off. The force throws me back against Z's chest. His muscles bunch and move against me, and it steals my ability to focus on anything else. That is, until I notice Fury approaching the end of the walkway.

I tense as he takes a massive leap off the dock into the dark water full of man-eating monsters, only for the sensation of the jump to wash over me. We reappear in a land of contradictions.

We're surrounded by lush, vibrant green that seems to coat everything in sight, even encroaching upon the cobblestone road we're on. Moss-covered branches reach across the expanse of the road, meeting in a viridescent canopy above us, as though the trees desperately crave the comfort of their own kind amidst the surrounding destruction. The branches' embrace blocks out the sunlight. Z slows Fury to a walk as we continue forward.

Through the greenery lining the road, I glimpse brick, wrought iron, stucco, and lumber. The broken-down estates have been reclaimed by nature. Moss and vines have overgrown much of the damaged structures remaining, leaving a beautiful contrast of the old world's ruin against the healing power of nature. Even the trees have moss and vines growing up their trunks and limbs. The climate is still warm in that heavy sort of way, and I am beginning to crave a crisp breeze.

Z stops Fury every so often and either stares at the building in front of him or dismounts and heads inside to inspect it. Each time, he comes back, remounts wordlessly, and we continue moving forward. From what I can tell, at one point, this must have been a quaint historic neighborhood, complete with cobblestone roads and grand two-story houses. A place that was old even before the world went dark.

Why the world exists in this state and how humans survived, eking out a rough existence, is unknown. Information like that has seemingly disappeared, as if plucked from the minds of those who were once told the stories as children. Even Mama had no recollection of the time before this. Now there is nothing but vapor and cobwebs where knowledge was once commonplace. Almost as if something or someone didn't want that part of our history to be remembered.

As I look around, nothing but war-torn remains exist—hopelessly abandoned. It should feel sad, but with nature overtaking the devastation, it seems a bit magical to me. Like we are in another world. A world where new life burst forth out of the destruction, and together, the two exist in a harmonious understanding.

Finally, Z returns from his latest house exploration and seems to have found a place that suits his unspoken requirements. He helps me dismount before leading me through the front door. The inside bears the fingerprints of what must have once been a regal and beautiful estate, complete with marble tile floors, high ceilings accented with elaborate molding and curved archways, and an abundance of windows that line the walls and even ceiling to let in streams of trickling sunlight. Vines and moss creep along the walls, and the sunlight makes the place feel like a faerie wonderland from the old stories Mama would tell us when my brothers and I were children.

Z leads us into a room with dark wooden walls. An old fireplace sits in the wall, overrun with greenery. Old bookcases with dirt- and dust-coated books are built into the walls. In the center of the room lie two leather sofas that are in surprisingly decent shape given the state of everything else. It's warm and cozy, and I could happily live here forever.

I sober at that thought.

Z grabs my hand.

"Check this out," he says, leading me down the hallway. The sound of trickling water grabs my attention as Z takes me into an old bathroom. The ceiling is missing, as well as the roof from the second floor, giving a view of the sky and the peeking branches of the surrounding tree canopy. From somewhere on the second floor, an old broken or burst pipe pours a small but steady stream of water from the ceiling directly into the tub, where it drains away.

Our own makeshift waterfall shower, complete with a

hefty layer of algae coating the tub. Even in here, nature is taking over.

I try to muster as much excitement as I can for his efforts, but it's hard to feel anything knowing I won't be around long enough to enjoy any of this. Now that I've made my decision, everything feels muted. "This is incredible, Z." My tone doesn't match my words.

"Yeah, it should work pretty well for a bit. Fury will be our guard at night, and we can camp in the study." He eyes me with a furrowed brow, but says nothing as he returns to the study and gets to work taking the packs off Fury's harness.

Itching to explore, I head out the double doors at the back of the house that lead to what must have once been a beautiful stone patio, but now has been overtaken with greenery. There's no fence, so the space leads straight into the jungle-like wild that has commandeered the area. It will be tricky to navigate, but that just means Fury, with his enormous size, will find it difficult, if not impossible, to forge a path through. Seems like the best option right now. I don't know where I am or where I am going, but in the end, it doesn't really matter. All that matters is that I get away—alone.

I heave a sigh, trying to avoid the doubts that keep popping up, questioning if I am doing the right thing. But all I need to do to steel my resolve is remember the image of Z with a blade through his chest. I will not cause the demise of another person I love.

Thankfully, Z falls asleep uncharacteristically early. The injury is still taking its toll on him, I imagine. I lie on the leather sofa in the library for an additional two hours, just in case, my mind replaying my plan on a loop. I still have the tracker in me, which means that in order to avoid capture, I will need to be stealthier than I ever have before, and keep constantly on the move. I don't have much hope for success, but there's no other option that will keep Z safe.

Orphaned at infancy, it seems I was always destined to be alone. At least I have Roy.

I tiptoe as quietly as I can with my prosthetic leg across the floor to the sliding pocket doors of the library. Grabbing a pack that contains some provisions Z stored for us and a canteen of water, I locate the pocket knife and the flint and steel, squeezing them into the pack with the food. I open the doors slowly and just enough to slip through the crack.

Fury stands in the entryway, appearing asleep, but snorts at my entrance. He tracks me as I pretend I am going to the bathroom. Seemingly satisfied, he turns his head back toward the front door and resumes his sleepy sentry post. Lucky for me, the back doors are down this same hallway.

Carefully tiptoeing toward my exit, I allow myself one look back at the life I had hoped was mine and then let it go as I head out into the all-consuming darkness of night, with only an albino hawk soaring in the sky above as my companion.

CHAPTER 9

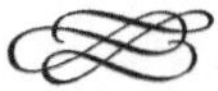

ZION

She's gone.

I know it before I even open my eyes. It's just barely dawn, but the part of my soul that latched onto hers all those years ago aches in a way it never did before I met her. I suppress the thought that this is a grief that comes from losing the bonded half of my soul. She was never mine in that way, but that doesn't mean that I won't dedicate my life to seeing her safe and made whole again.

I don't understand why she would leave me. Leave us.

I skim through my memories of her yesterday, trying to recall anything that could have predicted this decision. She was unusually somber, but I didn't think much of it considering the horror she had to live through at the bayou's cabin. It couldn't have been easy, given her history. But if she knows how dangerous it is out there, what could she possibly gain by leaving? Can't she see she's safer with me?

Fury snorts and stomps his hooves just outside the doors of the library I now stand in, and I know he senses my grief and fully understands what has taken place. She left him, too. I strap my twin blades across my back and leave everything else. Without her, nothing else matters. I send the pocket doors flying open, and Fury looks like he could breathe fire right now. I walk into the entryway and pause. Closing my eyes, I attempt a deep, steadying breath. I need to mute my panicked energy if I am to connect with that deeper part of me where the Ruach of Elohim is my guide. It takes a few breaths until I feel my heart rate slow.

"Elohim, help me find her," I whisper.

I open the front door and head out into the morning sun —Fury on my heels. Once we reach the derelict cobblestone road, I turn and leap onto his back and take off down the road. He runs with the same urgency I feel in my gut. We reach a fork with three choices: left, straight, or right. As I sense a strong pull to go right, I see Roy in the sky, soaring from that direction toward us. She screeches and circles before heading back in the direction she came from. Fury picks up his pace as we follow.

Thank Elohim for that loyal bird. This part of the town somehow looks even more forsaken than where we stayed overnight. As if even before the destruction, this was the less desirable side of town.

There's a small path that leads into the woods, which Roy ducks down and flies into, and we immediately take the left turn to follow her. It's not long before I see a set of old train tracks that cuts through the wooded area. Something in me screams this is significant as we follow the tracks from the cover of the tree line. A few miles later, I hear voices up ahead.

"Baim Lyy," I whisper, and Fury disappears from beneath me, back into my seal. I drop to the ground on one knee simultaneously, staying low to ensure I am covered by the foliage. The two male voices get louder as they head down the tracks, back in the direction of town.

"What do you think he wants to do with her?"

A rock sits heavy in my gut.

"Use your imagination, Baz. I know you are young, but you can't be that stupid. I mean, you saw her! She's like an angel that fell into our laps."

"I don't know, it doesn't seem right. I mean, she's already been hurt—" The thud of a fist hitting flesh sounds, followed by an oof.

"Don't even finish that thought. It's a dog-eat-dog world, and you have to take what you want. No one is going to look out for you but you. You chose this, Baz. No one forced you to join us. Be glad Rufus didn't hear you. Now let's hurry and get this errand taken care of so we can have our turn with her."

I can no longer control the shaking, which emanates from deep within my bones. The roar of blood in my ears fuels the rage rolling off me. My blood demands justice as I step out from my hiding place.

Both men freeze at the sight of me, and I know my eyes are black. I pull a blade from my back, and the younger of the two wets himself at my approach. The other one is trembling, but tries to puff himself up for a fight.

"Where is she?" I almost don't recognize my gravelly voice.

"Who?" the wannabe Tough Guy asks.

"You know who. I won't ask again," I reply with a deadly calm.

And as I expected, that's when his true colors show, and he takes off down the tracks. Running as fast as his cowardly legs will carry him. Roy follows from above, an aerial assault of claws and beak as he flees. I look at the younger one, whose heart is not yet fully dark.

"Take me to her."

He swallows but nods, dutifully ignoring his urine-soaked pants.

He leads me up the tracks a ways before veering off into the woods again. As he brings me deeper into the forest, I see a clearing up ahead with an old farmstead in the center. The boy, who cannot be out of his teen years yet, points.

As desperate as I am get to Vale, there's something inside me holding me in place, something that won't let me go until I give it release. I place a hand on the boy's shoulder. He yelps at the contact, and his terrified eyes look back into mine, clearly expecting death. And yet this force deep within me pushes forward to deliver something very different.

"The path you are on is not the only way. Despite what you are being told, there is a better path that leads to love, truth, and purpose. It is not easy, but it will not destroy you. And you will experience life, and life abundant, when you find it. You are not too far gone. Seek with an honest, pure heart and you will find it. Choose wisely."

And then I leave him, pale and trembling among the shadows of the forest. But I am not much better. That encounter left me off-kilter. It was as if something reached deep within me and called on the power of justice woven through my soul and released it. It was innate, and I could no more resist than the waves of the ocean can resist crashing on the shore. Even though I know I have not accepted the bond, I wonder if this new ability is related to Vale's presence in my life and my seal changing.

The sound of male jeers has me picking up my pace. I

think of calling Fury, but I need to quench this wrath in my veins with my bare hands.

I lift the latch on the barn doors and send them flying open. What I see robs me of breath and sends an icy burn through my blood.

Vale lies in the dirt. A swatch of tape across her mouth, her hands tied behind her. She's dirty and disheveled, with a small cut on her forehead and a bruise forming on her beautiful face. The dark, faraway look in her eyes testifies to the horrors she's anticipating. She sees me, and a ragged whimper sounds in her throat. Her prosthesis is being mockingly tossed between the half dozen walking dead men that circle her. Their once haughty smirks fall from their faces when they lay eyes on me. They freeze, rooted in place.

Justice has arrived.

CHAPTER 10

The hostility emanating from Z in waves chokes the air, and his obsidian eyes are full of fire. Only the muscle tic in his jaw marks him as a living person and not a statue.

He's really here. And yet the misery of my immense failure hangs over me, drowning out any relief I might feel at seeing him.

"Which one of you is Rufus?" His deep voice promises death.

"Who's asking?" says the stout, balding one who looks like a living toadstool.

"Your retribution," Z says with lethal calm.

He approaches, and it's almost as if the sky darkens in anticipation of what's coming. Rufus doesn't move, even though the other men around him step back, but he does ball his hands into fists. He brings one back to throw at Z, and a flash of movement is all I see before Z has him in a chokehold. Rufus struggles and turns red, but Z stands firm and unyielding against his frantic efforts to free himself. He brings his hand to the side of Rufus's head, and Rufus's eyes go completely white and grey—the pupil and iris disappear and what looks like roiling clouds move in their place. He goes still in Z's grip, other than his trembling hands. Tears begin rolling down his ashen face. He whimpers and then wets himself before Z finally drops him to the ground like trash.

Nobody moves. Z approaches me and tears apart the thick rope at my wrists like it's a strand of sewing thread. He gently removes the tape on my mouth before lifting me carefully and turning on his heel to leave. He pauses just outside the barn door and whispers, "Lavo Veshuv." Fury appears before us and rears up on his hind legs before slamming his hooves down so hard, I swear the barn creaks in response.

"You know what to do," Z says. Fury storms into the barn, and Z closes the doors behind him. Z is walking away with me in his arms when the screaming starts.

"We can't leave him!"

"We won't. He's just teaching that trash a little lesson first. A few broken bones, shattered ribs, and horse bites should do the trick. He wasn't satisfied to sit this one out." Z's eyes avoid mine. We reach the shade of the trees, and Z sets me on a stump. We're only two feet apart, but miles lie between us.

"What did you do to Rufus?"

"I served his justice. I made him personally relive every evil thing he has ever done. The list was long and depraved. He will never be the same—a vegetable for whatever remaining life he lives." He pauses a moment. "I've never been able to do that before."

I sense there is significance in what he just shared, but I

have no response. The silence is strained and uncom-fortable.

"Are you hurt?" His tone is low, his voice rough.

I was lucky to walk away with only some minor bumps and bruises. It would probably be a very different story if Z had not arrived when he did. "No, not really. Z, I—"

"You don't owe me anything, Vale."

I wince at the use of my given name, weirdly missing the nickname he was so fond of before. He continues, "But I'm afraid I can't let you leave yet, no matter how much you want to. Your safety is my top priority. So I'm sorry, but you're stuck with me. At least until we get the tracker taken care of."

"Look at me, Zion," I demand. He hesitates before finally meeting my eyes. "I didn't leave you because I wanted to. I left because I had to." A gush of emotion works its way up my chest, getting stuck in my throat. I can't even get trying to save him right. And the fact that I am right back where we started causes my vision to cloud with mois-ture as utter helplessness takes root inside me. "I can't watch you get hurt and die for me. I won't."

His composure cracks. In the space between one heart-beat and the next, I am in his arms again. I wrap my arms around his neck, soaking in his incredible smell that feels like home, and the tears break loose, soaking his shirt. His warm thumb rubs soothing circles on my back, causing the tears to fall harder.

"So that's why you left, because of what happened in the swamp?" he says softly, tentatively.

I nod through tears.

"I am a warrior, Raindrop. Getting hurt is in the job description. And I would suffer that pain a million times over to ensure your well-being."

"You'd be safer far away from me," I murmur.

"Safety was never in the cards for me, and even if that were an option, I would take danger with you over safety without you every day of the week. I belong by your side."

I don't know how to tell him that it's more than that. That death is an ever-present companion that follows me. Never taking me—only taking everything from me.

"Plus, I am a lot harder to kill than you realize."

And even with my doubts, his words soothe the sharper edges of my fear. Maybe he's right. Maybe there's a reason Elohim paired me with him. If anyone can outlast the danger that seems to pursue me, it would be Z—clearly, he's built for it.

The fracturing of wood sounds in the distance, and I look over just in time to see Fury break open the barn door and race toward us. He is carrying something in his mouth. As he gets closer, I see he has my prothesis. Z takes it from him and Fury pushes his head into my space, his velvet lips moving against my temple. I bring my hand up under his nose.

"Thank you, big guy."

He nudges me in response. Z places me on Fury's back, hands me my prothesis, and deftly hops up behind us. Then the pull of the jump slides over me.

We arrive back at the old regal home Z found. Maybe I will get to enjoy this magical place after all. But right as I think that, Z leads me out the back door to the open grassy area that must have been a patio at one time. He turns to face me.

"Attack me," he demands.

"What?" I say incredulously.

"You heard me, attack me. As if your life depends on it."

"You must have a head injury, too. I am not attacking a man who had a hole in his chest a day ago."

"I am well enough now, and you won't get close enough to do any damage anyway, Raindrop."

My blood begins to boil at his implication, even if he's probably right.

He stands, unconcerned, as I approach him. I lift my knee to slam into his groin, and he blocks, grabbing my arm and twisting it behind my back so that I am forced to turn. He wraps another arm around my shoulders.

"Good thinking, but if you want to get a man there, you'll need to distract him first. Now, how would you get out of this?"

I twist and squirm, but his arms are like metal clamps around me. I try to drop my weight but he just holds me in place.

"I've got nothing," I huff.

"Okay, I am focused on holding you in place, so I am hunched over a bit in order to get a good grip. The easiest way to escape would be to send your head back into my nose or chin. It can momentarily blind your opponent, but will definitely shock them enough to loosen their grip so you can get away."

He releases me from the hold and then throws me over his shoulder, so my head is dangling down his back.

"Now what?" he asks, a hint of smug humor in his tone.

I do the same squirming and flailing, but again, his grip on my thighs is a steel band and no amount of punching his back makes it loosen. Not to mention, his injury is back here, and I don't care what he says, I'm not about to make it worse. Instead, I sit upright in his arms so my hands are on his shoulders and his arms are around my upper thighs. I lean back slightly, bending my right leg at the knee, then reach a hand around to remove my prothesis and mimic beating him in the face with it.

A full smile works its way onto his face, and a bright laugh erupts from him. It is as if the heavens opened up at the sound, and everything is given new, vibrant life around us. His eyes glimmer, and his gorgeous dimples are on full display.

I'm speechless at this reveal. I have never seen anything so beautiful as Z in this state.

His hold on me loosens, and I slide down his body before his arms tighten again, this time around my waist. The smile is gone now, and I can feel the loss of it in my bones. How have I gone this whole time without experiencing that?

He visibly swallows as he sets me on my foot, his hands on my waist for support. He grabs the prosthetic limb from my hand and bends down on one knee to put it on me while my hands rest on his shoulders.

Once he's done, he lifts his eyes to mine from his kneeling position in front of me. Boldly, I reach up to touch his jaw and bring my thumb across his lower lip. He freezes, then closes his eyes and releases a soul-deep sigh, slightly pressing his face into my hand. It is a heady moment that I want to freeze in time. It feels pivotal in my understanding of this connection between us.

As much as I am his, he is also mine. And apparently, I have the ability to bring the same calm to his storm as he does to mine. But all too soon, he clears his throat as he stands and practically jumps away from my reach.

"That's enough for today," he says over his shoulder as he swiftly heads into the house, leaving me to watch him go.

And it's not lost on me that I always seem to be in a position of watching him leave. Despite his earlier words that he belongs at my side, I sense a time is fast approaching when he won't be able to keep such a promise. I just wonder if I'll know when he's walking away from me for the last time.

CHAPTER 11

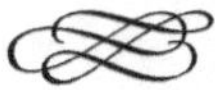

VALE

It's been four days of self-defense lessons and weapons training. Z is relentless, like a man possessed. After my failed attempt to strike out on my own, it's like he feels some sort of unspoken timeline pressing down on him. And the pit in my stomach says all this training is more than just cautiousness . . . he's preparing me for a life without him. Despite insisting that he belongs at my side, he is still intent on holding himself back from me, and it's maddening. He's been more stoic since our moment on the porch. I struggle not to let despair win.

At my request, or begging, we stay in our nature-reclaimed estate for a day longer than Z is comfortable with. But my heart breaks to leave this place, and I get the sense that things are about to change in a way I could never be ready for. Out of desperation or hope, I can't say, but I pray that Elohim strengthens me for what lies ahead, even as I tell myself it's probably wasted breath.

"Ready?" Z asks from the back door of the house.

One of my favorite places is now the verdant back porch where Z first decided to train me and where we've spent so much time together. It's the place where my heart has grown more attached to the broody Horseman who resists this thickening connection. He's a yo-yo of contradictions and emotions, and I am constantly on the lookout for cracks in his defenses. It's an unspoken dance we play each day, and I crave the glimpses of the side of him he shows to no one but me.

"Not really. I don't want to leave this place," I say somberly.

Z sighs as he comes to sit next to me on the steps, looking out at the lush landscape. Does he think about all the moments we've shared together out here like I do?

"I know, I've come to love it too. Maybe even more than the swamp."

I lean my head against his shoulder. We stay like that for a while until he clears his throat.

"You could always come back one day."

And what's meant to be a comforting statement is only a glaring confirmation that he means for me to be without him one day. Not *we*, but *you*. I could come back . . . alone.

I sit up, turning to face him. I don't hide my emotions from him this time. I open the floodgates and let the grief, heartache, and bone-weary exhaustion from his constant resistance pour from me. Tears well in my eyes, and I am helpless to stop their overflow.

"Raindrop . . ." Z says as his eyes soften and something akin to pain bleeds from his expression.

"Why are you doing this, Z? After assuring me that you belong by my side. Even your seal shows proof of our connection. And I don't want to hear some lame excuse that you are not worthy. Do I not get any say in this at all? You once said that I am yours and that it was your honor to protect me. If that's true, and we are going to take the risk of staying together because you are 'harder to kill than I realize,' then why do you insist on pushing me away like this?"

He tears his gaze from mine, staring at his clenched hands. His jaw tenses.

"You don't understand. I am not trying to hurt you. But unworthy as I am, I cannot be what you need in that way. No matter how deeply I wish otherwise. I failed you. My only mission must be to keep you safe and bring you justice. Otherwise, how can I live with myself?"

"Don't you see? I was a ghost before I met you. You gave me life again. And now you threaten to return me to the aimless wanderings of a specter." I grab his hand, but he fails to bring his eyes to mine. As if he can't bear to look into them right now. So I get up and move to kneel in front of him on the stairs. Both his hands rest in mine.

"I love you, Zion Cascus."

His eyes squeeze shut, and he tears his hands from mine as he jerks them up to his head. He is the picture of tortured agony.

"You can't," he says, so softly I almost miss it.

"You don't get to control my heart," I say, resolute.

I stand to move past him into the house, letting the shackles fall off me as I go. I no longer have hidden secrets. I can let this place go now that my heart is finally fully exposed. I head through the house to the front door where Fury waits for us. He comes up to me and urgently presses his head into my chest. He must feel what Z feels.

"I love you, too, big guy," I say as I kiss the soft spot between his eyes.

Z appears in the entryway, and he looks a mess.

I never meant for my words to do that kind of damage, but he needed to hear it, at least once.

"I finally heard from Elias," Z says. "He found a solution for the tracker. We're going to meet them now, and then you'll finally be free."

And the gravity of those words releases a torrent of emotions, the last of which is dread. What he means is that I'll be free of him.

We arrive at an obscure small town, void of life. Partially dilapidated buildings, abandoned rusting vehicles, old tires, a flickering lamppost, and an abundance of tumbleweeds are the main inhabitants. As we make our way down the quiet street toward a large building in the center of town, a lone deer jumps in front of us, pausing to look at us. Every bit as surprised to see something living as I am, I imagine. Roy circles above, having taken flight right as we arrived, just as uneasy about this ghost town. As we get closer, I make out a large red horse and three figures standing beside her.

The excitement I feel at seeing familiar, friendly faces is quickly squashed by the somber and serious looks that greet me. Elias stands next to Cai and Ansel, who strokes the red horse's nose. Despite their expressions, it's so good to see the familiar faces of my friends and rescuers from my time trapped in The Wastes, I have to fight the thickening emotion threatening to close up my throat.

"Why the long faces? Isn't this a happy occasion? Bye-bye tracker day!"

At that, Elias, the leader of the Prophets of The Way

and sort of guide or father figure for the Horsemen, gives me a slight smile.

"It's good to see you both in one piece," he says genuinely.

Z dismounts and helps me off Fury. His expression is guarded, and I feel like I am missing something.

"Okay, what's going on? Something is clearly off." I scan the faces, waiting for someone to crack. Elias seems to be intently studying Z and me.

"Let's go inside, and then we can go over the details of this plan," Elias says.

I get the feeling I am not going to like this. Apprehension hangs heavy in the air. Z's strong, calloused hand grabs my own, and I bring my eyes to his.

"I won't let any harm come to you." He means physical harm. He intends his statement to be a comfort. But the glaring truth is that my heart aches with the harm he's already brought about by his rejection. And it's hard to fear physical harm when I am living with the pain of heartbreak.

I swallow and tear my gaze from his.

As we get inside and take our seats in a small waiting area near the entrance of the building, I begin to see that this facility was once a hospital of some kind. I swallow the dread threatening to rise.

Z sits on one side of me and Ansel on the other.

"I love the new leg," she says with awe. "You look like a fierce warrior."

I smile at the genuine joy in her expression. I missed her, even though I barely came to know her before I was whisked away. Must be something about the Core connection we share.

"Thanks, it was a gift from Z."

Surprise flits across her expression. And it isn't lost on

me how misunderstood he is—so practiced at keeping himself apart.

"Okay," Elias says on a heavy exhale, the burden of his discovery clearly weighing on him. "I am going to give you all the details of the plan first. Please save any questions for the end."

He looks at all of us, and every head nods in return.

"Vale, your tracker is in your blood. It is not a single, solitary tracker, but a large quantity of microscopic transmitters that have spread all over your body. It's a revolutionary technology we've not seen yet." Elias pauses, and his eyes meet mine. "Whoever injected this into you was definitely working with the Amilign." It had to have been Lyle. I never had any up close encounters with the Amilign, but Lyle had become so demented and twisted—it's the only thing that makes any sense. What I don't understand is why. What did they promise him to make him sell his soul?

Elias's voice draws me out of my ruminations. "The most important thing to note is that because of the sheer number of transmitters and how they are constantly moving through your body via your blood, they cannot safely be removed. After some experimentation on the samples taken, one of our Prophets with a penchant for science discovered the only way to stop the transmitters is to short-circuit them with a sudden electrical jolt."

Z's hand in mine tightens, and I know he isn't liking where this is heading.

"Ansel recently discovered that her heavenly gift from Elohim is the power to wield lightning. With a small but strong zap from her power, we believe we can destroy the tracker. And since her power is a gift from Elohim and you, Vale, are a Core of Elohim, we believe that will offer you additional protection from the destructive nature of the lightning. As an additional precaution, we have Z nearby to help with healing. But we really don't believe that will be necessary."

Z's hand in mine is trembling. I look at him, and his eyes are flickering between honey brown and black. He stands abruptly.

"You want to electrocute my Core." The air around him stills as his words settle in the silence. Ansel and I exchange glances.

Elias's expression changes, his brows furrowing. "You're not bonded." The words come out like an accusation.

I flinch.

"That's none of your business," Z says with a deathly calm. "And that's not the issue at hand."

"Actually, it is my business when it comes to both of your safety, Z. And your bond would offer Vale added protection against any effects of the lightning."

"You said you found a solution, Elias! Electrocuting Vale is no solution!"

"Trust me, if there was any other way, we'd be pursuing it," Elias insists. "And with the bond's unique ability to heal each other, there would be no risk to her."

"NO!" he yells, his voice echoing throughout the space. His chest is heaving, and aggression pulses from him in waves. He's barely holding it together. "I will not risk her life!"

His eyes flash black as he storms from the room.

"I will talk with him," Elias says resolutely. "He needs to come to terms with this solution. And understand that denying the bond is only hurting you both."

"No, please don't. You don't understand," I say with a sigh. "Not only will he never accept anything that puts me in harm's way, but he's determined in his refusal of the bond. And the last thing I want is to force him. He believes he is unworthy because of my leg—that it would be an injustice to accept the bond because of his presumed failure to keep me protected. If there's one thing I have learned during my time with him, he will never willingly allow what he deems to be an injustice."

I don't share how my heart is a parched desert that can only be quenched by him. That his rejection of the bond is an open wound that feels like my failing as much as it is his. It's all too private, and the pain of it is too raw.

Both Cai's and Elias's expressions fall, as if they understand how unyielding Z is when it comes to injustice.

Ansel looks at me, and marked grief fills her eyes—clearly seeing the pain I am incapable of hiding.

"Well, we just need to convince him otherwise," Ansel says as she stands, ready to take on the world on my behalf.

"It's no use," I say softly.

Cai grabs her hand and pulls her closer to his side, like he needs the comfort only she can give. My heart cracks further as misery sweeps through me, acute and searing. This is what Z is denying us. I can't stop the tear that tracks down my face, and suddenly Elias is on his knees in front of me, his hands holding my own.

"My darling girl, this path you are on seems bleak, but a dark cloud is not a sign that the sun is gone. You have been through so much and there will still be more you must persevere through, but that is what you are—the Core of Perseverance. Perseverance is the piece of Elohim's love that has been gifted to you—grafted into your very makeup. You have been created for such a time as this, and you do not go alone, remember that. The Ruach of Elohim is your guide."

I let his words sink in, waiting for the peace that I so desperately need to follow them. But instead, I just feel tired. So very tired of having to persevere through everything. And I am done with it.

"I want to do it. Now. I don't want to wait."

Surprised faces stare back at me as they look between each other hesitantly.

"I can go talk with Z and . . ." Elias begins.

"No," I say firmly. "He has made his decision, so he has no say in this. It's my life, so it's my choice. And you said that the protection of the bond was only a precautionary measure, right?"

"Well, yes . . ." Elias draws out the last word, his thumb and forefinger holding his chin.

"So Ansel's lightning shouldn't be able to hurt me because it is from Elohim, and I am Elohim's Core, isn't that right?"

"Yes, but . . ." Concern shines in Elias's eyes.

"She's right, it's up to her. We can't take that from her." Ansel looks back at me, her expression resolute.

"Okay, if you are sure. We have a space set aside for the process," Elias says. "It has some things that may come in handy should we need them. But we're not anticipating any problems."

I swallow around the nerves that are building and nod.

Elias looks at Cai, and though no words are spoken, something is being communicated.

My brow furrows.

"No secrets, boys, we can handle whatever it is you two are sharing," Ansel says, walking up to my side. "We owe Vale the truth."

Elias nods. "I am not trying to hide things from you, Vale, only trying to protect you from the burden of details that can't be avoided. I merely told Cai that he needs to be the muscle to prevent Z from doing anything rash."

My eyes grow wide. I hadn't thought of Z's response. Hopefully, we can be done before he even knows.

"Even though he's not on board with the plan, the fact is that you and Z are connected, even if it's not a full bond. So it's safe to assume he will probably know when we start the process. And I imagine his response will not be pleasant."

"Should we warn him?" Cai asks. "Maybe do a little damage control."

"No," both Elias and I say simultaneously.

"He will try to stop it," I say.

"Either way, he will be an obstacle," Elias provides. "He knows the plan, we didn't hide it. And in the end, it is Vale's decision."

The sooner I am no longer a slave to these transmitters, the better. So I follow them, Ansel by my side, and pray that the life I've been waiting to live exists on the other side of this step of faith.

CHAPTER 12

VALE

Dingy, white walls and stale, moldy air greet me as I walk down the hallway to wherever our destination lies. This place feels clinical and ominous, and I begin to second-guess not having Z with me. Despite his stubbornness, he's been a constant at my side, and it feels foreign and chafing that he's not here now, like rubbing your hand against the grain of wood.

We wind our way up a dark stairwell to a heavy metal door. Cai pushes against the bar, and the harsh light of day breaks through the darkness of the stairwell. We press into the light and emerge on the roof of the building.

"We thought the rooftop patio would be the safest place to conduct this," Elias says. "Plus, there's an old generator up here that Cai was able to test still works, just in case we need it for the scanner or any medical equipment that might require power. We made sure to gather some precautionary equipment, like a heart monitor, from other areas of this old hospital."

Well, I suppose there is no better place to die and be reborn than an old hospital.

"So, how's this going to work?" I swallow the lump in my throat at the question.

"You are going to lie down here." Elias gestures to a makeshift bed. "Ansel will send a small bolt into your body, and I will use the scanner to test if the transmitters are inactive. If not, she will repeat her efforts with a stronger bolt. Ideally, only once will be necessary."

My heart races, but I nod.

"Now remember, we believe that Ansel's lightning will not have the damaging effects of normal lightning because its source is Elohim and you are one of His Cores. We believe that will protect you and the lightning will only work to destroy the instrument of evil in your blood. But, it is a direct source of true power, so it might not be . . . ah . . . very comfortable."

I stare at him, incapable of forming any sort of response. Suddenly, Ansel steps into my line of sight and put her hands on my shoulders.

"This is still your choice. We can keep running with you, if that's what you prefer. I am with you, either way."

Her words soothe something inside me. But there was never really a choice. I have been running for far too long. And no matter what happens, I will be free of this chain if I can only muster a small amount of courage.

"I'm ready."

Ansel nods, and I take my position on the bed.

"Cai, stand ready by the door," Elias says to him.

Cai looks fit for battle. He is wearing a set of leather armor and has a sword strapped across his back. A massive contraption that resembles a gun is propped against the generator, but the opening is far too big to house a bullet. It has some sort of bracer—for holding against your shoulder, I would assume—and a trigger, but that's where its similarities to traditional weapons end. It seems to be some sort of special-purpose weapon, but I am too nervous to ask if they are expecting an attack. I don't want anything else attempting to distract me from doing this.

"Close your eyes," Ansel says gently, and I obey.

"Elohim, protect your Cores and guide us," Elias prays. "Bless this endeavor, and free Vale from the chains of this evil. Protect her."

"Breathe," is the last word I hear from Ansel's mouth before a pain like nothing I've ever felt shoots through my body. I am being burned alive from the inside out. My back arches with the force of the energy, and an earsplitting scream erupts from my throat. Roy's furious screech fills the air in response.

A dark wrath that does not belong to me grabs hold of me like a clawed hand. And then the pain is gone, yet the wrath remains. Violent and desolate. I hear banging, the sound of metal on metal, yelling. I struggle to pull myself from the lingering effects of the pain. As if I am underwater and everything is happening on dry land just beyond me.

Slowly, things start to clear.

"The lock," a voice yells. "Get the lock!"

"There has to be another way."

A horse screams in the distance.

"He cannot be allowed to take Fury into his seal. Now, Cai." I recognize Elias's voice.

More sounds of metal on metal and men grunting in exertion.

"MINE." An unrecognizable, pain-filled bellow fills the space, and my heart squeezes. I manage to turn my head toward the source of the sound, and my eyes connect with deep, twin pools of endless obsidian. The warm, honey brown I love is gone, and not even the whites of his eyes exist in Z's once warm gaze.

Solid black—the color of the leashing.

The foreign claw of wrath within me begins to tear its way free. It feels as though my chest is being torn open while my head is trying to explode. I scream through the pain and hear Z's roar echo my own.

My gaze captures him for a moment as I try to take a breath through the agony. And in that moment, I know that the pain is from the small piece of his soul that latched on to mine years ago during my amputation—it's trying to tear itself free. Despite the agony, I cling to the piece of him that's still connected to me.

Z is distracted long enough for Cai to aim the giant weapon and shoot something into Z's back.

Z screams, an agonized, heart-wrenching sound, as his back arches and chains shoot out from whatever was shot into him, wrapping over his shoulders and crossing his torso before meeting again at his back. He falls to his knees, heaving painful breaths that I feel in my very soul.

Tears flood my face as I lie immobile, too weak to do anything but watch the horror unfold before me. Ansel stands slightly before me with her lightning flickering in her hands, ready to protect should she need to. But suddenly, it's extinguished, and she drops to her knees. She turns to look at me, and tears collect in eyes filled with grief and pity. It's all too much.

I close my eyes and let the oblivion of darkness claim me.

CHAPTER 13

VALE

Everything hurts.

As if I only exist in a fog of dull, aching pain. I lie still, afraid any movement will only add to the discomfort, but my mind is starting to pick up whispered conversations near me.

"Will she be okay?" Ansel's familiar voice says.

"I believe so. They formed a unique connection years ago when she lost her lower leg, but it wasn't a full bond. This partial connection saved him from being completely lost to us, even if it was agony for Vale." Elias's calming tone fills my ears.

"Is there any hope?" Cai asks.

"There is always hope, Mordecai, even when things seem darkest. We were able to activate the lock, and while it's in his seal, he will be unable to call Fury to him. That's preventing the full leashing."

"But the pain of it, I can almost feel it as if it's my own.

To be separated from Fury—it's an unspeakable hell." Cai's wavering voice betrays his pain for his brother.

"It's the only way, for now," Elias confirms.

A small *chwirk* sounds above my head, and I open my eyes and look up to see Roy on the headboard, standing sentry over me. Every channel of my brain feels like it's short-circuiting trying to make sense of what happened and what I overheard. I look around the room to see three figures standing apart from my bed. I slowly sit up, but they're so engrossed in their discussion they don't notice me.

"What happened?" my voice croaks out, raspy from screaming.

"Vale!" Ansel rushes to my side, but pauses as she cautiously eyes Roy on the headboard. "Oh my gosh, I was so scared for you. You've been out for two days. Are you okay?"

"I feel like I've been run over by a herd of stampeding cattle, but otherwise I'm alive."

Ansel throws her arms around me. Roy lets out a screech that has her jumping back from our embrace.

"I think Roy hates me now." A corner of her mouth quirks up, but it doesn't reach her eyes. Tears begin to fill her green gaze. "I'm so sorry," she whispers.

"Don't be, you only did what I asked." I turn to Elias. "Tell me. Everything."

The grief in Elias's expression is enough to make me want to lie back down and retreat once more into oblivion. But avoiding the truth will not solve anything.

"I'm so sorry, Vale. We had no idea of the effect the procedure would have on the partial connection you and Z share, or the pain you would endure because of it." Elias pauses, as if mustering the strength to continue.

"Zion is leashed, at least partially so. I'm not sure how much Sida shared with you in your time together, but the leashing means he no longer has free will and is controlled and essentially owned by the darkness. The good thing is that your partial connection helped anchor him and gave Cai time to shoot his seal with a lock that was designed as a protection to block the full leashing. The lock is not a permanent solution, but it will help to delay the process for a while.

"However, eventually, the lock will not be strong enough, and the darkness taking control of Z will be able to override it. When that happens, he will call Fury into his seal and he will be lost to the darkness. Fully leashed by hell."

I can't draw breath. This can't be happening. I only wanted to be free of the tracker. And now I've lost everything. I really do bring death and destruction to everyone I love. It was foolish to hope things would be different with Z. I close my eyes against the pain in my hollowed-out chest, and tears track silent streams down my cheeks.

"This feels like my failure," I confess. "Maybe I should have pushed him more. I guess I hoped that eventually the small connection we shared would grow into a full bond. I never imagined that something like this would happen before we'd even have a chance."

"This is no one's failure, Vale," Elias reassures me. "Least of all yours. Z is wired for justice. It was always going to be a struggle for him to accept what he deems his failing, and understand what true justice looks like in this situation. But the beauty of Elohim's gracious love is that through this journey into suffering, much will be revealed. Suffering shines a penetrating light into our souls to reveal our weaknesses so that Elohim may develop His strength within us. It's where all growth and pruning happens."

Elias grasps one of my hands in his as he looks into my eyes. "Stay strong. This is the time to stand firm on the rock of Elohim and persevere. You are not alone."

I nod, desperate to believe Elias's words, but the reality of my present predicament blocks out any light his words could provide.

"You should know that it worked—the tracker is deactivated," Ansel says softly, but there's no joy in her voice. She must know that nothing like that could possibly matter now.

Despite Z's stubborn and infuriating resistance to our bond, we did have a connection. It was fraught with frustration, but amidst the contention, we both felt passion, even if it was resisted. And despite the restraint, there was a fierce loyalty and care for one another. If Elohim defines love as being patient and kind, always protecting, always trusting, always hoping, and always persevering, then I know without a doubt that what I have with Z is love, even if it was unspoken on his part.

I have known for a while, though he did his best to deny it.

Z has driven me mad, but he has always been there. He devoted himself to my protection and care, and to giving me joy in small moments and experiences. Even at the expense of his own heart, however mistaken that mindset turned out to be.

I will not abandon him now. No matter how dark things look. At the very least, I owe him my help.

"Take me to him," I demand.

They all exchange looks, hesitation written across each face.

"Vale, you don't want to see him like—"

I cut Elias off. "I can promise you, I have seen and experienced worse in my life. I will not abandon him now."

"Very well," Elias says. "But be warned, he is not the same man. He is chained up right now, yet have caution and keep your distance. I know Z would never hurt you, but the same cannot be said for what he is becoming."

I nod as I follow him and Cai down the stairs, deep into the bowels of the building, to a concrete basement filled with old machinery and a network of piping everywhere. The dank smell is heavy in the air. The faint drips of a leaking pipe are a steady accompaniment to the pounding of my heart. After passing through a bulky door, we wind our way through the industrial maze until I finally see him, chained to large pipes in the corner. The darkness makes itself at home around him.

He sees Elias and Cai, and growls before lunging to attack them. His arms are tied tightly around the pipes so there's not much damage he can do, but his rage catches me off guard. What's left of my heart breaks further at his state.

Z would never willingly hurt his family.

I wipe a stray tear from my cheek. Now is not the time for grief.

"Please leave us."

"But—" Cai starts before I interrupt.

"He is mine. It's not a request," I say firmly.

The door clangs shut, and it's like the sealing of a tomb.

I stand still, waiting. He hangs from the chains, breathing heavily, but no longer straining against them.

"Z," I say softly.

He doesn't even lift his eyes to mine. I take a step closer, and he stiffens.

"Look at me, please."

He doesn't move. Mustering my courage, I move another step closer. And another.

"Don't come closer," he finally speaks. His gruff voice

cracks as though he's been screaming for hours. And hearing his voice, despite everything, is a balm. There's an undercurrent of strain in his tone that is unfamiliar, but overall he sounds like the Z I know and love.

"You won't hurt me," I say, taking another step.

"You don't know that."

"But I do, Z. I have always known that. You may drive me crazy and infuriate me at times, but you will never hurt me. I am yours, just as you are mine. Whether you accept it or not."

And then I am standing right before him. I lift my hand to his jaw and raise his face. I fight to hold back a reaction to the solid pitch-black of his eyes.

"I love you, and I will not leave you like this. Together, we will figure this out."

"There is nothing to figure out. I am lost to you, can't you see that?" He pulls his face from my hand, the action causing him visible pain. His eyes, which hold a defeated expression, look away.

"I do not accept that. And if I have to fight the forces of hell to get you back, then that is what I will do."

"You don't get it," he says, and I sense the anger rising in him.

He turns slightly in his chains, as much as they will allow him to.

"Look at me!" he barks. And it's then that I see the metal-bladed contraption in the seal on his back. It's buried to the hilt, and blood slowly oozes down his back. Chains from the lock wrap tightly over his shoulders and around his chest, holding the metal in place and preventing its removal. I gasp and reach out to comfort him.

He pulls away, as if my touch would burn him.

"Don't you see! If I was unworthy of you before this,

there's absolutely no hope of redemption now. I will not have you watch me drift further and further into hell."

"But Z . . ."

He lifts his dark gaze to mine, and the cold fury I see there forces me back a step.

"Your presence here is a torture to me. GET OUT!"

His voice is gravelly and unnatural. I can't stop the tears as I turn to leave. The door clicks shut behind me with a finality that echoes in the damp, dreary hallway, leaving Z alone in his prison of pain.

VALE

Z's final words to me play on repeat in my head as each step takes me farther from him. That, coupled with his current state, all but confirms the hard truth that I've tried to ignore or dismiss for years—death and destruction follow me like a shadow. And it pushes me to the breaking point.

Feeling like I am drowning on dry land, I take off. Past Cai and Elias, through the dark, confining pathways of the old hospital that feels more and more like a tomb for the remnants of my fractured, fading heart. Tears carve persistent and heavy tracks down my face, leaving a trail of my sorrow as I wind through the corridors.

I burst through the main doors into the golden sunlight, but none of the usual warmth caresses me. I am an ice storm inside—glacial and violent. My thoughts are jagged pieces, smashing through my mind, slicing as they go. At any moment, I fear I will shatter, fragments of me carried away on the wind. Scattered about this already desolate place.

The pain-infused scream of a horse breaks through my turmoil.

I take off in the direction of Fury's raucous protest. Rounding a side of the old hospital, I find him in what was probably once a lush, peaceful garden courtyard—a place of respite for the suffering. Now, it is unruly and overgrown. Another man-made place reclaimed by nature. Tall, wild grasses and hostile-looking weeds abound amidst the cracked and shifted pieces of the remaining concrete path.

In the midst of it all stands Fury—gorgeous yet grim. He stomps at the dirt, then rears up on his back legs and comes down hard enough to crack the stone beneath him. His bleak desperation mirrors my own.

I walk toward him, and he comes to meet me. He lowers his head to press firmly into my chest. If a horse could hug, that's what this would be. I throw my arms around him and let my tears soak into his ebony coat.

He's all I have left of Z right now. And, I suppose, I am all he has too.

I stroke his jaw, trying to soothe the turmoil in him, as I take in the grey, desolate space around us. I need to get out of here, even if just for a moment. I get the feeling Fury does too.

I walk over to a low wall and climb onto it. Fury follows me eagerly, understanding. He lines his back up with me so I can easily climb onto him. I grab the withers at the base of his mane like Z showed me.

"Let's get out of here." I barely get the words out before he takes off. I faintly hear my name on the wind and dare a glance back to see Ansel and Cai standing just outside one of the sets of doors. But right now, I am too desperate for an escape from the pitying glances and weight of despair.

The wind chills the damp tracks of moisture on my face

and tears at my hair and clothes. The thrill of Fury's speed is a momentary distraction. I imagine that if we just go fast enough, all the anguish, heartache, and failures will not be able to cling to me any longer. They will be ripped off and left in the dust of Fury's pounding hooves.

We ride for an hour until Fury slows and turns, as if he hears or senses something. The signature red hair of Ansel and Ginger appear hot on our trail. They come to a stop in front of us, and the pity in Ansel's gaze makes me want to flee again.

"Vale, please don't run. You are not alone. There's still hope!"

Fury stomps his hooves, reflecting my own distress. I wasn't actually going to run, I just need some air and space. Truth is, I have nowhere to go. Not that it should matter; it's becoming all too clear I am meant to be alone.

"You don't get it, Ansel." I sigh and squeeze my eyes closed, preparing to speak the truth I've always kept hidden. "Everyone would be safer if I did go. Death and destruction are the only constants in my life. And they follow me everywhere."

My voice cracks on the last word. I let my statement settle between us before lifting my gaze to hers. Her open expression is free of judgement and filled with empathy, and it's the permission I need to release everything I've kept locked up tight for so long.

"My mother and youngest brother were shot and killed in front of me, because of me, then I woke up in a moving wagon, my right leg missing, and my older brother gone. Sida was steering the wagon and insisted on taking care of me and helping me. And what did that get her? She was trapped in The Wastes with me for months on end, struggling to survive, and was eventually shot and on the verge of death. Then Z took over, and look where he is now."

My chest heaves in relief and exhaustion. My shoulders fall, and my throat thickens. If Ansel knows what's good for her, she'll turn around and run.

Instead, she blinks slowly, her expression pained. She urges Ginger closer so that she is right next to me, the green of her eyes blazing with that fierce protectiveness that always seems to shine out of them.

"Just because you have been the victim of atrocities does not mean that you are a slave to them, or that is all your future can hold. Yes, you have an enemy that seeks your destruction, but even better, you have Elohim, who placed a calling on your life and created you to reflect an element of His very love. He's given you a purpose and a hope that will redeem every part of your story. Take it from someone who has walked a similar road."

She reaches out and grips my hand gently.

"Do not listen to that lie any longer, Vale. Death and destruction are not your destiny. You are playing right into the hands of darkness when you believe that lie. The blame for Sida's injury lies solely on the shoulders of the evil beings who attacked her, and she is healing beautifully and back home, reunited with Lucia, who is like a daughter to her.

"As for Z, you are not his destruction, but you can be his deliverance from it. *That* is your true destiny and purpose—Elohim's design for your life. It's time to stop believing lies and rewrite the script. You are a gift, to Z and to this world. And despite the evil that tried to destroy you, you have persevered every time. With Elohim as your guide and fortress, you cannot be shaken."

Ansel's words are cool water to my dry, parched soul.

Something akin to hope begins to grow inside me. Could she be right? And do I have it in me to believe her words? I'm afraid that the letdown I'll feel when her words prove false will break me irreparably.

But something in my soul urges me to grasp that thread of hope with both hands. And I get the sense that Elohim is behind the urging. So, despite my hesitation and fear, I will try to take a step of faith—for Z. At the very least, I can do what needs to be done to try and save him. After all, there is no future for me without Z by my side.

"Thank you, Ansel." I smile warmly.

The lilac- and flame-colored hues of the sky herald the coming of night. Ansel and I ride back to the hospital. Back to Z. Fury's steady pace exudes a comforting confidence, as if he is of the same mind as me. It's ironic to think that this incredible horse, with whom I was at first so hesitant, is now a lifeline for my sanity—a guardian and my friend.

Back at the half wall in the garden, I slide off Fury easily, and then sit down to hop off the concrete. I have barely touched the weed-ridden ground when Cai rushes out the door with Elias close on his heels. Cai reaches Ansel first and pulls her into his arms. That's when I notice his eyes are darker than usual. He bends down to whisper something in her ear, and her eyes widen before she turns to me.

The temperature around me drops. Elias reaches out a hand to my shoulder as Ansel comes to stand closer to me, tugging Cai with her as she clings to his arm. Something pulls taut in the air—an eerie sense of anticipation that feels like dread. Elias's solemn eyes all but confirm it.

I close my eyes and brace myself for his words.

"Z's escaped. He's gone."

<h1 style="text-align:center">CHAPTER 15</h1>

I recoil as Elias's words hit their mark. A deep breath shudders through me while I fight to maintain my resolve.

"When? How?" I ask.

"Right after you and Fury left," Cai responds. "We thought maybe he was going after you, but then you and Ansel came back alone. It appears there was a weak area in one of the pipes—which have rusted over the years. He managed to break it." The grief shining in his eyes is painful to look at.

I glance at Elias. The air thickens with all the words unsaid. I ignore the nagging inner voice that says all is lost.

"He still has the lock on?" I ask.

Elias gives me a nod, but his somber expression does nothing to calm the erratic beating of my heart.

"What is it? There's something you aren't saying." My arms are crossed in front of my chest as though I can shield my heart from what's coming.

"The lock is a blessing and a curse," Elias explains. "A

blessing, because it is preventing Zion from being leashed by him being unable to pull Fury into himself." He pauses and visibly swallows. "Did you see the lock?" he asks gruffly, looking deep into my eyes.

I nod. I have no words for the torturous contraption.

"Then you have an idea. Part of the reason it's a curse is because it is an unimaginable agony. The shortblade is shot into the seal of a Horseman and then releases curved barbs that extend from the blade itself, designed to prevent its removal. And on top of the barbs, the chain that wraps around the Horseman and locks it in place further secures it. Only someone with a key can remove it. Because it is in his seal, he will also be unable to use any of his Horseman giftings, including his ability to heal rapidly. The seal is like the heart of the Horseman, and the lock will weaken him.

"As time goes on and he continues to grow weaker, he will reach a point where even the lock cannot save him. His body will weaken to the point where his spirit begins to give up and then the darkness will have him, or he will die—poisoned by the evil threatening to take control and the heartbreak of a split from his soul." Elias's face is ashen as he finishes. Cai's expression is stoic, but the white-knuckled grip with which he clings to Ansel betrays the storm within him.

Elias's words pierce my very soul, threatening to rend it in two. I reach a hand out for something, anything to steady me. With my other hand, I rub my forehead, trying to bolster myself against the onslaught of my thoughts. Every channel in my brain is searching for a solution—grasping for hope. My confidence is like thin spring ice. Even so, I will not give up on Z.

"Do you know where . . .?" I trail off, because all of a sudden the answer is staring me in the face. The one thing that kept coming up over my weeks with Z was what he deemed his failure and source of inadequacy—The Ruination. And the common theme of every discussion was his need for justice.

"I think I know where he might be headed." All three pairs of eyes are on me.

"Please explain." Elias motions for me to continue.

"One of the things that Z mentioned during our time together was that his sole purpose, apart from seeing me safe, was bringing justice to those who hurt me. Do you think he could be headed to the town I grew up near? To bring those evil men to justice?"

Elias tenses and goes still, and I feel as though I am missing something. He reaches a shaky hand out to the wall to steady himself.

"If we were only dealing with Zion, the Black Horseman of Justice, then I would agree with you. But since he's partially leashed, he is not himself. He will be seeking a twisted, dark form of retribution." He pauses, as if he is hesitant to speak his thoughts aloud. "What he will be seeking now is revenge. And if he gets it, there will be no hope of redemption for him."

My pulse thunders away, sounding ominously loud in my ears. Words cannot escape past the knot in my throat. Elias's hand on my shoulder draws me from the spiral of despair and back into the present. His determined gaze creates a spark of hope in my chest.

This is not over yet.

"We have the Prophets combing the ancient texts for solutions. But we know it all comes down to the bond that Elohim gifted to you both, Vale. Which is tricky when it was Z who chose not to accept the bond." Elias pauses, bringing his hand to his chin as he starts pacing.

"I guess the good thing is that he doesn't necessarily know where the town is, right? I mean, it's not like he's ever been there before," I say, searching everyone's eyes for confirmation.

Elias's gaze is unseeing, and from what I know of the man, that means he's having a discussion in his head with another Horseman. Considering Cai is standing right next to him and looking at me, it's most likely Nic, the White Horseman of Conquest, who's back at The Refuge with his Core, Lucia, and all the Prophets.

So I look back at Cai, waiting for him to confirm my assumption. But his grimace dashes my hopes.

"As you know, we've been here for over a hundred years," Cai says, "and the thing is, we've spent much of that time familiarizing ourselves with the land. I'd be more surprised if he didn't know the location of your little town."

Before I can respond, Elias turns to us, and the hope in his eyes is a lifeline.

"The Prophets found something," he says urgently. "There is a substance—specifically, a tree resin—that they believe will be able to help draw Zion forth from the darkness, hopefully allowing him enough presence of mind so that you can reach him and complete the bond."

"What? How? Where do we find it?" Cai says, grabbing Elias's arm.

"It's called olibanum resin. Through their research in the ancient texts, the Prophets believe its ceremonial and holy uses in ancient times point to its unique and specific link to Elohim—that is, it's a substance marked by Heaven. Its unique properties may help to form an anchor for Z and draw him from the darkness that holds him captive. They believe it could grant him enough clarity for the bond to be completed." He pauses, forehead wrinkling as he looks up, still deep in thought.

"It will be tricky to find." Elias rubs his chin. "It's a rare material, a resin produced by a tree that is not from this part of the world. And, once found, it will need to be ground to a fine powder so that it can be blown or thrown in his face. He needs to inhale it, you see."

"We should start with the mountain apothecary. If anyone would have this resin, it would be him," Elias says to Cai.

"I suppose you're right, even if he can be miserable to deal with. He's the closest to our current location." Cai gives a reluctant sigh.

"How far?" I ask.

"About a day and a half journey on horseback, but we can take turns distance-jumping everyone," Cai responds.

"And Fury can do that?" I ask, wondering if Fury might require his Horseman to jump.

"We'll see," Cai says, "but considering I can jump with a passenger, I'm hoping that if Fury stays right next to Ginger and I have a lead rope connecting us, he'll be able to jump with us. If not, Ginger and Fury are still faster than normal horses so we'll just meet you guys."

"Okay, let's go! No time to wait," I urge them.

"Look, the thing is, this apothecary is a quirky character and it's been a while since we've seen him. Elias is the only one who has a decent relationship with him, and I can only take one, maybe two other passengers in a jump. Additionally, other than a small area directly in front of his shop, most of the surrounding terrain is densely packed and rocky. So we will need to jump a short distance away, and wait until we are all together to traverse the area before approaching him carefully." Cai says in his brotherly way.

"Vale, you must know," Elias says, "the closer that we get to each Core finding their Horseman, the harder evil will come at us to stop it. You and Z are the third pair. The battle ahead will be fierce. And we will be safest if we stick closely together. With Z out of the picture for now, it's important you remain right by our side and we take this as slowly as necessary to ensure your safety."

I nod.

"Cai, Ansel," Elias says, "will you two gather any supplies we may need?"

They both nod and leave me standing alone with Elias.

He steps directly in front of me and places his weathered hands on my shoulders. The comfort of his bracing grip is overshadowed by my anticipation of the news I sense he's getting ready to deliver. His brows draw together and he purses his lips, as if this next part is hard to say.

"Vale, depending on the state in which we find Zion, if we can reach him in time, you may need to deliver the justice that Zion so desperately craves, before he is able to exact revenge in its place."

My stomach drops, and an icy chill coats my skin.

I am going back home. And not only that, I will be confronting the man who took everything from me.

I will be going back to Lyle.

CHAPTER 16

VALE

I clench my teeth in an effort to keep from airing my frustration at our snail-like pace. I know I should be grateful that Fury was able to distance-jump alongside Cai and Ginger. We're far closer to our destination than we would be if we had to wait for them to travel the distance one hoof-beat at a time. But Cai distance-jumped us about a mile outside of the apothecary's location due to the dense forest and rocky terrain that surrounds it—hence the snail-like pace. That, and the unpredictable nature of this recluse apothecary requires a more indirect approach than popping up right outside his door. Once we get close enough to see the place, Elias will make first contact with the man.

For now, Fury's hoofbeats create a steady crunching through the underbrush as we weave and meander through the thick vegetation and rocky landscape. I try to let the feel of his coat and smooth rock of his gait calm my agitation. Ginger is back in Cai's seal, but Fury doesn't have that option. So everyone walks ahead of us, trying to find the best path forward for the large horse and his rider. I could have walked, but they all insisted I might as well ride. In any other situation, I would probably argue, but I am so eager to get there as quickly as possible, it was easy to agree.

Cai brings us to yet another stop as he contemplates how to get Fury around a massive boulder in our way. I try and fail to quell my irritation—which is stupid, really. After all, we got here faster than we would have without Cai's handy distance-jumping ability. Plus, it's probably smart for this guy to have his place in such a hidden location. But it's knowing that every hour, minute, and even second is added time Z has to survive the torture he's living through that makes me want to crawl out of my skin. I heave a sigh as I consign myself to our meandering amble.

Ansel looks back at me and gives me an empathetic half-smile. It's a bit uncanny, the way we can read each other at times. Like we've been sisters our whole lives, instead of for a few moments. I am so grateful for her presence these past few days.

Fury snorts loudly, and I stifle a grin. I guess I am not the only one acting like a petulant child at our predicament.

We continue forward and I instinctively search the skies out of habit. No sign of Roy. She's been disappearing more than she's been around lately. Back at the hospital, she was gone for large blocks of time, only showing up right before we left. And the minute we landed here, she took off again. I haven't seen her since. But I have an inkling that she is keeping an eye on Z for me. She may be just what I need to find him when the time comes. I hope I am right. I say a quick prayer to Elohim that I find him in time.

"Almost there, everyone," Elias says, and both Fury and I perk up. One step closer to saving Z. "Stop here a moment."

I barely muffle a groan.

"I will go in first, as Dugal doesn't like or trust many people," Elias explains. "He's been hardened by the world and his experiences, but deep down, he has a good heart. Which is why he owns an apothecary, I suppose. He won't be thrilled to see you, Cai."

Cai nods, unconcerned, like he already knew this.

A frown tugged at my lips. "Why?"

"Well, Dugal's past has made him a very bitter and skeptical man," Elias says. "He avoids any person or situation that may bring violence to his door. And he sees the Horsemen as harbingers of such things. He claims detachment from a world that took everything from him, but in the same breath, works to make medicines to help and heal people. Really, he's a contradiction and his moods are as unpredictable as the shifting sands of The Wastes."

As much as I can empathize with the poor man feeling the way he does, I am not thrilled at the prospect of another obstacle. I pray that this "Dugal" is willing to help us.

Elias leads us around a hill to a humble little cottage that sits in a small clearing with a massive rocky outcropping that looks like the aftermath of a rockslide from the small mountain looming behind it. We wait at the tree line as Elias heads toward the cottage.

When he gets close enough, the door opens, and a small blue ball hurls from the opening, landing a few feet in front of Elias. It explodes in a sizzling crack, and blue dust fills the space. Elias staggers on his feet, surrounded by the blue smoke, before dropping to his knees and toppling over.

Horror unfurls within me.

Cai's eyes are black as he runs toward Elias with his sword drawn. The blue smoke starts to dissipate, revealing the figure of a man standing in the doorway. He holds a green ball in his hand and fidgets with some sort of lighter in the other. That's when I realize he plans to light another one of his bombs and throw it at Cai.

I look to Ansel, but her murderous gaze tells me she's already seen.

She moves a few paces in front of us, and lightning starts roping rapidly around her arms, legs, and through her hair.

"Plebeian swine!" A hostile voice fills the smoke-laced air. "I defend this estate unto death! You have unleashed hell by your trespass."

Ansel holds her hands out in front of her and a bolt of lightning strikes the ground between the man and Cai's crouched position as he checks on Elias. The man in the doorway of the cottage is knocked off his feet.

"Enough!" she yells into the aftermath.

I urge Fury forward. Elias is on his hands and knees coughing, and Cai stands with his sword out in a defensive position by his side.

"It's me, Dugal!" Elias yells through his hacking. "You infernal lunatic."

"I will not fall for trickery—only a lesser fool would even try!"

I roll my eyes. Good grief, this guy is dense. And he's standing in the way of me saving Z. I urge Fury toward the doorway.

The man—Dugal, I assume—is attempting to rise on shaky legs after witnessing Ansel's light show. We need him on our side, so I decide to try a different tactic.

"Please, sir, we need your help. We haven't come to bring you harm. If anything, we have come to bring about the redemption of this world. And we need your skills." I figure a little ego-stroking never hurt.

But what seems to catch Dugal's attention isn't my words, or my behemoth of a dark horse, but my prothesis. He approaches me and, without permission, takes my leg in his hands. He flicks his head to drop his glasses from his forehead back onto the bridge of his nose and resumes his rigorous inspection.

"Absolutely exquisite craftsmanship," he murmurs to himself. "I've never seen anything like it. And what of this metal . . . tungsten? No, too heavy . . . an alloy, perhaps? And the suspension design allows for compression and yet reduces the force on the residual limb—impressive." He pokes and prods the prosthetic limb, and I should be insulted at his manhandling, but I am completely distracted by the state of his hands. The majority of his fingers have been reduced to stumps at various heights, and he has only four full, undamaged fingers left. Two thumbs, a pointer, and a ring finger.

"The technology is beyond anything I've seen," he says wistfully to himself. Finally, as if realizing a person is actually attached to the prothesis, he raises his bulbous eyes, magnified by his thick glasses, to mine. "I say, where did you get such a fantastic limb?"

I am so taken back by his exuberance and question that I almost don't answer. I clear my throat. "It was a gift."

Elias stumbles up next to us, one of Cai's arms around his waist to offer stability.

"Dugal," Elias says flatly.

"Elias, old chap, whyever would you try to come through the front door? Do you have a death wish? You should know to enter through the rock."

Elias heaves an exasperated sigh. "Dugal, the last time I was here, the rock entrance was only an idea. I thought I would use your secret knock, like always."

"Ah, yes, well, out with the old and in with the more secure, I always say. Gotta keep the degenerates guessing."

His back is bent, either from injury or years of working hunched over, it's hard to say. The hair on his head is sparse and mussed, as though he has roughly run his hands through it one too many times. But despite his frail appearance, there's a keen and sharp intelligence behind his eyes. He may be quirky, temperamental, and aloof, but I sense that exterior conceals a brilliant mind. He turns and hobbles his way around the back of the cottage.

"Everyone, meet Dugal," Elias says with a dry look, followed by another hacking cough. We follow Dugal as he meanders down a little path that leads up to the rocky outcrop.

"The horses will have to stay here," Dugal says.

My heart sinks. I can't abandon Fury. If anything happened to him while he was in my care, it would be like losing a piece of Z—a piece of my heart.

Cai is suddenly at my side with his hands lifted.

"Need some help getting down?"

"Cai, I can't leave him out here. He's the last piece of Z I have. What if something happens to him?"

Cai's gaze softens. "Don't worry, Vale, he is not some soft flower. You must remember, he is also supernatural. I pity anyone who thinks they can get the better of him. But I'll leave Ginger out here with him for company."

I nod my thanks and lean forward to grasp his shoulders as he helps me down.

I follow Cai, Ansel by my side, down a tight, hidden path through the rocks. We traverse around tight corners for a few minutes before it finally opens up into a giant, cavernous space. It's genius—no one would ever know the rocky outcrop is hiding this vast space deep within.

Dugal is already well inside, showing Elias around. Not quite as homey as The Refuge, but this place has its charm. Wooden workbenches line the walls, and there are open cracks along the wall of the layered rocks that let in light and air. Along one wall is shelving lined with glass containers filled with all manner of herbs and liquids, even some questionable things that resemble parts of animals or sea creatures, soaking in a murky fluid. I don't let my eyes linger on those too long. Drying plants hang from a line above the shelves. In one corner sits a makeshift hearth, complete with a pot hanging over the crackling flames, and in the far back of the cave are three beds.

Three? To whom do the other two belong? I feel Ansel's questioning gaze on me, and I glance at her and shrug. Dugal doesn't seem like the kind of man to keep slaves or abuse people, so maybe he has helpers? Who knows? Maybe they're for his imaginary friends. It probably gets lonely being a quirky, cave-dwelling medicine man.

"Now, while I appreciate the visit, Elias, I am not thrilled you brought guests to my home. Especially that loose cannon." Dugal flicks a hand at Cai.

"Come on, Dugal, I always thought us good friends," Cai says wryly. "Plus, you know I am the most steadfast of my brothers." Cai holds his hands out, as if pleading innocence.

"Maybe so, Mordecai, but you are still a Horseman, a harbinger of destruction. I have no doubt death and pain follow you."

Dugal's familiar words reverberate inside me, and Cai flinches slightly at the comment. I'm indignant that anyone could say such a thing about him. Cai and Ansel saved me and Sida in The Wastes, and before finding us, he rescued Ansel, even though she'd been intent on killing him. He doesn't deserve this treatment. If it weren't for him, two of the four Cores might never have been found.

"How dare you!" I blurt out, and four sets of wide eyes turn to look at me. "Cai cannot help that he is pursued by darkness, and he has done everything he can to fight it. He stands for what is good, despite his circumstances, and clearly he seeks to do good. Only a coward holds evil acts against the victim instead of placing responsibility solely where it belongs."

I seethe at Dugal. My words ring true not just for Cai, but for the way I've treated myself all these years. And I realize my words mimic the words Ansel spoke to me after Z's partial leashing. A tear rolls unbidden down my cheek, and I angrily wipe it away. It's like a window with years of built-up grime being washed clean, and I can finally see clearly.

"How can you speak of this ancient being with such familiarity, girl? Who is Cai to you?" Dugal asks.

I meet Cai's soft gaze, and Ansel holds his hand in silent support, smiling at me encouragingly. I turn back to Dugal.

"He's my brother," I declare.

Dugal says nothing in response, but his astute gaze takes in Cai and Ansel. He turns to Elias.

"The Cores . . . how many have been found?" Dugal's rough voice betrays the emotion and urgency in his question.

"Three," Elias responds. "But that's why we are here. We have hit a snag, yet have what we believe is a solution that you can help us with."

Dugal gestures to the table, where we all take a seat as Elias fills him in on the situation.

"This is more than a snag, Elias," Dugal says with a dry

look after he finishes. He turns his penetrating gaze to me. "And you, girl. You are Zion's Core, then?"

I lift my chin and stare him down. "My name is Vale, not girl. And I am."

His gaze is intense and assessing before turning contemplative. "Maybe you are right, Elias. With Vale as his Core, this may indeed be nothing more than a snag."

Dugal turns back to me.

"You will need strength and perseverance for the task ahead, Vale. It will not be easy," Dugal says. "I am not prone to false hope, as Elias will confirm." Elias nods from his seat at the table. "But I can see that you were created for such a time as this. I do believe you will prevail. Elohim has given you the strength and perseverance necessary to bring Zion back from the brink of destruction."

CHAPTER 17

I am at war.

What is left of my will battles against an infiltrating darkness that gains ground within me every moment. My body is becoming an enemy. My mind cannot be trusted. Even my memory of my life is riddled with holes.

Confusion is a fog that won't lift.

Only one thing I know still, one thing that both sides of me agree on. Justice will be served to those that hurt Vale before my end.

I run doggedly in the direction of Glennlyle. My body is weak and only getting weaker. This bladed contraption in my back beats out a rhythm of agony with each pound of my feet on the ground. Yet the darkness pushes me forward —urging me not to fail this time. To do something right for Vale. Even if she is lost to me forever. And that is a worse pain than any I could physically endure.

The darkness I battle is made blacker and stronger without her light.

But I can still make things right. And something whispers that I can even be made worthy.

I can give her a world free of the evil men who harmed her.

My mind gives me an image of Vale, lying helpless while monsters remove her leg. The thought of the fear and pain she must have felt makes me see red. Then the memory of the pain I felt in my leg from across the vast distance—I knew something bad had happened.

Murderous vengeance burns through me.

An eagerness to make them pay—make them suffer.

A warning bell tries to sound within me but something quickly smothers it. Instead, fuel is poured on the flame of my rage as I approach the town of Vale's nightmares.

CHAPTER 18

Dugal explains the detailed process of grinding down the olibanum resin. Apparently, it is a tough material once it hardens, almost like rock, and must be ground to a fine powder. But brute-force has been shown to lessen the effects of the olibanum resin. It must be done slowly, with delicacy, until it reaches a fine powder.

Dugal likens it to the way water cuts through rock—steadily and consistently over time. The slower process also allows for unwanted contaminants in the resin to be left out of the powder, locked in the harder portions of the rock-like resin that are resistant to powder form. Thereby creating the purest and most potent form of the powder.

Why does it always seem to be time that we need more of? It's the one thing we don't have. Why does everything seem to be testing how long Z can last in this battle?

I'm grateful that Dugal wasted no time getting the grinder set up. He has a small amount of resin left and it's nearly impossible to get more of, so it will have to do. Apparently, it comes from an unusual tree native to the deserts on the other side of the ocean. These trees only grow along an ancient pilgrimage trail taken by people seeking an encounter with the Ruach of Elohim. Only a few ships still operate to import materials from that part of the world. At this point, I am just thankful he has any at all. When this process is finished, I will have only two tablespoons of powder. And it will take two solid days to produce that tiny amount.

He dumps the hardened resin into the grinder. A round stone basin, topped with another, slightly smaller round stone that has a small bowl in the middle where the resin is placed. A metal handle sticks out of the top stone with a round metal disc that has grooves attached near the base. What looks like a bicycle chain attaches to the metal disc and leads to another metal disc that is attached to a very homemade and sketchy pair of rusted metal handlebars and a set of bicycle pedals.

"This is my own invention, and it will make this work much easier," Dugal says with an air of pride. "But the speed with which you need the powder will still make this tricky. It must be constantly ground if we are to get the powder to the consistency we require in two days, which means we will have to take shifts. There will be six of us, so every five hours, each of you will have your hour-long shift."

We all watch as Dugal sits on the stool in front of his homemade contraption, placing his feet in the pedals before starting to pedal at a steady pace. The chain connected to the contraption turns the handle of the grinder and gravity presses the top stone into the resin sandwiched between both stones, slowly grinding away at it.

It's going to be a long two days.

And something Dugal said sticks in my head. Six of us.

But before I get the chance to ask, Ansel voices the question.

"Who is the sixth person?"

"Oh, my assistant," Dugal says over the sound of his pedaling. "She should be returning any moment. She was out collecting some herbs for me."

Well, that explains two of the beds. And just then, a small, mousey woman with short brown hair and large, doe-like eyes appears at the entrance of the cavern. She gasps at the sight of the newcomers and drops her pack. Her eyes scan us until they land on Dugal, still pedaling away, and fondness enters her expression. She claps her hands once, and Dugal's gaze finds her. And then her hands start moving, making signs in what I assume is a language all her own.

Dugal nods at the girl.

"Yes, yes," he says placatingly. "All is well, my dear. Meet my friend, Elias, and his companions. We are helping them with some powdered olibanum resin."

Her eyes somehow grow even bigger, and she begins moving her hands rapidly again.

"I know, I know," Dugal responds. "But it can't be helped."

Her hands move again, and frustration pours from her jerky movements.

"Dee!" Dugal shouts. "These people are with the Prophets of The Way. They are fighting against the darkness, same as us. And they need our help if they are to succeed."

Her hands hang by her side, frozen. She reminds me of a deer being hunted—like any minute, she will bolt.

Dugal gestures for Cai to take his place pedaling and

approaches Dee carefully. He grabs her hands in his as he looks into her face.

"You are safe, my dear. No harm will come to you. You have my word."

Dee gives a slight nod, but her stiff posture and skittish expression suggests his words do little to reassure her. She turns and slips back into the darkness of the cavern's rock entrance, leaving her pack on the floor where she dropped it.

Dugal sighs. "Dee has had a rough life. Partially because of what was done to her, and partially because of choices she made. Mostly, regret weighs heavy on her, more debilitating than the physical scars she bears."

I can sympathize. But as I glance at the others, Elias's face gives me pause. He wears a serious expression, and his rigid posture and guarded eyes speak volumes.

"You trust her?" Elias asks.

Dugal's expression changes in an instant. His nostrils flare, and his body tenses. He pulls himself as upright as his bent frame will allow, chin lifted, and crosses his arms in front of his chest.

"With my life," Dugal replies sharply.

"What do you know of her? Where did you find her?" Elias presses.

"What is this about, Elias?" Dugal asks, his gaze searching. "I think the real question is what do you know about her?" Dugal lifts one brow at him.

Elias approaches Dugal, grabs him by the arm, and walks him to the area with the beds, just out of earshot. The two men seem to have a heated discussion filled with gesturing hands, shocked expressions, and even a finger poke to the chest by Dugal.

Elias must be the most patient man on the planet.

Dugal leaves the cavern and quickly returns holding Dee's hand. The girl looks resigned, as though she is headed to the gallows. As he brings her beneath the main light of the room, I get a glimpse of the scars mentioned earlier. Small slashes cover her arms, neck, and face. And one especially gruesome slash down the side of her face leads from her temple to her chin, beneath her ear and down her neck. It's puckered and red, as if it still bears the malice of the evil who left it there.

Elias returns from the corner and wastes no time getting to the point. "Are you the Dee that betrayed our Lucia?"

Ansel gasps, Cai's eyes grow big, and for a moment, he stops peddling before continuing.

A tear rolls down Dee's cheek as she nods and hangs her head. Her entire frame seems to fold in on itself, as if she wishes to disappear entirely. Dugal stands next to Dee, his hand on her shoulder.

"Where does your allegiance lie?" Elias asks firmly, but not unkindly.

Dee looks up at Dugal and begins signing with her hands, her movements less frantic than before. More wooden and surrendered. Elias is the only one of us who doesn't look confused by the interaction as he intently watches Dee's hands. I wouldn't be surprised if he is versed in this unique language too.

Dugal turns to the group when she finishes. "She said her allegiance is to me and any who have suffered at the hands of evil, and she offers her aid to any who aim to rid the world of the darkness."

"What brought you here?" Elias asks. "According to Lucia, you offered yourself up as a vessel to a demon host. They don't let go easily."

Dee's cheeks flare red, and she trembles. Dugal turns

red, too, presumably for an entirely different reason as his nostrils flare and his expression tightens.

"Enough, Elias, she has already been through so much. You—" Dugal stops when Dee grasps his arm, drawing his attention. She starts signing her response, and Dugal nods. Then she continues signing while we all wait. Elias again intently watches her hands.

Dugal turns back to the group to translate. "After she gave up Lucia, the demon had no use for her frail form. It had used her to get what it wanted. It promised her a purpose and gave her voice back to her, but then took it all away, leaving her more damaged than she was originally." Dugal pauses, then continues, "I found her near the mountain ashram, wounded and clinging to life. I brought her here, healed her, and she's been helping me ever since. That was a few months ago."

Dee approaches Elias and begins to sign directly to him. We all stare on, lost, but Dugal translates for us.

"She wants to know what happened to Lucia. Her betrayal of her only friend has haunted her these past months."

Elias looks at Dee, and he is so quiet, I begin to think he won't answer. Tears flow down Dee's face, but her earnest gaze seems desperate for news.

"She survived," Elias says, and Dee lets out an audible sigh. "One of the Four Horsemen was able to find her before the Amilign fulfilled their corrupt goals for her. She bonded with her Horseman and is now safe and happy with us."

A weight seems to lift from Dee. She smiles and closes her eyes, putting her hand over her heart.

Dugal glares at Elias.

"I'm sorry, Dugal, I had to know. I can't take any risks

with Vale and Ansel, not after knowing what happened to Lucia. And thank you for your honesty, Dee. I am truly sorry for what you suffered."

Her eyes open wide at his words.

He places a hand on her shoulder. "When one is not grown on love, in their desperation, they can seek it in lies instead. One of the darkest evils is a man who can no longer see truth because he's been consumed by lies. Make no mistake, you were spared the consequences of your choice for a greater purpose, Dee. No longer can you wallow in shame and regret. You are only listening to the lies of evil when you do. Evil tried to destroy you once; do not give it the power to do so again. Elohim is in the business of redemption and second chances. He has always been the answer to what you've been seeking."

Dee's eyes have a light in them that was missing earlier. She signs something, and Elias nods to her. Then leaves the cavern.

"I know Dee," Dugal says. "Until she can make amends with Lucia, she will always be a prisoner of her past."

"I understand, but if I know Elohim, I am sure that's already in His plans for her."

Dugal pushes his glasses up on his nose and sighs. "Must you always stir things up whenever you come for a visit? Good assistants are hard to find, you know."

Dugal makes his way over to a pot that hangs over the fire and begins to ladle out a thick black liquid. "Come, let's get you all some of my special brew to give you the energy for our endeavor."

He passes mugs full of the stuff around. Ansel looks into her mug a bit too intensely, as if it's a foe she's trying to puzzle out. Cai catches my eye and ever so subtly shakes his head no—a warning. I look into the sludge-like concoction.

The scent of earth, cloves, and something that vaguely smells of rotting garbage assaults my nose. I feign a sip out of politeness, and the gritty texture of the drink accidentally touches my lips. It tastes like it smells, and my stomach roils. I do my best to stifle any expression of disgust. If there's one thing my mama aimed to teach us as kids, it was kindness and manners.

Elias takes a hefty swig, seemingly unaffected by the viscosity and aroma. That man is made of tougher stuff. Dugal takes a deep sip and sighs in relief, as if that mug holds the solution to all that ails him.

"The clock is ticking—let's get to it."

CHAPTER 19

VALE

Thirty-six tedious hours have crawled by, each of us rotating shifts every five hours on the pedaling contraption that's quickly become known as Bane, short for the bane of our existence, much to Dugal's dismay. But I will say, other than needing to be oiled a few times, Bane has been a steady, albeit obnoxious and exacting companion in our assignment.

Dugal attempts to fill us with his special brew multiple times, but even the mention of the concoction causes my stomach to heave. I have a hard time believing anyone could stomach drinking it daily.

Fatigue hangs heavy off all of us except Cai, who looks like he could run up a mountain side for a bit of fresh air if he felt a hankering. He's even doubled up shifts to give the rest of us more rest, taking two hours to our one. He offered to take my shifts completely, but the look I gave him quickly shut down that idea.

The breaks also allow us to eat, clean up, and rest. I

found a white sundress that fits me, and I was quick to slip into the familiar comfort of the soft cotton. Not the most practical, but I've found, especially since getting my prothesis, that I prefer the ease and simplicity of a simple, knee-length dress.

It's night, and everyone rests in haphazard piles around the cavern. Probably lulled to sleep by the sound of Bane grinding the resin.

I can see the finish line—we are so close.

Dugal offered me a turn in one of the three beds in the corner, and I am not ashamed to say I accepted it without protest. Every part of me aches, and it is nice to sleep on something soft for a change.

Cai is nearing the end of his shift, and my turn approaches. I stifle a groan as I sit up and prepare to put my prosthesis back on. My left foot accidentally kicks a small piece of wood that was lying next to the bed. I bend down to pick it up, and time stops. A wooden carving of a bird sits in my hand.

There is only one person I've ever known who could carve animal figurines like this, and I watched him die. But if this is one of Rain's carvings and it's here in this dank little cave, lying next to this mattress—

It couldn't be. I am not that lucky.

But still, my heart beats like a hummingbird's wings, and my breath stalls in my chest.

"Ash?" I whisper the name I haven't spoken aloud in over three years like a prayer.

Dugal lies on the mattress across from mine. I look up and find he's awake, and his eyes study me curiously.

"Who does this belong to?" I say a bit too loudly. I feel additional eyes on me. I've only spoken to Z and Ansel of my past. No one else knows anything about it—about me.

"My primary apprentice." Dugal tilts his head in a dog-like manner, his brow furrowed. "He's out making a delivery right now."

"What is his name?" My shaky voice betrays my emotion. Ansel makes her way over to sit beside me on the bed; her hand on my arm offers her solidarity. Elias stands close by while Cai's gaze is pinned on us from his place atop Bane.

"Ash," Dugal says matter-of-factly. "Why? Do you know the young man?"

I put my hands around my middle, hunching over slightly, struggling to calm my breathing. Darkness presses in on the periphery of my vision. This is too much to process. Ansel's soothing hand on my back helps anchor me and reminds me I am not alone anymore.

I slowly pull myself together and lift my eyes to Dugal, and Elias, now standing beside him, concern etched on his face.

"I do . . . he's my brother. I lost him the day I lost everything—my leg included. He's the only family I have left."

It's so quiet, you can hear the slight whistle of the wind between the cracks in the rock face. And despite Dugal's usual gruff manner, his expression softens.

"I should have known when you said your name. He doesn't like to speak of what happened to him, but he did once share his story, about a year ago. And his desperate yet fruitless search for his baby sister, Vale. I think he feared you were dead, because he said this world was too intent on snuffing out shining stars like you."

I try to cover the sob that bursts from my mouth as I curl in on myself. My brother is alive. And he looked for me. Maybe he doesn't blame me for what happened. All these years, a secret part of my heart believed he sent me away because he, too, knew that death followed me—despite Sida's attempts to assure me it was only for my safety.

But he tried to find me. He called me a shining star.

The knowledge is a solace for the wounds left behind by the lies I've believed for far too long.

Ansel leans her head against mine, her arms around me as the waves of my emotions crash over me unchecked. Finally releasing after years of being pent-up. When the sobs slow, she helps me to my feet, linking my arm with hers.

"I am sorry he won't be back for a while yet. He's gone to deliver an order to one of our primary clients," Dugal says. "It's a long and treacherous journey, but he has made it a few times. However, I don't anticipate his return for another few weeks, possibly longer. But you're welcome to leave a letter for him to read on his return. He will know where to find you now."

I look at Dugal as if I am seeing him for the first time. This is the man who offered my brother a refuge. Gave him a purpose after he'd lost everything. And if Ash has been here at least a year, potentially longer, then he must be fulfilled by, if not happy with, what he's doing.

Releasing Ansel, I stride toward an unsuspecting Dugal, whose eyes widen with my every step, and I throw my arms around him. An "oof" comes out of him with the intensity of my hug, but slowly, his arms come up for his mangled hands to pat my back.

"Thank you," I say softly. "For taking care of him when he had nothing. For giving him a place and purpose. For being the family he desperately needed after losing everything."

When I pull back, emotion shines in Dugal's eyes. He

clears his throat. "No thanks are needed." His voice is gruff and wavers slightly. "He saved me as much as I saved him."

After taking a moment to recover from the earth-shattering news that my brother is alive and well, I head over to Cai to relieve him. He glances down at my leg, almost like he can see the blisters and sores under the prothesis from the pedaling. Bane is not designed for a prosthetic leg.

"It's okay, Vale," Cai whispers, careful not to wake those who have fallen back asleep again. "Just rest—I can take your shift this time."

He's already been riding for two hours solid. And even though I know his intentions are kind, I can't let him take this from me. It may be harder for me to pedal Bane, but I will still take my turn in this effort to save Z—I need to. I can't sit here and do nothing.

"No, Cai, I must do this." My tone leaves no room for argument.

He nods and slows to a stop, giving me his seat. I take my place on the bane of our existence and begin. Cai makes his way to Ansel, lying down beside her, curling his body around her back, and pulling her into his chest. She smiles in her sleep.

I look away and try to ignore the pang in my heart at the sight of an easy familiarity I never had with Z. My vision blurs at the thought of him out there, alone, battling an internal foe that seeks his destruction. My pedaling increases in fervor.

I am coming, Z, I promise.

I am nearing the end of my shift when Elias and Cai sit

upright simultaneously, eyes wide and skin ashen. They look at each other before jumping to their feet.

Something has happened, I just know it. Cai wakes Ansel while Elias heads to Dugal's bed. They tow their sleepy companions over to where I sit with Bane. Probably so they only have to deliver the news once.

Elias visibly swallows. "The Refuge is under attack."

Gasps fly, mostly from Ansel and myself.

"Cai and Ansel will leave immediately to help Nic and Lucia defend it. When it's possible, one of them will return for me."

My stomach sinks as I think of all the innocent people that make that place their home.

Elias looks at me. "Vale, you will stay here with Dugal and continue to work on the powder. Hopefully, we can make fast work of the situation and return to you before the powder is ready, or at the very least, not long after. When we return, we will help you find Z and bring him home."

I give a wooden nod, struggling to suppress the panic that tries to take hold of me. Z cannot wait. And I will not linger one moment past the time the powder is ready. Even if I must go alone. I can't risk him—I won't.

But Elias and Cai don't need to know that. They need nothing more to worry about at this moment. So instead, I leave Bane to hug Ansel goodbye.

"Be safe and go kick butt," I tease her. "Show them what happens when they mess with those that belong to Elohim."

She smiles, but the expression falters as she pulls away to look at me, a question on her brow.

"Vale—"

"Don't worry about me. Keep your head in the game. I'll see you shortly." I give her the brightest smile I can muster.

Whatever it takes to avoid her looking too closely. Sometimes I think she can read my mind.

She nods and gives me a half-smile that doesn't meet her eyes. Then she follows Cai out of the cavern.

I turn to get back on Bane, but Elias sits in my place.

"It's not your turn yet."

He pedals steadily. "I don't expect to be here long, Vale, and then it will be up to you, Dugal, and Dee to finish this work. I'd like to help while I am here. Go rest."

I nod and head off to my makeshift bed area. There's no way I can sleep, but I lie down anyway and look at the rocky, cavernous space as my thoughts drift to a dimpled grin, honey-brown eyes, and the smell of cedarwood and an earthy lake breeze. And I say a prayer that Elohim will strengthen him until I can get there.

CHAPTER 20

The powder is finished, and Dugal is packaging it for me. I requested two separate pouches, because it seemed foolish to put all my hopes in one. This way, I have a backup, should I need it.

We've had no word from anyone from The Refuge. I know they all expect me to wait for their return, but there's no way I can. And if our roles were reversed, Z wouldn't wait to come save me. But there's the little problem of me having no idea where I am, exactly, or how to get to Glennlyle from here.

Leaving the dingy cavern, I take a deep breath of forest air to clear my head. I am restless now that everything is finished.

Fury trots up to me and pounds his left hoof repeatedly into the dirt. He clearly feels as I do. He prances around me, and I get the keen sense he's trying to communicate with me. I wish I could understand him.

"I'm sorry, boy, I don't know what you want. I am sick of being here, too."

A familiar hawk's cry cuts through the sound of the wind moving through the trees. I scan the skies and glimpse white feathers. Roy glides down to land on my outstretched arm.

"Roy, you clever thing, what have you been up to?"

I pet her feathered head with my knuckle. She flies to my shoulder and stays there only a moment before taking flight and circling overhead, letting out a shriek. She, too, seems restless.

Dugal appears at the entrance of the cavern holding two pouches, a satchel, and a canteen that I hope is filled with water instead of his special brew.

"Here you go, my girl." He hands me the items. "May Elohim guide you on your journey and keep you safe."

I raise a brow at him. "You're not going to tell me how dangerous it is and that I need to wait for the others?"

He glances down at my leg. "Something tells me that I don't need to tell you of the danger that awaits you. That, and I doubt you'd listen if I asked you to wait."

One side of my mouth quirks up.

"I didn't think so," he says with a wink. "So much like your brother. Is there anything else I can do for you? Do you need directions? The canteen contains water, but I can get you some of my brew if you like?"

I stifle my cringe and feign a smile. "No, this is more than enough, thank you, Dugal."

I glance at Fury, who's trampling the ground, and Roy, circling in the air, and something tells me I won't need directions. Elohim has given me what help I need in these two furry and feathered companions.

"Do you have a message you'd like me to relay to Ash?"

My heart stutters. I would write him pages upon pages if time allowed. I meet Dugal's penetrating gaze.

"Just tell him I said thank-you, for everything he did and sacrificed that day to save me. I am okay, and I love him." I wipe away the stray tear that escapes. The grief that my brother is so close and yet still so far away sits heavy on my chest. Hopefully, one day soon, I'll be reunited with him and truly heal the wounds Lyle inflicted on what's left of my family.

Fury heads over to a cluster of rocks and stands sideways against them before turning to look at me. He's trying to help me mount him. Now, I know without a doubt what he wants. I clamber up the rocks and get situated on Fury's back. Roy circles above and starts heading in a southern direction before circling back again. I'd bet my new leg that she knows where Z is and she's going to lead us to him.

"Thanks for your help, Dugal." I wave a hand at him in farewell.

Dugal nods. "Our hopes and prayers go with you."

When we pass the tree line, Fury's pace picks up. I grab onto his withers and do my best to squeeze him with my thighs. But I am no experienced horsewoman, and I don't know how long I can last at this pace.

Just when I feel like the jarring pace will shatter me, the telltale feeling of a jump pours over me. Before I can wonder how we're jumping without Z, we appear in a field.

I look behind me to get my bearings and see the edge of the forest in the far distance, probably a few miles behind us. In the sky, now slightly behind our position, Roy soars, gaining altitude to get in front of us more easily. Fury's pace slows again. Somehow, and I have no clue how, Fury is still able to jump. But from what I can tell, he can only jump short distances.

My heart soars. We can reach Z faster now. I throw my arms around Fury's neck.

"You beautiful, brilliant horse!"

He whinnies in response.

I sit up, and the sun beating down on my face feels like a warm hug. A confirmation that I am not alone. I am being equipped for what lies ahead. And Elohim is my guide.

Fury picks up his pace again. I get the feeling he's trying to give me breaks between jumps. He must be as unsure about my ability to keep my seat as I am.

He gets up to speed, and then the feeling of the jump glides over me before we appear somewhere else. He gives me less of a rest this time before he accelerates again and ready for another jump.

Six jumps later, it seems ridiculous that I should be exhausted in any way—all that's required of me is to hang on. But the tension in my muscles from the effort to stay astride Fury is rapidly wearing me out. Not to mention that multiple jumps in a row is highly disorienting.

But Fury is a steady and confident force beneath me that gives me the encouragement to continue.

I sit in anticipation for Fury's pace to increase into another jump, but instead he heads over to a large downed tree and comes alongside it. He whinnies and turn his big head back to me, side-eyeing me.

I guess it's time for a break.

I dismount, and my legs want to crumble beneath me. I collapse onto the log and attempt to stretch away the tension. Taking a hefty swig from the canteen, I glance around—there's not much out here. I can still see a hazy image of The Range, the vast stretch of mountains that spans a large portion of the continent, in the far distance, but other than grass and the occasional copse of smaller trees and bushes, it's a fairly bland and even landscape. The Range was never visible from Glennlyle, so the further we get from it, the closer I get to Z.

I pull the satchel Dugal gave me off my shoulder to see if it conceals something edible that might lessen the hollow feeling in my stomach. Suddenly, a searing pain explodes within me and I scream, grasping my middle and curling in on myself. Fury's velvet nose nuzzles my head but I can't move. What is happening to me?

The sharpness of the pain subsides, leaving a dull ache in its wake. It suddenly dawns on me: This has to be from my connection with Z. It's the only thing that makes sense. My rasping breaths seem to echo in the silence.

Z is running out of time.

I stand on the log and practically throw myself onto Fury's back. Then he's off, as if sensing my urgency. My mind offers no reprieve from the pain that writhes like a snake in my chest. What is this agony Z must be enduring? Is this the leashing? Or is something else going on? What if in his weakened state, he was captured? What if Lyle has him? Will I lose someone else I love to Lyle's darkened soul?

"Faster, Fury," I yell over the rushing wind. "He needs us."

CHAPTER 21

Pain.

My only constant. Time is unknowable. I exist in a cold, dark place of constant agony. Ever resisting the clawed blackness that weaves and thrashes inside me—fighting for control.

My breaths are frantic and short, never deep enough to fill my lungs. My heartbeats are shallow and erratic—my heart as desperate for escape as my soul is. My thoughts are disjointed and crumbling, like trying to hold a sandcastle in your hands. I only get small glimpses of faces and faint, fleeting emotions that quickly get snuffed out by the dark beast within.

But a glowing azure gaze and ethereal, white-blonde hair stands out the most. I grasp for a name, something to call her, but names were the first thing to be suppressed.

Something nudges against the vault of my mind.

Something to do with water . . . but not a tangible thing, a title? No, a nickname . . .

Raindrop.

My heart pounds out a forceful beat in confirmation. My Raindrop.

I remember. She was hurt. Badly. But she's strong, so she lived, despite the injury.

My blood begins to boil. Remembering—

That's why I am here.

I need to make it right. To make those that dared to hurt her pay. My Raindrop.

I will bring about their destruction.

I will have revenge.

Something sharp tears across my chest. A growling bellow breaks loose from my throat. My arms pull on the chains holding me in place.

"I thought that might draw your focus," a nasally voice cuts through the fog of pain.

But first, I must escape. I blame my weakened state for my current predicament. That, and the constant battle against an unseen foe that craves my destruction by any means necessary. Even if it is at the hands of this sadist.

He leans in closer, and I lunge, snapping my teeth at him. Not my typical response, but the dark influence is dominant in me now. I get a backhand for my effort. I spit the blood onto the floor in front of me, adding to the pool that appears to contain more of my lifeblood than what remains within me.

"I know you are special," the voice chuckles maniacally, "which is why I will take my time with you. You will earn me a special reward if only I can crack open the safe inside you." He smiles, a sinister smile that oozes greed.

"Let's begin, shall we?"

And the scream tears from my throat as I am set ablaze anew.

CHAPTER 22

VALE

Two solid days of jumping, and I am dead on my feet. I don't know how Fury seems unfazed. He really is not of this world. And yet, somehow, he still manages to behave like a big babysitter at times.

Last night, he stopped and wouldn't budge. Insisting, in his nonverbal, dead-eyed horse glare, that I rest. Even lying down like he did the night on the beach so I would have somewhere warm to sleep. I swear he's more stubborn mule than horse at times. I was only able to sleep for a few hours, the nightmares quick to claim me. I suppose that with the dull ache of pain still in my chest, I should be grateful for any rest. The fact that I could sleep at all is just a testament to how truly exhausted I am.

Now, we wait just outside the town's boundary, hidden in the forest, while Roy scopes it out. The familiarity of the woods and the scent on the wind that used to smell like home do little to ease the pit of dread in my stomach. My memories of this place are a tangled web—pleasant memories full of joy and love are twisted with the barbed nightmares of loss and pain. It's not the same.

I am not the same.

Roy flies in low from the opposite direction of town, careful not to give away our position. Clever bird. Being an albino hawk, she's very recognizable. I wouldn't be surprised if she were spotted and led them on a wild-goose chase. Maybe if they are out looking for us, this will be the distraction I need to infiltrate the town and find Z.

Back from her mission to lead the guards away, she lands on my shoulder and grabs a few strands of my hair in her beak in a preening behavior. I know she's attempting to comfort me. She knows what happened here last time. She was as helpless to stop it as I was. I think we are both different now.

I am done letting my past dictate my future. I can't control what will happen in the coming times, but I will fight for the future I want. I can see now that I was made for such a time as this. Elohim has equipped me, and I will stop at nothing to save Z.

Roy takes flight, keeping low, and flits around in front of Fury before leading us through the trees. I say a prayer for strength and steel myself for what lies ahead.

Roy flies over to the old, two-story parking garage that's next to the town hall building. It's sat abandoned for years, seeing as none have the resources to operate vehicles, but Lyle and his cronies loved to make use of it for their little club of losers.

Roy circles overhead.

If Z is here, this is most likely where he'd be kept.

I clumsily twist onto my stomach so I can slide off Fury's massive frame. We stand at the edge of the forest, cradled by the darkness of the tree canopy.

"Please stay here." I stroke his velvety nose.

He snorts and stomps a hoof.

"I know, but we may need you to be our secret weapon. And right now, the garage entrance is blocked off and I am going to have to sneak in over the sides. You are just too big."

He lets out another snort but seems to begrudgingly comply. I make a beeline for the garage.

I avoid the main entrance, which is blocked off by old, rusted vehicles, and slip in by one of the concrete support pylons, sliding over one of the guardrails that line each level of the garage.

A shiver tiptoes down my spine. It's eerily quiet. Not just in the parking garage, but the town in general. It's as though this place has been bled dry of all life.

An awareness in me pulses, and I sense Z is close. I reach the center support wall and peek around the corner. Nothing. I run to the end that winds around to the next level, a little more experienced with my prothesis, thanks to Z. Still nothing. I run up the ramp of the next level and peer around the corner of the concrete wall. What I see stalls the breath in my lungs. The rush of blood in my ears makes me feel as though I am underwater.

Z is at the end, in the center of the aisle. His arms are restrained above him in a Y position, chained to opposite hooks in the ceiling. He's kneeling, or more like sagging in the chains. Even from this distance, I can see the glimmering pools of what I can only assume is blood all around him. Blood drips steadily from wounds on his chest into the growing pool.

He's been tortured, for who knows how long. A prisoner of the very man who took everything from me. My blood boils with a murderous rage that is like nothing I've ever felt before.

I run to him. He must hear my steps because he raises his head and solid black eyes greet me. In my haste to get to him, I almost forgot.

I am not just dealing with Z anymore.

"Z," I say softly.

He tilts his head, his eyes unblinking. So animal-like—curious and cautious.

"It's me, Vale. Do you remember?" One step closer. His muscles tense, and his stare is so icy, I can almost feel the frost in the air. Everything about his body language is preda-tory. Nothing of the Zion I love looks out of those black pools at me. My vision blurs.

I can't be too late.

I pause, pulling one of the pouches of olibanum resin out of my pocket. There's still hope. I just need to get close enough for him to breathe it in.

I take another step.

He pulls on the chains, leaning toward me. That's when I see his feet are shackled to the concrete. I hate to see him like this, but I might not be able to get close to him if he weren't in chains.

"Well, well, well," says a voice from my nightmares. "What a sweet surprise. My long-lost fiancée has returned."

Z growls at the newcomer. I swallow as I turn to face the architect of The Ruination.

He stands before me, a half dozen of his "followers"

behind him. He looks much like I remember. His head is now shaved, but the oily grey pallor of his skin and the dark circles under his eyes are just as I remember them. My mind flashes back to him standing in the town square, raising a gun to take from me the things I loved most. I shake my head to clear the image, unwilling to relive the horror that defined the course of my life for so long.

"What? Are you incapable of speech in my presence?" He glances around at his crew, who eagerly provide the tittering laughter he clearly expects. "Or did you lose your voice as well as your leg? Although it looks like you aren't doing too badly without the leg. Who did you whore yourself out to for that replacement?"

I don't respond. He doesn't deserve it. He's nothing but a pathetic worm who feeds off the misery and torment he causes others. Like a kid who pokes a wounded animal with a stick, eager to cause pain in a desperate attempt to ease the pain inside him.

"No matter, I have ways of getting you talking. Just ask the brute." He gestures at Z. "But for now, we can't have you running away again." He turns his head to speak over his shoulder. "Boys, bring me her leg."

Two of his lackeys move toward me, and out of pure instinct, I run the rest of the way to Z. If I can just get this powder in his face, then not all will be lost.

I fumble with the small bag, opening it. I am about two feet away, readying to empty the pouch in his face, when one of the guys grabs my arm. The powder disperses into the air, harmless and ineffective.

My eyes connect with Z right as the other creep comes up to my back, sliding a hand around my waist, and lifts me off the ground in front of Z. I reach for him while the first miscreant bends down to tear the prosthetic limb from my leg.

I am being hauled away when I hear Z speak something so softly, I almost miss it. And the word sets hope alight in my chest.

"Raindrop."

CHAPTER 23

I wake to a pounding headache, my cheek pressed into the cold concrete floor. The last thing I remember is the bite of a needle in my neck, and then the lights went out. My hands are bound behind my back with a scratchy rope.

But that's it. I don't know if I should be insulted or grateful that they think me so harmless and inept. I suppose they figure that without my leg, I am not going anywhere. And last time I was here, I was a flighty, harmless, naive girl. But that girl died when her family was torn apart.

I've spent the last three years barely surviving, and yet, somehow, growing into the Core of Perseverance I was destined to be. I had to reach the end of myself for the power of Elohim inside me to be fully realized. And it's in that realization that I see the overarching truth of my life—Elohim was always with me. Always faithful. I am a ball of clay that never left the hands of the potter. And He is faithful to complete the work He started in me. What darkness meant for my destruction, Elohim used for my strengthening. None of what happened to me was wasted. And that truth fills me with a bold confidence.

The silence tells me I've been left alone. I sit up to take in my surroundings and realize they dumped me in front of Z. Lyle likes to play with his victims, mentally and physically. He either witnessed me reach for Z and is trying to discover more about our connection, or wants me to see how dark Z has become and how helpless I am to help him. Or worse yet, he has no clue of our connection and is trying to intimidate me or scare me into his arms. The fact that he called me his "long-lost fiancée" makes me think it's the latter. Little does he know, I would snuggle up to one of the monsters in the dark, brackish water of the swampland if it meant avoiding him.

Z hangs from his chains, his eyes closed, head drooping. Everything in his posture screams defeat.

Hanging from one of the exposed pieces of rebar in the ceiling, directly above him, is my prothesis. Lyle must think himself so clever to taunt me with my prosthetic leg out of reach. I couldn't care less, if it weren't for the fact that I hid the second pouch of olibanum resin in it, thinking I was being clever by not keeping it in a more obvious place like a pocket.

I sigh. One problem at a time.

Grateful for my flexibility and my missing right lower leg, I open my arms as much as the rope will allow and squirm and wiggle my butt through, pulling my right leg after it, followed by my left, to bring my tied wrists together in front of me. On my hands and knees, I crawl a bit closer to Z and kneel in front of him. The iron smell of his blood permeates the air around him.

I bring my tied hands up to his face, maneuvering them

so I can cup his cheek with my palm. He jumps at the contact, but doesn't lunge at me. I raise his face to mine.

"Raindrop," his gravelly voice grates out.

"My Zion."

He closes his eyes, pressing his cheek into my hand. Seemingly relishing the contact as much as I do.

"You must go, before he comes back," he urges.

"Surely, you must know by now that I am not leaving you. Where you go, I will follow. Even into hell itself."

His black gaze pins me in place. "Can't you see it's hopeless? I am lost to you."

"I know it seems that way. But it's always darkest before the dawn. Your Prophets found something—a resin—that will help anchor you so you can resist the leashing and accept our bond." I glance up at the prosthetic limb hanging from the ceiling. "I just need to get it from my prosthesis so you can inhale it."

"Some resin can't fix me. I am filled with darkness. I can feel it, even now, fighting for control. It's like trying to swim through mud. It's relentless, and I am so tired. I don't even understand how I can be here with you now, other than I saw your eyes and they called me out of the depths of the pit that was holding me captive. But it won't last. If I was unworthy of you before, it would be reprehensible to bond with you now."

"Zion, you listen to me, and you listen good. The darkness you fight is not your identity, it does not define you. It can only win if you let it. Your identity is what Elohim gifted you. It's love! I know it's scary. Love is not safe. People leave, willingly and unwillingly. But you are a warrior, Z. So use that wild and beautiful spirit of yours to fight. Fight for your life. Fight for good. And fight for us.

Because I am with you, through good or bad. Even this moment together is better than an entire lifetime apart."

His expression is pained. I use my thumb to soothe away the lines on his forehead, trailing my fingers down his face to his stubbled jaw. I lean closer. He can do nothing to push me away. His black gaze is empty, but I feel a thousand emotions in the tension and anticipation that emanates from him.

"I love you," I speak into the hairsbreadth space between our lips, before I softly press my lips to his. His lips are soft but frozen beneath me. Either due to the shock of our first kiss, or he's still resisting. I am not eager to pull away, but I also won't take what he isn't ready to give. I begin to lessen the pressure of my lips against his, dreading the cool absence, but then he presses forward and his mouth takes mine with an urgency and desperation that rivals a man fighting in battle. I grip his neck as much as I am able with my tied hands and press myself against him, craving the comfort of his nearness. Even under the heavy tang of blood in the air, I can detect the scent of cedarwood and a fresh lake breeze that is all Z.

Something new smolders inside me at the passion of his claiming kiss. Z slows his lips, and the tenderness in his final kiss has me pressing in for more. My tongue grazes his bottom lip, and Z makes a low sound in his throat.

A hand fists in my hair and yanks me back from Z. I scream, and Z lunges against his chains. A guttural roar tears from his chest.

"You two-bit whore!" Lyle screams in my face. The stinging bite of his backhand across my face resounds in the air and blurs my vision as I fall to the floor. "You'd choose the monster over me? I have all the power here, woman!"

"YOU are the monster! How can you not see it? What

did the Amilign promise you to get you to sell your soul, Lyle?"

"You think you have it all figured out." He smiles fiendishly, his crazed eyes darting around. "But you know nothing about what it takes to secure power! The Amilign offered me a place with them and access to some of their resources if only I would take control of this town and be an extra set of eyes as they search for something. I merely report any strange findings to them and thus prove my value.

"So, when I told them about my newest prisoner with the black eyes, much to my delight, they knew exactly who and what he was. He is my final test—I am to break the Horseman, slowly, so he falls to the darkness. Then I will have proven myself and earned a place among them. Finally a part of the ultimate power in this world."

At least he doesn't seem to know about my role in all this. I get the feeling that the Cores are the "something" the Amilign are seeking.

At that moment, a familiar hawk's screech rends the air. Roy swoops into the garage, claws extended, and dives at Lyle, scratching, pecking, and tearing at his skin. He yells, and his cronies run to his rescue. He slaps at the air with his hands, desperate to keep her away.

One of his younger lackeys pulls a slingshot from his pocket.

"Roy!" I scream, praying she will flee in time. She turns at my warning, but instead of flying away, she heads to my prosthesis. She pulls it from the rebar so it falls to the ground, and as she turns to leave through the open sides of the garage, the slingshot releases. I hear a thud and see a burst of feathers before she tumbles out of the opening in the parking garage and spirals down toward the ground.

"NO!" I scream. Warm tears flood my face. I don't hear her little body hit the dirt, but my heart stutters in my chest as if I did. I get another slap across my face, and I spit blood onto the ground. Lyle fists his hands in my hair again and pulls me to my knees.

He leans in, and his putrid, rotting breath assaults my face. "You are MINE! You have always been MINE!"

"I have NEVER been yours, and I NEVER will be. No amount of force can change that."

A dark shadow passes over his face. And he leans close to my ear, despite my squirming to get away from him. "Who said I cared about what you want? Power is all that matters. And you, the rare beauty that you are, will be my chosen queen. The fact that you fight me only proves you are the right woman to be by my side. So please, fight harder, it only makes me want you more. Once I break that Horseman fully, I will have proven myself to the monks and I will receive a great gift of power bestowed only to those who are worthy. And I am definitely worthy. I have always been destined for greatness."

The maniacal desperation in his eyes is like a final nail in the coffin of his insanity. And I can't help but wonder at what point his bleak existence broke him so fully?

Hooves hammer against the pavement, and a horse whinnies from the ground. The yells and screams of men tell me Fury is doing his best to diminish Lyle's forces from outside the garage.

"Go," Lyle says to the few men in the garage, "see to the situation."

They leave to do as he says. Suddenly, Lyle forces his lips onto mine. I push and hit him to escape the vile assault. He pulls away with a sneer, and I smack him across the face with my tied hands. Lyle stands from his crouched position and pulls a gun from his belt, aiming it at Z, who's still straining against his bonds.

"No," I scream, and throw myself around Lyle's legs, causing him to fall back against the concrete and lose the gun. I scramble after it, but he grabs my leg and hurls himself onto my back, slamming my head into the concrete, stunning me. He stands up and retrieves the gun, giving me a swift kick in the stomach for my efforts.

Z's mournful howl echoes in the dingy garage. I lift my head, fighting against the dizziness that makes it hard to focus, just in time to see Lyle raise the weapon at Z. Lyle turns to me, gives me a sinister grin, and pulls the trigger.

CHAPTER 24

Lyle misses.

But he immediately prepares to fire again. His pistol appears jammed, and he curses while he fiddles with it.

Thank Elohim. Desperate, I look around for something, anything, to help me. In the drainage grate next to me, a tiny piece of old rebar sticks out. I grab the end and pull. I'm rewarded with a decent-sized metal pole.

I use it to help me stand, and then, with all my might, I swing it at Lyle's head while he's distracted. The impact and my instability on one leg sends us both flying. I crawl over to his unconscious form and pat him down. The thick lump in his jacket pocket conceals the keys to Z's chains.

I crawl over to Z.

"Raindrop." The nickname is a plea and an oath on his lips. "Your face."

I bring my hand to my cheek but resist touching it. The throbbing ache and my blurred vision tells me all I need to know about how I probably look.

"It's okay," I lie.

Z raises one eyebrow at me.

"I've had worse."

He flinches at the reminder.

I crawl behind him to unlock the shackles at his feet first. He stays still while I move around to his front. I stand and lean against Z for added stability to unlock his left wrist. Once released, he stifles a moan at the change in position, but brings his arm around my waist, holding me to him —clinging to me like a man to a life raft. I unlock his right wrist. Soon, both of his arms engulf me, and his face presses into my stomach. I bring my tied hands around his head. He looks up at me from his kneeling position. He says nothing and everything in his reverential dark gaze.

The cocking of a gun draws my attention. And before I can even turn my head to look over my shoulder, Z stands swiftly, lifting me in his arms and spinning so that his back now faces the danger and I am cocooned in the safety of his body.

The deafening boom of the gunshot echoes in the space, and Z's body shudders against me. He looks down at me, a valediction in his eyes.

"You have been my awakening. And my reckless heart has loved you, silently yet endlessly, all this time."

His feet stumble in his fight to stand as a barrier between me and Lyle, but he fails and crumbles to the ground, taking me with him.

A violent scream erupts from inside me, burning as it goes. As though it plans to rip everything to shreds on its way out of my throat, leaving me a cracked, empty vessel— hollow and without purpose. The scent of Z's blood on the air thickens, threatening to choke me.

I raise my eyes to Lyle. Rage rolls off me like the waves

of a wild storm that beats against the shore. A dam abruptly breaks inside of me, and an immense power floods my veins. I am an overflowing container as the power surges and swells within me. It's soothing and caressing, yet strong and unyielding. Steadfast and patient, yet determined and destructive.

Lyle aims his gun at me. On instinct, I raise my hands and notice small streams of water weaving around my wrists and fingers. The water glides between the rope and my skin, stretching the rope around my wrists, and gently loosens the knots so my bonds fall harmlessly to the floor.

Lyle is rooted in place with his mouth ajar.

I feel the nearness of my lake like a hum just under my skin. The sensation is familiar and comforting. It longs for me, and I instinctively call it to me. The water, vast and dominant, yields to me and obeys my command. It comes in the air on streams, gliding around me like a favorite blanket. Using this power feels similar to releasing a breath I've been holding for far too long.

First, it lifts me from the ground by Z, who lies too still, his breaths shallow and uneven. With only a thought, I fashion a liquid prosthesis for my leg that is soothing but somehow has a corporeal strength despite its fluidity. It moves with me as if it were always a part of me.

Lyle shifts on his feet.

With my stance grounded, I lift my hand again at Lyle.

He seems to remember himself as he cocks the gun again. Before he can pull the trigger, I send a jet stream of water at him. It gushes from the air all around us, pouring in from the open air outside the parking garage. It collects around Lyle in a fluid prison. The gun is maneuvered from his grip and ejected from the collection of water to fall harmlessly to the ground. Lyle flails and kicks, trying to get free, but there is no moving against the will of this living water.

My hands outstretched in front of me, I hold and manipulate the sphere of his watery prison. And when Lyle's form starts to jerk, in desperate need of oxygen, I send him flying out of the second story of the parking garage, softening his landing in the street with a liquid cushion but allowing just enough of a hit to render him unconscious.

I run to Z, falling to my knees next to him in an ever-growing pool of his blood.

"How do I help you, Z?"

"You . . . can't," he says too softly. "T . . . too late . . . for me."

This can't be true, not after everything we've overcome and fought for. I remember the resin and grab the prosthetic leg lying near Z. But the leg is drenched. With dread, I pull the soggy pouch of resin from where I hid it. It looks more like a chunky paste than a powder for inhaling.

No, this can't be happening. This was my last shot at saving him. This can't have all been for nothing. And I have been gifted Elohim's power now. The power of living water. Ancient words, unspoken, flow freely in my mind—*the river was her defense, the waters her wall*. I don't know how I know them, but something in my soul connects with these words, like a puzzle piece locking in place.

Maybe I don't need the resin after all. If I have this power, then that means Z has finally accepted the bond. I know what I need to do. Ever so gently, I call the water to lift Z and imagine an almost microscopic stream entering his gunshot wound. He stiffens slightly and moans, but otherwise lies still. I feel the water as it moves through the damage, finding the foreign object that tore into Z's back. The water begins to reverse the bullet through the path of destruction until it pops out of his wound and drops to the ground.

I manipulate the water to lay Z down again. Thanks to Ansel, I know only one thing can heal him right now. I just pray that the lock still in his seal will not interfere. I lie next to him, leaning my upper body over him. I draw his face to mine, and he looks at me through half-lidded eyes.

I bring my lips to his, and my love for him starts like a trickle before becoming a torrent that pours out of me. This kiss is a prayer, a claim, and a haven. I will him to be restored. The water that I am one with weaves around us both. It gently caresses Z's skin, cleaning away the remnants of his torture and pain. It continues its ministrations, flowing and surging around us both.

I keep kissing him—I won't stop until he is whole. But he feels as cold as the water around him. And in my desperation, I failed to notice his utter stillness. My heart seizes. My warm tears mix with the cool water that lazily flows around us. The anguish building in me bursts free, and the water scatters at my despair. It splashes against the concrete and flees into the open air.

I sit, my back against Z's prone form, and finally fall apart. Sobs rack my body, and I hold my head in my hands, as if I can keep the grief from tearing me apart.

Something moves up my back, and I quiet. It couldn't be. But it is—somehow. A hand reaches my neck and moves my hair over one shoulder. Then lips press against my shoulder. I turn and throw myself around him. I sob, releasing the pain, the fear, the dread, and the exhaustion, and letting the relief that Z's okay and it's all done wash over me.

I unbury my face from Z's neck, and the warm, honey-colored eyes that stare back at me cause my tears to start afresh.

"Raindrop," he says, picking up a strand of my soaked hair. "You really earned that nickname."

A laugh erupts from me, and Z leans in, stealing the sound with his kiss. One of his hands fists in my hair and the other comes around my back, holding me to him, even though I already sit in his lap. It's as if he can't get me close enough to him, and I am fine with it because I feel the same. The cold drops of water do little to cool the smoldering heat growing inside me. Everywhere Z's skin presses against my own, sparks ignite. This kiss is a declaration, and it's heady. He slows his assault on my lips and presses his forehead to mine. My chest heaves, and I try to catch my breath.

He looks down at my leg, his brow furrowed.

"What is it?"

"It didn't work," he says, "It was a fool's hope, anyway. I think I always knew it wouldn't work."

"What do you mean? What didn't work?"

"The healing? I had hoped my kiss would be able to heal you like yours did for me, and it didn't." He gently grabs my right knee in emphasis.

I didn't even think about that. Now that I have been gifted with the power to wield water, I'm not the least bit concerned about my missing lower leg. Elohim has made up for everything. Z just doesn't know it yet.

I lift my hand to his face, and his sad eyes meet mine.

"Don't you see, Z? I am already whole. I don't need any healing."

His eyes shine, and he kisses me again. Each time steals

my breath. He pulls away, presses a kiss to my forehead, and smooths my hair behind my ear.

"You better get used to that, Raindrop," he says with an air of mischief. "I need to make up for lost time." The twinkle in his eyes sends a thrill through me. And in a dingy, partially-decayed concrete garage, soaking wet, my joy is made complete.

CHAPTER 25

ZION

Despite Vale's protests, I carry her cradled against my chest as we wind our way down the ramps of the garage. I simply need her near—touching me. She is the remedy to the darkness. I see it plain as day now and I am kicking myself for ever resisting the gift she is to me—to this world really.

Not to mention, without full use of my powers with this damn lock in my seal, I am on high alert against any threats. I am still not sure how we are both alive. My memories of the events in the garage after I was shot are hazy—something I'll need to evaluate later.

Her hand presses against my chest over my heart, like she needs the reassurance of its steady beat, ignoring the chains that bind the lock in my seal. I place a kiss to the top of her head, and she sighs and snuggles in closer. To think, all along, I've possessed the ability to elicit such responses from her. That this connection is as much a gift to her as it is a tool of my redemption.

What a stubborn fool I have been.

She's healed now, but the memory of her swollen cheek from that monster daring to lay a hand on her—again—has me holding her a little tighter. I am absolutely bloodthirsty over what she's suffered. I almost fear the moment I see Lyle again. My desire for retribution threatens my reasonable judgment, and the most concerning part is . . . I don't care. For her, I would do anything—become anything.

"Z." She pulls my focus. "Your eyes are black again." An air of hesitation fills her voice.

"I'm sorry, Raindrop, I let my mind wander to things best avoided."

At my words, she stiffens in my arms, and a tear rolls down her cheek. "Roy," she says softly, choking on a sob. "She fell . . . defending me."

My wide eyes drop to hers. The grief shining out of them is a knife in my heart.

"I need to find her. I need to see her for myself. At the very least, I owe her a proper burial."

I hold her a little tighter, wishing I could take her pain away.

"She fell out of the west side of the garage," she says as we clear the dreary prison that was my home for far too many days and enter the open air of the town. We begin to head around the corner of the garage to where she saw Roy fall, but what I see roots me to the spot and enflames the rage I am trying and failing to dampen.

Lyle's cronies have somehow gotten a few ropes around Fury. Over a dozen men hold down the lines, and a few poke at him with pitchforks.

"Put me down, Z," Vale says in a voice I almost don't recognize.

I do as she says out of pure shock, forgetting we left her prosthesis in the garage. I hold onto her waist, expecting her to realize she's at a disadvantage without it, but then, before my eyes, water begins to collect beneath her stump, forming a watery prosthesis. She walks forward as if this is her new normal. I watch in awe as she raises one hand and jet streams of water begin shooting from all directions, sending men flying off into the distance. It's only a few moments before all the men are gone, leaving the ropes to hang from Fury's neck.

He trots up to Vale and pushes his head into her chest as she throws her arms around him. She plants a kiss between his eyes and whispers to him. Then he turns and takes off for me.

A warmth begins to pulse in my seal on Fury's approach, filling the cold, aching hollow that previously existed without him. I press my head against his and close my eyes, inhaling his scent. He's like a missing piece of my soul that's been returned. I am not me without him. But it's not finished yet—I can't call him to me until I get this lock out.

My eyes find Vale, and what I see incapacitates me. She stands in the sunlight, a simple white sundress accentuating the blue in her eyes. The fluid movement of her watery prosthesis only adds to the ethereal, otherworldly beauty that is naturally Vale. A mist seems to hover around her, as if drawn to her and ready at a moment's notice to be her defense.

She looks at her hands, at the streams of water she wears like bracelets, moving languidly around her wrists. She must sense my gaze because she looks up at me and smiles.

I am seeing the true Vale. Her purpose and identity are plain now, no longer hidden treasure waiting to be found. She is a beacon of light in the darkest of nights. And somehow, by the grace and gift of Elohim, she is mine and I am hers.

With Fury free, she takes off around the corner of the garage, and I follow. We round the corner, and there in a small patch of dirt lies a white-feathered body. Vale runs to it, and as we draw close, the feathered head lifts.

"Roy!"

Vale kneels down, gently lifting the hawk into her arms. Roy's wing seems injured, but she's alive. Thank Elohim. Tears shine in Vale's eyes as she brings her head close to the bird and Roy burrows against her cheek.

"Thank you, my sweet friend," Vale says.

Cradling her injured hawk in her arms, she heads toward me, and her beautiful smile radiates love for me—it is arresting.

Somehow, despite everything she's been through, her light has not dimmed—if anything, she shines brighter than ever. The awe I feel, that this incredible woman somehow loves me and chooses me, is humbling. Something wet and warm rolls down my cheek. Vale stands before me and lifts her free hand to wipe away the falling tear.

"I'm so sorry, Raindrop, for everything I put us through."

She gives me a smile that is wrapped in love and acceptance. "There's no need, my love. It was our journey. There were things we both needed to learn. Elohim did not let our pain be wasted."

My lips respond with a kiss in place of words I don't have. I splay my hand in her hair, holding her to me, and let the love, adoration, and passion I feel for her consume the kiss.

Roy lets out a squawk of displeasure at being in the

middle of our love sandwich, and I chuckle. I bring a finger up to stroke the loyal hawk who sacrificed her safety for Vale's. "And thank you, Roy."

The sounds of hoofbeats and a horse's snort fill the air behind me. Fury is standing next to us, so I instantly tense and pull Vale behind me, even though she's probably more dangerous than I am at this point. My innate sense of justice will never allow me to stop protecting her.

A red horse with two riders stands just past the garage, in the center of town, and I relax.

"We missed a lot, huh?" Cai says with a knowing smirk.

Vale peeks from around my arm. "You have no idea," she says with a wink. She walks around me, and the audible gasps bring a grin to my face.

Ansel's hands cover her mouth, while Cai's mouth hangs open.

"Your heavenly power is water," Ansel says with wonder. "It's absolutely beautiful, Vale!"

I lean down to Vale. My arm wraps around her waist as I bring my mouth to her ear. "You were always beautiful." She looks up at me, and unshed tears rest in her eyes. The world seems to fall away. I could spend forever in this moment.

A throat clears, and I'm beginning to loathe Cai's presence.

"Yes, Mordecai?" I say without breaking eye contact with Vale, making it clear who my priority is.

"I figured you might want the lock out of your seal," he says knowingly.

Vale and I both look to him and the key to freedom that rests in his hand. They both approach on Ginger's back. Ansel looks down at Roy in Vale's arms.

"What happened to Roy? Is she okay?"

"She's injured. Her wing, I think. She fell defending me." Vale gazes lovingly down at her wounded friend.

"I am pretty sure Dugal can help her. He seems to have an affinity for collecting and healing broken things." Ansel smiles. "If you think she'll allow it, it would be my honor to take Roy back to him for you. You know, while you deal with Z's lock."

I can see the hesitation in Vale's face about letting Roy out of her sight, but she must know it's what's best for her loyal friend because she nods. "They're going to take good care of you, and I'll be right behind you." Vale says to her feathered friend as she presses a final kiss to her head. She hands her off to Ansel, who carefully cradles Roy against her chest. The fact that Roy goes without complaint is a testament to how injured she is.

Cai raises his hand over his head and chucks the key to me. I snatch it out of the air.

"We'll leave you to it," Cai blurts. "Meet you back at Dugal's when you are ready." There's something unusual in his tone, but I am too distracted to dwell on it. And then they're gone, and I turn to Vale, placing the key to my freedom in her hands.

"You've already saved me in every way a man can be saved. It's only fitting you help restore me fully."

She blinks away the tears welling in her eyes.

I turn my back to her and drop to my knees. She rests a trembling hand on my shoulder. I sense her hesitation and cover her hand with my own.

"It's okay, you won't hurt me. Nothing can hurt me now that I am yours."

"If you're sure . . ." Her voice wavers. I feel the press of the key, and then the small spikes retract back into the main blade, pulling free from my flesh. To save her the unpleasantness, I reach over my shoulder and yank the blade free from my back. It scrapes bone on its way out, and I grit my teeth against the agony.

"Z!" Vale gasps.

Hot blood pours from the wound, but I am unafraid. I meant what I said. I sit in the dirt, legs crossed.

"Come here, Raindrop." My voice is rough with the anticipation of what I know will happen next.

She comes from behind me, and I pull her down onto my lap.

"You have the power to heal me."

A spark lights in her eyes, as if she suddenly remembers who she is and what she is capable of. Her lips crash into mine, and my hands trail up her back and the slender line of her neck. She shivers in response, and I feel it deep in my chest. Her skin is warm and silky in contrast to my battle-toughened skin, but it brands me like a hot iron pulled from blue flame. I feel the wound knitting itself back together. The blood has stopped pouring down my back, but I never want to feel space between us again. I take over and place reverent kisses on her cheeks, chin, nose, and finally on her forehead before resting my forehead against hers.

And like an arrow of truth shot from the heavens into my soul, I realize that this is true justice. In the face of unimaginable pain and grief, new life and new love has been born, made stronger and better having risen from the ashes of a past life wrought with devastation. What I wanted when I first arrived here, overcome with the darkness I was fighting, was revenge. My own retribution. I thought if I got it, I would be made worthy of Vale.

But, in fact, the opposite was true. Justice is seeing Vale whole, healed, and walking out her purpose in strength and confidence—a new creation. True justice is always intertwined with love, for justice without love as the anchor only paves the way for revenge.

CHAPTER 26

Being held by Z like this is a dream brought to life, and even though it came about through healing the wound to his seal, I never want to leave his arms. I've craved them for so long that now I am like a bear who's finally gotten her honeycomb.

We sit in the dirt, our foreheads pressed together while our breath intermingles. It feels like this precarious pause is a gift to finally allow us both to catch our breath after too long running. Running from something or running toward something—it's been a bit of both for me at different times. Probably Z, too.

Z's reverent touch, gentle and adoring, skims down my cheek to my neck. My hands are on his chest, cherishing the drum of his heartbeat—steady and strong—against my palms. This moment feels surreal. Like at any minute, I will wake and return to the nightmare that was my life.

"I'm afraid that if I move, you will disappear," I whisper,

afraid to speak the words too loudly and make them a reality.

"I'm not going anywhere. I will never willingly be far from your side ever again." The promise is laced with sincerity.

The familiar *thump thump thump* of a helicopter blade cuts through our reverie. I gasp at the recollection of what follows that sound.

Z stands with me in his arms and runs for the tree line.

"Baim Lyy," he whispers, and I watch over his shoulder as Fury disappears, once again a part of Z. He lets out a sigh at the merging. I reach my hand up to his jaw, and his eyes gaze down at me.

I smile at him. "You know I can walk now, right?"

"Old habits die hard," he says with a half grin. "Plus, I kind of like the feel of you in my arms."

Begrudgingly, he sets me down, and we duck behind the foliage to watch the black metal beast land in the center of town.

Eventually, Lyle makes his way, limping, to the helicopter. He's supported by two of his lackeys. We can't make out words, but a man in a dark brown robe climbs out of the machine, followed by a Silent. The wind whips his hood back, and I see he's bald and pale, with what looks like burn scars all over his face. But it's his inhuman, solid white eyes that have me shrinking back.

Words are exchanged, and the scary monk's demeanor changes, his face filling with rage. In one fluid movement, he pulls a blade out from under his robe, slashes out, and sheathes it as he turns to leave. The two men holding Lyle drop him and step back, clearly in shock, as blood flows from a wound in Lyle's throat. They tuck tail and flee as the Silent steps forward, picks up Lyle's body, and dumps it into the helicopter, like an old bag of junk. Then they are gone as quickly as they arrived, and I finally release the breath I've been holding.

I lean up against the tree, tilting my head against the rough bark, allowing the sensation to ground me. I close my eyes and take deep breaths. Then I feel Z's hand on my cheek, right before his lips press against mine. And I am reminded that we are safe and together, and that's all that matters for now.

"Are you okay?" He smooths the hair back behind my ears as he holds my face gently.

I nod. "It's strange, I should feel relief that he's gone. But instead, there's nothing. Just a sort of emptiness, and the old, familiar grief that surrounds any thoughts of him is still there."

Z nods knowingly. "Death never brings a relief-filled justice. There's a finality to it that may feel like relief, at least from the fear related to that person, but the utter permanence of it without hope for redemption or closure creates a sort of sadness. Not necessarily a sadness that an evil person is gone, but sadness that a life was lived the way it was and any hope for choosing a different path is gone."

I nod, somewhat dumbstruck at how Z so adeptly puts my thoughts into words. He's so in tune with me now that our bond is complete, but it gets me thinking.

"Why did we hide instead of fight, especially now that I have this gift?"

"Again, I blame instinct. It's hard for me to suppress the urge to keep you out of harm's way. It will take some adjusting on my part, if you'll just be patient with me." He pauses, glancing down before his gaze returns to mine. "Plus, after everything we've just been through, the thought of having to go through another battle, with so many unknowns, including a new power you're still learning to use, just felt like an unnecessary risk." His eyes implore me to understand.

I nod.

"I don't want to keep you from being who Elohim made you to be, but I also want to ensure your safety."

It's impossible to resist touching him, especially when he says things like that. I reach out to caress his stubbled jaw and move my thumb across his full lower lip.

His breath catches, and then his lips press against mine. The passion and love in the gentle caress sets my blood aflame with yearning. Z moans deep in his throat and pulls back, breathing heavily.

"This bond is going to kill me!"

"What do you mean?" My brows furrow.

"Now that our bond is solid, I can feel you. Not just here," he gestures to his head, "but here as well." He points to his heart. He stands, pulling me to my feet, and the water instinctively creates a prosthetic leg for my stump with barely a thought from me.

Z's arm comes around my waist, and he leans down to whisper in my ear.

"I can feel your emotions—your need and your desire— and it's like fuel on the smoldering embers in my veins right now."

I gasp at the revelation, and he pulls back to look at my reaction. I bite my bottom lip and feel the flush of my cheeks.

Z tips his head back and groans.

"What?"

"You really are trying to kill me, Raindrop."

I laugh. "Little ole me? Never! Did you ever stop to think that this is your fault anyway, big guy?"

Now it's his turn to look puzzled.

"You've resisted me for weeks. Building this need, anticipation, and craving." I walk slowly around him, trailing my finger across his chest, purposefully manipulating the water in the air to leave a trail of moisture behind at my touch. I trail it over his bicep and around the muscled expanse of his back before facing him again.

"I am the monster you created." I wink, and the honey in his eyes turns black.

On instinct, I gasp and step back, but trip over my feet. Z reaches for me, but before he can grab me, the water in the air collects and rushes around to prevent me from hitting the ground. It cradles me and lifts me to standing again.

"Never fear me." Z reaches for me, not to grab, but with an open hand, pleading—asking.

I take his hand. "I don't, truly. I was just surprised. Your eyes are black again. I thought the darkness was gone."

He pulls me to his chest. "It is, but there's something new in its place. I feel it, like an unending well of power. Ready to be commanded. And I sense it activates with high emotions or danger."

And suddenly, like floodwaters, the feelings of desire, need, adoration, and love slam into me, and if Z's arms weren't around me, I would've fallen over again. I inhale ragged breaths at the onslaught, and my eyes connect with his. This is what Z was talking about—those were his emotions he sent down the bond.

"Oh, wow." It's all I can say as my wide eyes absorb this incredible man who feels such intense emotions about me.

He leans in closer. "Yeah, wow." He winks and then presses a kiss to my forehead. And I feel a tad bereft that it wasn't my lips that received the gesture.

Z looks at me and tips his head back as a deep belly laugh erupts from him.

"Needy, much?" He smiles, and those glorious dimples I love are on full display.

"You have no idea." I scowl at his back as he turns to walk out of the trees.

He looks over his shoulder at me. "Yeah, I do, and that's the problem."

And now it's my turn to laugh. Oh, this is going to be fun. And after all we've been through to get here—the loss that has marred both of our lives—we're finally free of the chains that had us bound, and we're able to freely choose each other.

As we head back to the center of town, there's a stillness in the atmosphere and it seems as though all of Lyle's cronies bolted the moment the life was bled from him. Z suddenly pauses in front of me, tense. A lone figure stands in the entrance of a building, and I'm preparing to call the water to be my defense when a familiar voice pulls on the threads of a long-suppressed memory.

"Vale, is that you?"

Arlo stands, nervously wringing his hands. He's older, much older than his age should make him look. Like the burden of living in this place has stolen his life force.

"Arlo?"

He nods and comes out of his father's shop. He walks with a limp that he didn't have growing up, and I get the feeling his story is marked with grief, too.

I close the distance between Arlo and myself and pull him into my arms. He was my brother's best friend growing up, and seeing him again flings wide the doors of the memory vault I had locked tight. I can't control the tears that flow down my face.

Arlo clings to me in the same manner. "I'm so sorry, Vale, for everything. I never got to tell you, but I wish I would've said something that day. Stood up to him."

Sobs shake his frame. This is clearly a grief that's been weighing him down all these years. I remember looking back and wishing someone would've said something against Lyle, stood up to him. But they would've just ended up dead right alongside Mama and Rain.

"It's okay, Arlo, there's nothing to forgive."

He pulls away, vigorously wiping away the moisture from his face and trying to collect himself.

I grasp his arm and smile at the boy who grew up with me. "I'm so glad you're okay."

He hangs his head and sniffles again. "Yeah."

"Really, Arlo, you would've just been killed along with Rain if you'd tried anything. Lyle was unhinged. Nothing would've changed what happened. It took me a long time to put the blame where it belongs. Don't let him take anything else from you, my friend."

He nods at me. "Where's Ash?"

"I don't really know, but I hope to see him one day soon," I say.

"Wait, did Ash never find you?"

I shake my head, and he sighs.

"My mother helped heal Ash's injury and get you stabilized as much as she could, but as you know, her knowledge of healing is limited. I was with you and Ash at your home until Ash woke up. He was distraught and sent me away, saying he just needed to be alone. I went back the next day to check on him, and you were gone. He wouldn't tell me where or with whom. He barely spoke to me."

Arlo sighs and hangs his head again. "We both knew the only reason Ash was left alive was so he'd be leverage to keep you obedient once you were healed. So as soon as Lyle came to check on you, Ash's life would be forfeit. I watched him pack a bag and leave without a backward glance. That's the last I saw of him. Lyle killed Dad a year ago. I got shot trying to stop him. Mom's been bedridden since then. I fear she'll follow him soon."

My heart squeezes in my chest at what he's endured at Lyle's hands, and I am glad it's over. But I look around and realize this place is a ghost town now. A forsaken remnant of a life long ago extinguished.

"You need to come with us." I look back at Z, knowing that even with the distance between us, he's heard everything. He nods.

I turn to Arlo. "Both you and your mother. Are there any others we should bring with us?" I ask.

"None who are innocent," Arlo says. "All the others fled or were killed over the years. I tried to get Dad to leave, but he didn't want to abandon his store. He remained hopeful that things would get better until the end." A pained expression gathers on his face.

"There's nothing more for you here," I say, reaching out to grasp his shoulder. "It's time to bury the past."

A light begins to shine in his dull eyes, and I sense hope rising within him.

"Lavo Veshuv," Z says, and Fury stands before us.

"Um, what just happened? Who is that guy? Vale, are you sure you're safe?" Arlo rapid-fires his questions as he scowls in Z's direction.

Z's eyes flash black as he turns his back to us. I get a flicker of grief down the bond before he shuts it down. Arlo's questions about my safety probably hit Z harder than I could've expected. I let the love, adoration, and above all, the immense safety I feel in his arms fill me up, and I release it like a tidal wave over him. His hand reaches out to Fury, as if to steady himself against the barrage, and I know he got the message.

"Yes, I am a hundred percent sure, Arlo. This is Zion, the Black Horseman of Justice, and he is my providence."

Arlo stares, slack-jawed.

"Get some things together and tell your mother. Z will return for you in an hour's time. Will that be enough?"

Arlo nods, speechless, as he continues to stare at Z. I walk back to Z, drawn like a magnet. His back is still to me, and I reach my arms around his waist, pressing my face into his back and placing a kiss against his spine. His free hand comes to rest over the top of my hands.

"Let's get back to the apothecary," he says over his shoulder. "Then Cai and I will return for your friends."

Z lifts me onto Fury's back, hops up behind me, and we take off. And I watch as the place that left so many scars on me blurs into streaks of pale colors and disappears before my eyes.

CHAPTER 27

We reappear back in the shady, cool forest outside Dugal's apothecary. Only this time, no bombs are thrown at us and a mass of people bustle about the grounds, carrying goods and organizing supplies, it seems.

Something significant has happened.

Z jumps from Fury's back and looks around. He gets that unseeing look in his eyes that tells me he's communicating with his brothers. Nic and Cai both come running from inside the cavern.

"Z!" Nic yells before yanking him into a punishing hug. I never realized how close they all are. I don't know why—it makes sense, them having been together for over a hundred years, living in each other's heads at any moment, and enduring this same battle against the darkness. It must have been torture for them knowing that Z was partially leashed and hoping that I could fix it. Cai stands next to them, arms crossed over his chest.

"We're so glad you're okay, brother," Nic says. He walks

up to me as I sit atop Fury. "And you, Vale. Thank you for saving him."

I have never heard more than a handful of words out of Nic's mouth, and his sincere gratitude is so unexpected, I can only nod and awkwardly smile.

Z walks up next to him, pats him on the back, and then holds his hands out to help me down. I call the water to my stump instinctively as he lowers me to the ground. All the peripheral movement freezes, and everyone stares at us—me and my watery appendage, specifically. Lucia stands with Dugal, who is cradling Roy in his arms at the mouth of the cavern—both of them appear gobsmacked. Ansel stands with them, a knowing grin on her face.

I flinch. Maybe my powers were supposed to be a secret? I don't see Lucia and Ansel flashing their gifts around. But I don't have much of a choice if I am to walk. My gift is also my restitution. Z takes my hand and squeezes it reassuringly.

"Everyone," Dugal announces, "meet Vale, Core of Perseverance, mate to the Black Horseman of Justice, and, apparently, gifted by Elohim with the power of water. Let us honor her for her sacrifice and endeavor to save Zion and bring him back!"

Heat rushes to my face, and I know it's beet red. I bite my lip as cheers go up and claps reverberate through the air. I look at Z, and he kneels before me, but not before he winks, his lashes shielding a dark gaze. I sense his attraction through the bond. He places his fist over his heart as he bows his head. I feel his love, respect, gratitude, and devotion, and it brings tears to my eyes.

I couldn't talk if I tried, so I send my need for Z down the bond and he immediately stands and engulfs me in his embrace—hiding me and my tears from spectators. The din slowly dies down as people return to their tasks.

"Nic, do you have a second?" Z says as he turns to face Nic. Cai gives Nic a slap on the back on his way back toward the cavern.

"Yeah, what do you need?"

"We left a friend and his mother back at the town. I need you to jump with me to pick them up quick."

Nic nods, appears to mumble something, and suddenly a giant white horse stands before him. He's atop his mount in a blink.

Z is mounting Fury when I remember something.

"Z, would you bring back my prosthesis?"

He looks a bit puzzled at the request. "Sure, but why?"

"It's the first gift you ever gave me." I blush at the girlish sentimentality.

He nods and gives me a grin that highlights his adorable dimples before they both take off. There's a lightness in Z that hasn't been there before, and it gives my heart wings to see him like this.

Dugal heads my way with a smile on his seasoned face and cradling Roy, as if he knew I'd need to see her right away.

I bring a finger up to her head. "How is she?"

"A rare albino hawk—she's absolutely exquisite."

Roy chirps, as if agreeing with his comment.

I smirk at his quirkiness. "Her injury, Dugal, how's she doing with that?"

"She's doing well. Fortunately for her, it just so happens that I have a special love of birds. I made a brace for her wing. I also mixed up a special remedy to aid in her healing."

"Really? Oh, thank you, Dugal! I can't tell you how

much that means to me. I raised her as a hatchling, she's my oldest friend. She helped guide me to where Z was captured and even fought for me—that's how she got wounded."

The way she rests so contently in Dugal's arms tells me she knows a bird lover when she sees one. I breathe a sigh of relief at seeing her healing and well-cared-for. I bend down to kiss the top of her head.

"I'll come see you soon," I say to Roy. Dugal nods to me and heads back into his cavern with her.

I head over to Ansel and Lucia, who seem to be waiting for me. Ansel throws her arms around me before I can get a word out.

"I am so glad you're okay! And you saved the day all by yourself, too." She pulls back from our hug to look at me. "You fierce badass!" She winks.

I laugh. "Hardly. More like reckless and stubborn. But Elohim was with me, and it all worked out." I haven't really had time to contemplate everything that happened, but suddenly the vivid memory of Z hanging from chains, bruised and bloodied, fills my mind. When I try to force it away, it switches to the image of him shot and dying.

"Vale, what happened?" Lucia says next to me. She reaches out to my upper arm in a gesture of support. "You have that look."

"What look?" My brows pinch.

"The thousand yard stare that comes from remembering horrors you'd rather forget." The empathy in her eyes loosens my tongue. I get the sense she's experienced her share of horrors as well. It seems to be a common thread among us Cores.

"I found Z hanging from chains. He had been tortured by the man who took my leg."

Lucia gasps and covers her mouth with her hands. Tears

well in her golden eyes. Ansel looks absolutely murderous, and the slight crackling of lightning in her eyes suggests she might be struggling to control her emotions.

"With some difficulty, I was able to get him free. But Lyle caught us and shot him." All the emotions surrounding what we endured come rushing forward. Tears flow down my cheeks. "He was dying, and I knew hardly anything about how the bond worked. Only that he was partially leashed and I was the only one who could save him. I got my powers after he was shot, and I could only hope that it meant the bond was complete. After commanding the water to remove the bullet, I tried to heal him. At first, it seemed I failed. But here we are."

"Where's this Lyle now? I'll kill him," Ansel practically snarls.

"You can't, he's already dead. The Silent arrived with some creepy, robed bald guy with burn scars and white eyes—"

"Drystan," Lucia murmurs in a hushed tone. Her eyes are wide, and her skin turns pallid.

"He was quick to cut Lyle's throat and haul his body away."

"Wait," Ansel blurts, her forehead wrinkling as she begins pacing. "Why would he take the body?" The question seems rhetorical. But then her gaze snags on Lucia, and her demeanor shifts.

"Lulu, you good?"

"Uh-huh." Lucia's gaze is faraway. "I'm just going to go sit down for a bit." She wraps her arms around herself, as if she can hold herself upright, and wanders off into the trees.

Ansel heaves a sigh.

"Is she okay?" I watch as she leaves.

"Yes and no," Ansel replies. "She bears scars like all of

us, but the one involving Drystan is most recent and haunts her nightmares most frequently. He's a special level of depraved monster."

"Yeah, I think I got that from my brief observation." A chill runs down my spine at the memory of him.

"He held Lucia captive for a brief time. Nic found her and saved her before any permanent damage could be done, but the mind is a funny thing, and nightmares can resurface at the most unexpected times."

My gaze wanders back to the forest path Lucia disappeared down.

"She lived with monsters and got very good at blending into the shadows, but after she escaped and then was recaptured, things were different. She'd discovered that they planned to use her to breed their twisted demon offspring—"

Now it's my turn to gasp.

"And Drystan was the one that *prepared* her for the ceremony." Ansel makes quotation marks with her fingers on the word *prepared*.

I blanch at the revelation. She looks to where Lucia left, and a marked grief fills her eyes. She turns on her heel, picks up a box, and stomps off into the cavern. And I get the sense that Ansel is the type that needs to stay busy in the face of her grief.

I head off in the direction Lucia took, and it's only a few steps into the dense canopy before I see her sitting on a log in the woods. She's staring off into the distance, and I take a seat next to her. We sit together in silence. I am content to just be here for her—let her know she's not alone. Be the anchor I know I've needed when nightmares come to claim me. I twirl a blade of grass in my fingers.

"He's a vessel," she says so softly I almost miss it. "It's

why he looks the way he does. At least that's what Elias thinks. A vessel was once a human but is now host to the demon living inside them."

I nod, giving her space to continue.

"I am lucky, really. I have no permanent damage, not like what you went through."

I lean to the side and gently bump her shoulder with my own. "Let's not compare hardships. We both know there's different types of scars, whether visible or not. And I often find it's the invisible ones that cut the deepest."

A tear rolls down her cheek. "I'd almost allowed myself to forget that he's still out there. And I hate that just when I think I've put it all behind me—"

"—some newbie comes up and mentions him, and everything comes rushing back like it just happened," I finish for her.

She gives me a grin that doesn't reach her eyes. "Something like that. It's harder when Nic isn't around, not that that's very often."

I laugh. "Z has already informed me he won't be leaving my side willingly."

"Yeah, they are a protective and possessive bunch, aren't they?" She smiles, a genuine smile this time.

I reflect on my story and what I know of Ansel's and now Lucia's stories. "I find it kind of amazing that although Elohim created us to be a force for their redemption, I feel like it was Z who saved me. Maybe not in the most literal sense, but he saved me from living my life as the wandering wraith I had become. I don't know, maybe that's just me."

"No, it's not. Nic saved me in a way too. He did save me literally, but my life was a blank canvas before him. And he's spent the past few months we've been together filling it with color."

"I am sorry for what you went through, Lucia."

"Likewise, Vale." She gives my hand a squeeze, then bends down to pluck a blade of grass from the dirt and begins tying it in knots. "You know, it's stupid, really. I know Drystan can't touch me again. I would light him up like a bonfire if he even came near me." And the fiery glow emanating from her eyes tells me that's not just a metaphor.

"But I can't control the emotions that rush back at the memory of what happened. Those feelings of helplessness and terror."

"It's not stupid. I get it. Really, I do. Lyle took everything from me, and even though he's gone now, just the thought of him makes me sick to my stomach. It's a physical response that I can't control."

She leans her head on my shoulder, and we sit like that in silence. Sharing in the comfort of a sister who knows what that kind of pain and grief does to a person. The way it marks you. All of a sudden, Lucia sits up and looks in the direction of the camp.

"Nic," she mumbles.

A few minutes later, he appears on the path that leads to our current spot. Lucia gets up and rushes to him. She leaps into his arms and wraps herself around him. He holds her to him and buries his face in her neck. And it's like even the forest around us lets out a noticeable breath in the relief of their connection.

They leave the forest's canopy of tightly woven branches, and I stay on the log, closing my eyes and soaking up the peace that seems to be like a rare bird drifting ever closer to extinction. I feel the water all around me, an anticipatory presence. It's in the ground under my feet, in the air all around me, and flowing through a small brook about a mile away. I hold my hands out in front of me, the blade of grass forgotten, and call the water in the air to collect. It forms a thin tendril that snakes around my hands and weaves in and out of my fingers. It's almost effortless, the way the water obeys. I tell it to disperse, and it turns into mist before my eyes and dissipates back into the air.

A feeling of amazement comes down the bond, and I look around to find Z leaning against a tree, watching me. The shadows seem to cling to the Black Horseman of Justice.

"You're incredible, you know that, right?"

I smile and stand, instantly forming my new watery limb. "It's not me, Z. This gift from Elohim is incredible."

"No, Raindrop, you were incredible long before the gift of water was given to you. It's your steadfast determination in the face of impossible odds and an obstinate Horseman." He winks as he draws closer to me. "You amaze me. Even when I had long ago given up, you never did. You were the lifeline I didn't know I needed, and you dragged me back to myself with your sheer stubbornness. It's the most spectacularly implausible gift that someone as magnificent as you should be mine."

I close the distance between us and walk right into his chest, putting my arms around his waist and pressing my head against his heart. His arms come around to hold me, and I relish the ability to touch him like this whenever I want to.

Someone clears their throat, and we both turn to face Cai. "We need to talk." There's a seriousness in Cai that is rarely present. We follow him, hand in hand, to the clearing. Nic, Lucia, and Ansel wait with Dugal. Interestingly enough, I have yet to see Dee since my return. I can't help but wonder if she's made herself scarce now that Lucia is here. A somberness hangs over the group and it makes me wonder if maybe Lucia did find out about Dee. But then Cai turns his attention solely on me and Z.

"We wanted to give you time to recover after your ordeal, but frankly, we can't wait. There's no easy way to say this, but you both need to know. The Refuge fell to the Silent . . . and they have Elias."

CHAPTER 28

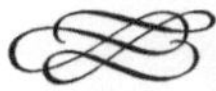

I glance up at Z and am unsurprised to see an obsidian gaze staring back at me. The deep agony coming down the bond has me pressing closer to him—anything I can do to offer my support. Remind him he's not alone anymore.

He gives my hand a gentle squeeze.

"Okay, so now that we're all together, it's time to strategize how to get him back. Throw out ideas—nothing is off the table." Ansel has that single-minded look on her face. Like a dog with a bone, she won't be deterred.

"What do we know about where he's being kept? And where's this mysterious fourth Horseman? Shouldn't we have the whole motley crew together for this?" Ansel looks around the circle at each of the guys.

"Mav can't help us," Nic states. "He can't even be reached. We think he's found the fourth Core, because that's the only thing that would keep him away. As for why he's unreachable, we don't know, and the only one who might be able to answer that is Elias."

"And we know nothing about where he's being kept in The Refuge, if he's even still there." Grief pours from Cai. "He surrendered himself to give us time to evacuate the others."

"I don't understand." My brows pinch. "There were two Horsemen and two Cores with heavenly gifts there, right? How did they even stand a chance against you?"

"They came with over two dozen Silent, relentless in their mission to raze our Refuge to the ground." Nic's inky black gaze pins me in place. "We took out a dozen of them while the people began trying to evacuate through the secret entrances. But then the Silent showed up with reinforcements. Elias said that our best bet was if he met them face-to-face, under the pretense of negotiating while we continued jumping our people to safe locations—his only priority was saving our people.

"He wouldn't hear of the girls separating from the Horsemen to use their powers to hold the Silent back; he thought the risk too great. He told us the plan was only to stall them. But when we came back for him, Legion had arrived with more Silent, and they were leading Elias into The Refuge. He used the mental link to tell us to keep our people safe and that this was his sacrifice to make."

My throat thickens at what Elias's sacrifice could mean for him. But something else Nic said stands out in my mind. "Who is Legion?"

"He's the leader of the Amilign, and based on what information we've been able to glean about him, he's an upper-level demon," Nic explains.

I swallow past the knot in my throat. This world almost doesn't feel real, and yet I've experienced too much already that I know it is.

"We came here with most of our people and to see if

you needed support, but you had already taken care of business all by yourself." Cai smiles in that brotherly way of his, pride in his eyes.

"So do we have an estimate on how many Silent are remaining at this point?" Ansel asks.

"When we left, our estimate was around thirty." A familiar feminine voice drops that number like a bomb, and we all sit in the silence of the aftershock as the newcomer with corkscrew white hair arrives, a few rolled-up scrolls of paper in her arms.

"Sida!"

She drops the scrolls right before I wrap her in a hug.

"Oh darling girl, I'm so glad you're okay."

"Me! You were the one who was shot. I was so worried about you."

"I'm tougher than I look." She winks and gives me that familiar smile, leaning close for only my ears to hear. "I see the fog has lifted from you. The light of Elohim has finally burned it all away. You have truth now, don't you, my dear?"

I smile at her and nod, unsurprised by her uncanny ability to see me and the things I never spoke aloud. She nods in return, pleased, before looking back at the group. "I brought a blueprint of The Refuge to help with the planning. A few of us were able to grab some of the important documents and scrolls when we were being evacuated. I figured these might come in handy."

I look around at everyone's faces—a mix of determination, frustration, and rage stare back at me. But no fear. Together, operating in Elohim's purpose and gifting, there is no place for fear any longer.

"I can't use my flames because they would not only destroy everything, but without being right in the room with

Elias, I couldn't ensure his safety." Lucia fidgets, clearly uneasy with the limitations.

"And I don't know if I could do much good inside The Refuge. I've never directed lightning inside of something or even wielded it inside."

Looks of deep concentration grace every face in our group, as if the solution that will save Elias lies just beyond their reach. And I suddenly realize, I am the only one with a gift that is both defensive and offensive. My gift gives life and takes it. It is not just a representation of Elohim's power, but it is a representation of His love and life—it is cleansing, healing, and redemptive in its nature, too.

The answer is glaringly obvious. I am the only one who can save him. Z tenses beside me as he senses my emotions. And he is trembling. Everyone's eyes seem to find him, detecting the change in his demeanor.

"No," he says softly, his expression pleading but resigned. As if he already knows it's futile to ask me not to go.

I reach my hand up to his jaw, and he presses his face into my hand. I smile at him. "With you by my side." That seems to calm him, and the shaking ceases.

"What are we missing?" Ansel blurts out, impatience evident in her tense posture and fidgeting hands.

"I can save him."

"Explain," Nic says without preamble. Sida smiles at me in that secretive way of hers that suggests she knew what I would choose all along.

"My gift is the only one that is not solely destructive. And when I was fighting to release Z, I held Lyle in the water until he reached his limits of holding his breath. With my connection to the water, I could sense his body's response to the lack of oxygen. I knew just when to release him so as not to kill him. I believe I can flood The Refuge, then use the water to isolate Elias and move him towards an exit. With a little help to understand the layout, of course."

Wide eyes and gaping mouths are what I get in response. But then they shift to smiles and eyes that are no longer black. Except for a certain stoic Horseman standing next to me.

"This just might work!" Ansel says, wringing her hands.

"We can review the layout of The Refuge for you and go over all the exits. That way, based on Elias's location, you'll know the best exit." Cai is practically giddy as he strategizes. "We will all accompany you to act as distractions and defense."

"Zion," Cai says, "you can communicate with Elias through our mental link as the events unfold." Cai slaps Z's back, totally ignoring the fact that Z's eyes are still black.

"I'll gather some supplies," Ansel says.

"As much as I hate to say it, I'll stay here and gather some of our healers and supplies to prepare for his arrival," Sida says.

"Darn right you'll stay here, you are barely recovered!" Lucia adds. "We'll also need some first aid supplies to take with us—we don't know what state Elias will be in when we get to him." She follows Ansel and Sida into the cave where Dugal is at work, and Cai and Nic huddle together next to a makeshift table as they pore over a blueprint.

With everyone focused on their tasks, Z turns, my hand still in his, and leads me past the tree line—out of sight from the group. He's blocked me from his emotions, but the tension in him gives me pause.

Once we are shielded from prying eyes, he lets go of my hand and takes a step away from me. His hands shakily slide through his hair that's grown out a bit since our first meeting.

"Z, I—"

Before I can say more, he turns, and his lips collide with mine in a kiss that's fueled by pure desperation and need. One of his hands tenderly cradles my head while the other snakes around my waist, bringing my body flush against his. He finally opens the bond, and his emotions hit me like a tsunami—panic, worry, shame, amazement, gratitude, dread, and longing. I cling to his neck and try to anchor myself—it's all I can do to endure the onslaught.

He finally pulls away and presses his forehead to mine, breathing heavily.

"I can't . . . I don't . . . " he stutters and stops, squeezing his eyes closed.

"Z, we can do this." I cup his jaw. "Together, we can do anything. That's the greatest gift Elohim gave us. This incredible and beautiful bond. Together, we are healed, whole, and a force of nature."

He lets out an audible sigh and opens his eyes. "I don't deserve you."

"Not true! And clearly, Elohim agrees with me, because I am yours—body and soul."

He gives me a soft, tender kiss that is adoring and patient, like a flower opening its petals to the caressing rays of the sun. It renders me speechless.

He pulls back with a smirk and runs a knuckle down my cheek.

"Let's go save the day, my champion."

CHAPTER 29

The plan is set.

Vale is confident, ready to walk out her purpose and make a difference. I sense this is about more than just helping Elias—she's proving something to herself too. Which is why I am doing my best to rein in my apprehension over this whole situation. I just became whole, after months, even years, of fighting, and now I am about to put this precious gift and my reason for existing back into harm's way. Vale has faced so much in her short life, and it feels wrong that she must do this now. It's eating me alive.

I lock the bond down a little tighter. She doesn't need to deal with my emotional state right now on top of everything else. I only want her head in the game.

We stand in the forest, just beyond the cliff's edge that hides the facade of The Refuge. Everyone knows their roles and positions. Each couple will take a position on either side of us, back from the cliff's edge, but close enough to see Vale and provide additional support with their powers as needed. That will also allow Nic and Cai to intercept any Silent that escape from the additional exit hatch hidden in the trees. I will guard the one we'll be using to rescue Elias. Vale is chatting with Cai as he gives her one of his warrior pep talks.

"Are you okay?" Lucia says with a hand on my arm, somehow sneaking up on me. Which only testifies to my distracted mind.

This is the first I've been able to speak with her since she helped me back at The Refuge. She was an anchor every time it seemed like the darkness was going to win. She helped me cling to my sanity as I moved ever closer to a line I wouldn't be able to come back from. And yet, because of Vale, somehow I did come back from it.

"I will be, thanks Lucia. And I don't think I ever adequately expressed my gratitude for what you did for me at The Refuge. If it weren't for you, I might not be living out this impossible dream."

Her smile brightens her face. "It was my great honor to help you." She pats my forearm. "She'll be okay, you know. Not only is she tough as nails, but she is one of the most resilient people I've ever met. I would hate to be on the other side of her fury."

"I know, trust me. But it goes against my nature to let her walk into the lion's den after everything she's suffered. I am the Horseman of Justice—and this is the opposite of justice."

"I get it, Z, but that's where you are wrong. This is what she was made for. There's no greater justice than her being able to live the life she was meant for."

The truth of Lucia's words lifts a weight off me, and I tug her in for a hug. "Thank you."

Nic heads over on Adira. "Any word from Elias?" He pulls Lucia up to sit behind him.

I shake my head. "I can't get through. I sense he's alive, but it's like he's not available."

He gives a grim nod, unsurprised. "Same, for Cai and me."

"Then we move forward without his knowledge of the plan. Let's take our positions."

Nic puts a fist to his chest, a sign of our dedication to each other and our mission, and rides away as Vale approaches.

"Are you ready?" she asks.

"If you are, then I am."

We are going for stealth, so Fury is with me—for now. Cai and Ansel jump, immediately followed by Nic and Lucia, and then we are alone.

We move past the tree line to the top of the cliff above The Refuge. Not only is it where one of the secret exits lies, but Vale thought it would be easier to move the water through the layout if she were positioned directly above it. I suppose it's like looking down on the blueprint.

She closes her eyes, and everything is still. She lifts a hand, and the rush of water replaces the silence. I look to the training field and forest just beyond the ancient indigenous facade that hides the entrance to The Refuge. Streams of water move from the direction of the river, but also from other directions—she must be calling water from even greater distances.

I glance at her and startle at the brilliance of her now open eyes. The blue appears to be glowing and looks fluid, as if it's actually water flowing around her pupils. A haze of mist surrounds her, and water weaves between her fingers and around her outstretched hands like threads of wool. She raises her arms to the sky, and the water holds in a wall directly in front of The Refuge—building and cresting.

Then, all of sudden, she slams her hands down by her sides, and the water surges forward, like the breaking of a dam, and crashes into the front of the cliffside. A look of concentration pinches her brows, and her hands are out in front of her. One looks like it's holding while the other makes a pushing motion.

"Well, that's something you don't see every day." Cai's voice slides into my head.

"Incredible." Nic's tone reveals his awe.

"Any movement from your vantage points?" I ask.

"Nope," Cai says.

"Nothing yet," Nic states.

"Z," Vale grits out through clenched teeth. *"It's working. It's slow with that sturdy front door, but I am pushing in through the cracks. It won't be long now."*

"Vale is in, be ready," I send to my brothers through the link.

"I found him! He's not conscious. And there's only six Silent in there."

Wrath ignites inside me, and the new power that I've been gifted with floods my veins, preparing me for battle. I hear the slide of the trapdoor from the clifftop exit, and I pull the sword from my back.

"Clifftop exit opened," I send to my brothers. Make that seven Silent, I think to myself, preparing to engage.

A cool resolve slides over my skin as a monstrously large Silent climbs out of the hole. He eyes Vale, and the covetous expression that fills his face has me moving to block his view of her. I am all that stands between him and Vale. Before he's even clear of the hole, I shoot forward, swinging my sword down at his head. He quickly drops back into the hole, and I connect with rock. In the seconds it takes me to lift my sword, the Silent jumps free of the exit as if propelled and stands before me, pulling two long, curved knives from his side. With dizzying speed, I lunge, slash, and slice. This power in my veins makes everything effortless, and I don't even break a sweat.

Another head starts to clear the exit in the ground. I need to end this guy now. Who knows how many more outran Vale's water.

"TAKE COVER," Cai's voice yells in my head as static causes the hair on my arms to rise. I dive behind a boulder right as lightning strikes the Silent, dropping his smoking corpse where he stood. Then flame suddenly erupts around the exit, making it nearly impossible for anything to leave.

I sheathe my sword and turn to Vale. She's dropped to her hands and knees in the dirt. I rush to her side.

"Raindrop!" The panic rising in me threatens to take control. I scan her for injuries.

She looks up at me, and the dread on her face almost knocks me over. "He's chained to a bed."

The words hit me like a rockslide, and it takes all my resolve to not let it topple me to the ground beside her. It's not just the fact that they would dare chain him and what that means for what he's been enduring these past few days, but no bed is getting maneuvered through the halls of The Refuge, let alone through the tiny emergency exits.

Elias is trapped.

CHAPTER 30

ZION

The realization slams into me—I need to go in and break the chains, then Vale can get him out. It's the only path forward.

"I'm going after him."

Wide, glowing azure eyes look back at me. But she doesn't speak. She knows we're out of options.

"Kill the flames," I send down the link. *"And someone get up here to guard Vale."* Almost immediately, the flames die and the sound of hoofbeats fills the air as both Ginger and Adira approach. Resolve steels my blood as I stand before the smoking ground around the exit hatch.

"Wait," Vale says, extending a hand. Her eyes flare a bright blue, and water fills the hatch, bubbling over. "I have all the Silent. Jump in, and I'll carry you to him."

I nod. Arms tight across my chest, I spare a final glance at her, with a perimeter of Horsemen and Core guards around her. I send my love, trust, and confidence in her down the bond. She sends the same back to me as I jump into the cold, dark water.

It's disorienting and nearly impossible to see. I know this is the storage closet, but with all the items from the closet, plus debris and dirt, floating around, I can't see through the murky water to get myself out. But suddenly, I am moving. A current wraps around me like a loving embrace and carries me, feet first, through the door. I pass a body on the way, one of the Silent. The current picks up, and I am rushed through the halls at a dizzying speed. Then I am unceremoniously spat out of the jet stream onto my hands and knees.

I look around the small bubble Vale created for me. Just to the right of me sits a metal bed frame holding Elias's prone, unconscious form. The mattress has been removed, and multiple cables connect the metal bed to what looks like a giant box with a switchboard.

A gush of emotion hits me in the chest—they were electrocuting him. My rage is a tangible beast, and I take a shuddering breath to rein it in. I allow the berserker power, as Nic likes to call it, to take over, and I break the metal chains that connect Elias's wrists and ankles to the bed. I check his pulse, praying that we aren't too late. A soft but steady heartbeat flutters against my fingers.

Thank Elohim.

Other than a few cuts and bruises, Elias has no noticeable open wounds. But that doesn't speak to any internal damage. I pick him up carefully, and just then, the bubble shudders and shrinks rapidly. The walls waver, and water splashes across my face. Watery walls ripple before solidifying and moving away from me to their original position.

What was that all about?

"Tell Vale we're ready," I say to my brothers, but the

message is blocked. The link is dark. That happens when they are too busy focusing on something to allow distractions, which can only mean one thing . . . they are under attack. Now the unstable bubble makes sense. I swallow my dread to focus on the task at hand.

Holding Elias, I look around, trying to discern which room we are in. It's one of the spare bedrooms, though that's not very revealing considering how many rooms this place holds. The bedroom is either nondescript or all the decorative touches have been cleared from the walls by the water. The only option is to trust that the minute I get in the water, Vale will sense it and be able to carry us to the exit. Which means I need to trust my brothers and their Cores to be able to handle whatever is happening out there.

Saying a prayer to Elohim, I take a deep breath and surrender myself to the water. It surrounds me as I push toward the door, half walking and half swimming with Elias in my arms. The hallway is dark and could be one of any number of pathways through The Refuge. I think of Vale and shoot a wave of love her way. The water current picks us up and begins moving, right as a much-needed air bubble appears around our heads.

She carries us to the northern exit that lies deep in the bowels of The Refuge. It hasn't been opened, which means that no Silent have come this way. I press the button on the wall next to the door, and it slides open. A long set of chiseled earthen stairs lead upward, but with no light, it's dark and seemingly unending. Vale holds the water at the door. It's not wide enough for me to carry Elias in my arms, so I gently maneuver him over my shoulder, hoping no damage was done to his internal organs, and step out of the water to begin the ascent.

Behind me, the water sloshes and roils as I imagine the

horrors that are potentially fighting for Vale's focus above-ground. I begin taking the stairs two at a time, trying my best to hurry without jostling Elias too much. But he doesn't stir.

This has to be the longest stairway in the world.

A slightly glowing button on the wall to my left illuminates the cramped space. I pull a knife from the sheath at my thigh and slam my fist into the button. The trapdoor slides open, and I climb out into the sunlight. Two bolts of lightning strike, one right after the other, directly behind me.

"Lavo Veshuv," I whisper, and Fury appears before me. I gently place Elias over his back and hop up behind him. We take off in the direction of the strikes. The clashing of blades soon becomes louder than the pounding of Fury's hooves across the terrain.

The trees thin, and I see the edge of the cliff that The Refuge resides in. Lucia stands, surrounded by her flames, sending fireballs at a Silent trying to work his way past her fiery shield. Ansel sends strike after strike down, succeeding at sending Silent fleeing, and causing rocks to explode, but not getting close enough to do any real damage. Cai and Nic fight with blades, engaging any foes that come too close to the Cores. They all fight with fierce determination to protect each other and Vale.

And it hits me, what a fool I was to think I was protecting myself and others by distancing myself from those I love. All I did was make it easier for the darkness to dig its claws in. The way an animal is most vulnerable when it steps away from the herd. It's not alone that we are strongest, but together.

Vale stands at the edge of the cliff, her blonde hair whipping in the wind. Her fluid prosthesis is luminous with sunlight, and her liquid eyes appear to glow. I am undone by her ethereal image. She has one hand pointing toward the ground, commanding the water inside The Refuge, and the other hand outstretched, controlling the jet streams that protectively weave around her in a complex and aggressive pattern. One of the Silent sneaks toward her, and just when I am about to yell and rush off on Fury to protect her, she sends a surge of water that sends him flying from the edge of the cliff.

Fury gets closer, and I hop down. "Keep him safe," I say to Fury, who moves carefully behind the foliage with Elias to keep him hidden. I run the rest of the way, trying my best to stay out of sight to maintain the element of surprise, but when I get close, I notice there are only two Silent left. One is simultaneously fighting Nic and Cai while Lucia stands ready with flames in her hands. A steaming body lies by Ansel's feet, and I am guessing she finally hit her target. The last Silent circles Vale in the opposite direction her water flows. And if it weren't my Core he were stalking, I might be impressed by the strategy. It'll be harder for her to hit a moving target with her concentration divided. And Ansel won't risk a strike so close to Vale.

If I could just get her to see that I am safe, that she doesn't need to hold the water in The Refuge any longer . . . I send that longing for her gaze down the bond, and her eyes lift, searching the area, and land on mine. Without faltering, she pulls her hand from the ground and toward the sky, palm up, causing water to erupt like a geyser out of the trapdoor by her side.

The Silent pauses at the display of power, and seemingly realizing he's the only one left standing, turns on his heel and runs—right in my direction. Staying behind the cover of a tree trunk, I grip the tip of my blade in my fingers, pull it back over my shoulder, and throw. The blade sinks right into the eye of the Silent, and he drops like a brick.

I step out from behind the cover and give a sharp whistle. Fury carefully walks toward me while the others head in my direction.

"You got Elias, thank Elohim," Nic says with an audible sigh.

Lucia rushes past him. "Is he okay?"

"His pulse is steady, but we won't know the extent of the damage until we get him back to Dugal's," I say.

Vale wobbles towards us on unstable legs. Her fluid prosthesis appears to be faltering. She puts her hand out as if she can brace herself. I open the bond wide. Sensing her extreme fatigue, I run to her.

Right as I am about to reach her, the water under her stump falls away, and she collapses into my arms.

"I've got you, Raindrop."

I cradle her to my chest, and she nuzzles her head into my neck, her breath warm across my skin.

"Rest now, you were incredible."

She sighs, placing a hand over my heart.

Nic is repositioning Elias onto Adira, and as we pass them, Vale lifts a shaking hand and pulls every drop of water from Elias until he's dry. Her hand falls limp as her head sags against me.

"She was incredible, I've never seen anything like it. And for someone with no battle experience, she never wavered." Pride shines in Ansel's eyes.

I look down at my fierce and determined Core, limp in my arms, with her pale skin, full lips, and long lashes fanning against her cheeks. An immense sense of gratitude overwhelms me. I am so undeserving of this gift, and despite it all, Elohim saw fit to bless me anyway. To save me and call me into a greater purpose. And that grace is a gift I'll never be able to thank Him enough for.

"We need to get Elias to the healers," Lucia calls from behind Nic, "so we'll meet you back at the apothecary."

And I am brought back down to earth by the gravity of what we just went through. The fight may be over for now, but I get the sense that Elias's is just beginning.

CHAPTER 31

I wake to the sounds of cursing and banging around in the darkness of the cave. I sit up, and my head throbs. I groan and lie back down.

"Here, drink this," Z says from a chair next to the bed I am currently melded to, holding out a cup. "You've been out for nearly twenty-four hours." I do as he says and instantly gag, but force it down my throat.

"Bleh, please don't tell me you just fed me Dugal's special brew?"

"Well, yeah—he said it'll heal anything."

"It tastes like hot garbage!" I hand it back to Z. "I think Dugal has convinced everyone it's healing when really they are just distracted from their pain by the putrid flavor and overwhelming desire to spit it out."

Z laughs, and those gorgeous dimples appear on his cheeks, but there's a shadow behind his eyes.

"How is Elias?"

"He's alive, thanks to you." He pauses, placing his

230

elbows on his knees and dropping his head into his hands. There's more he's not saying.

"What is it, Z?"

"He's awake, but the Silent tortured him by electrocution. I'll spare you the details, but his tongue is damaged to the point that he can't speak. He mostly sleeps." He lifts his gaze to mine, and grief spills from his eyes.

I grasp his hand. "I'm so sorry."

"He was the first person to be there for us, Vale. When we first arrived here, Elias had been here long before us. He came to prepare our way and be our guide. We've always known he's a supernatural being, but it's just this unspoken thing he won't talk about. I think we've taken it for granted, assuming him to be untouchable. It's shaken our reality to see that's not the case."

"He will get better, and we will stop this. Together. We were created to put an end to the infestation of darkness."

He smiles at me, his gaze a caress, and smooths the hair back from my face. "But first, I am taking you somewhere. Doctor's orders. Or more like quirky apothecary's orders."

"What do you mean?"

"Well, Dugal thinks you expended too much energy with this new gift you're barely familiar with. It's a lot of power, and until you become better adjusted to its ebb and flow, it could easily overtax you. He recommended I take you somewhere for a few days to rest, away from all of this. Somewhere that will help you recover, recharge, and reconnect with your gift. Lucky for you, I know just the place."

"And where might that be?"

"It's a surprise—you'll see." A corner of his mouth quirks up.

"Before we go, how's Roy doing?"

"See for yourself," Z says, gesturing to where Dugal

works. Roy sits, wings tucked in tight, on a cushioned bed next to his work station. Every so often, Dugal reaches a stubby finger over to stroke her head or grabs a piece of some kind of food to feed her.

I smile at the sight of her being pampered by him.

"So now that you've seen she's being spoiled rotten, it's your turn."

He lifts me in his arms and carries me out of the cavern, ignoring the looks of the people milling about as we pass by. Just outside the entrance to the cavern, Fury stands, wearing his harness that has a few bags strapped to it.

Z sets me on Fury's back and hops up behind me. His arms come around me, and his thighs cradle my legs as he settles in. The scent and feel of him everywhere short-circuits my brain. I press back into him, relishing the freedom of being near him and touching him whenever I want now that he's accepted the bond.

He presses a kiss to my temple. "Ready?"

"Definitely!"

We reappear in a grassy knoll, and the first thing I notice is the salty scent of the sea on the wind. My heart soars, and I sit upright. Z gives a soft chuckle behind me.

The water calls to me, and it's a balm to my weary body. It doesn't ask anything of me, but instead welcomes me home. A place of rest and respite.

We clear the top of a hill, and I am greeted by glittering waves and a warm breeze. Grass gives way to sand as we head toward the beach. Fury takes us right into the water, and it climbs his body, reaching for me. He starts prancing around, clearly not thrilled with the situation.

"Give me a hand down, will ya?"

Z lowers me from Fury's back, and the crystal-clear water rises to cradle me. It plays with my hair, the current combing through the strands, pressing in along the tension in my back and shoulders like a gentle massage. It holds me in an embrace while I float amidst the waves. I never want to leave.

I don't know how long it has been when I hear Fury snort from the beach, but as I open my eyes, I notice the sun has begun its descent and colors the sky in an orange-pink hue. Z sits on the sand, tracking me with eyes that never stray far. Next to him, Fury throws his head and repeatedly stamps at the sand. He's clearly had his fill.

I laugh and begin to sit up, but the water lifts me and floats me to shore, depositing me gently on the sand. It forms a prosthetic leg with barely a thought, and I stand on the wet beach. Every drop leaves my body, returning to the ocean, leaving me sun-kissed but dry as I head toward Z. The bone-weary exhaustion is gone, and I feel like a battery that's been recharged.

Z smiles and stands at my approach. "Better?"

"You could say that—I feel like a new person."

"I can see that. You're practically glowing."

"I'm sorry I made you wait." I step into his personal space, our bodies almost touching, but not quite. I tip my head back to look into his eyes.

"I'm not, it's been a long time since I've been that at peace." His softly spoken words are a caress against my lips, and goose bumps erupt on my skin.

He brings a hand up to my hair, grabbing a strand in his fingers. "Watching you in your element, filled with joy and peace—it's all I could ever ask for in this life."

I want to push up on my feet to kiss him, but he's quite a

bit taller than me. At that thought, the water builds up underneath my feet until I can press my lips to his. His taste fills me with warmth and creates a yearning in me I don't know what to do with.

He pulls back and grabs my hand, pointing inland. "Come, I have something to show you."

We take off in the direction he indicated, the water accommodating me as I need it. He leads me up a stone path to a bright yellow cottage. My last memory of a beachside cottage comes to mind, and I almost stumble. But I push it from my mind, determined to stay in this moment with him.

We reach the front door, and he turns to me. "Will you close your eyes for me?"

I raise one eyebrow at him, but do as he requests. He leads me forward through the door, and I am immediately hit with the scents of lavender, vanilla, and a slight thread of chocolate. I hear the door close behind us. He leads me in a few steps.

"Okay, open."

I do, and I can't suppress the gasp that flies from my mouth. At least twenty candles, in varying sizes, burn around the quaint little cottage. A small and simple but delectable-looking chocolate cake sits in the center of a table set for two. A fireplace glows to my right.

"I got some help from some friends while you were out cold," Z says from behind me. "Seb and Isa, two brilliant cooks from The Refuge, scraped together some ingredients to make the cake, and Cai and Ansel helped with the candles since I wouldn't leave your bedside."

I am speechless. Tears fill my eyes as I turn to Z, who kneels before me, next to the fire that illuminates the honey hues in his eyes.

"Vale," he says, swallowing as he wrings his hands. "You deserve everything good this world has left to give, and somehow, you ended up with me."

I open my mouth to reassure him, but he presses a finger against my lips.

"No, let me finish." He smiles.

I nod.

"I started calling you Raindrop, not because you brought the rain to my sunny life, like you sarcastically told me once," he smirks at the memory, "but because you are like the first drop of rain after a lifetime spent wandering across a dry and dusty wasteland. And despite keeping you at a distance and trying to deny this bond, I felt it deep within me—even from the very beginning. You were nourishment for my soul, and you brought my half-dead heart to life." He brings my hand to his lips and presses a soft kiss in the center of my palm.

"True to the nature of water, you seeped into all the darkest parts of me and cleansed me of everything that weighed me down and tried to steal my life. You gave me love when I gave you resistance, and you created a wellspring inside me."

Tears track down my cheeks. The words I was so eager to speak only moments ago fail me now.

"I want you to know that I regret ever pushing you away and making you feel like you had to fight for us alone." He pauses, taking a deep breath, as if he has to prepare himself for what comes next.

"From the moment I showed up in your life outside The Wastes and stole you away to The Refuge and then jumped all over the wilderness with you, you were always just along for the ride. Never really given a choice. So, in an effort to honor you and give you all the love you deserve, I have a question to ask you . . ." He pauses, pulling a small box from behind his back and opening it, revealing a small metal band that holds a small, pinkish-hued, uncut rock.

"It's a raw diamond—to remind you of your strength," Z says, taking the band from the box and holding the band out between us. "Vale, my Raindrop of redemption, will you do me the incredible honor of being not just my Core, but the greatest love of my life? Will you allow me to spend the rest of my life by your side, as your partner, your best friend, your confidante, your guardian, and your support?"

The image of Z blurs through my tears.

"Will you allow me the privilege of loving you, through the good and bad, utterly devoted to your joy and success? Will you allow me to spend the rest of my life making you feel valued and cherished in every way you deserve?"

His words are gentle and reverent and betray a softness he shows to none but me. I drop to my knees in front of him.

"Z, what you need to know is that when it came to loving you, there was never a choice. I couldn't breathe in a world where you no longer existed. I would've sacrificed anything and everything to save you. Whatever fabric souls are made of, yours and mine are cut from the same swath. I could no more deny you than pull my beating heart from my own chest." I smile and raise a hand to his stubbled jaw. "So there was never going to be another answer besides yes."

He places the ring on my finger, but before I even have a chance to admire the gift, his hand slips around my waist, pulling me to his chest. I can feel his breath against my skin right before his lips crash into mine. His kiss is possessive and consumes me. His hand sprawls across my lower back, holding me to him. His scent fills my lungs with every breath. Want unfurls deep within me—like molten lava, it ignites everything in its path until I am nothing but roaring flame. I am almost tempted to call the water to cool me, but this is a fire I don't want diminished.

My hands move to explore the hard landscape of his back while his lips leave my mouth to press a soft trail of kisses down my neck, sending shivers everywhere. A moan escapes me at his ministrations. He suddenly sits back on his heels, pulling from my grip, leaving me wobbling on unsteady knees. Dark eyes look up at me.

"Sorry," he says, rubbing his hand across his head to the back of his neck. "I didn't mean to let things get so heated. Should we eat? Yeah, chocolate sounds like a great distraction right now."

He goes to stand, but I grab his hand, holding him fast. His eyes meets mine with a question on his brow, and a boldness rises up within me. I know what I want, and I will no longer delay claiming it.

"I am not hungry for chocolate." My words are soft and breathless.

His eyes flash, and he visibly swallows. "What are you hungry for?"

"I think you know," I tease, and a burst of desire shoots down the bond. "I'm ready to test your commitment to giving me everything my heart has ever desired."

"Are you sure? There's no rush, Raindrop. We have all the time in the world." And somehow, his words only intensify my craving for him.

"Z, I've wanted this connection with you for so long, and for a while, I didn't think you'd ever be mine. Now that you are, I want nothing standing between us ever again. If you'll let me, I would choose this moment to begin our new life together, putting the past and the pain behind us. I want you to be mine in every way."

"Raindrop, I already am. Our bond is a deeper connection and a more unbreakable covenant than anything on earth. I am yours—forever."

I bring his open palm up to my face and press my cheek into it. "Then show me. Don't make me beg," I say, biting my lower lip.

His eyes flash before softening as he takes me in his arms and brings his mouth so close, I anticipate the touch of his lips.

"You never have to beg. I'm only and forever yours to command." His husky words caress my skin before his lips claim mine with an intensity that cuts off all thought. And he spends the rest of the night showing me what it means to be loved and cherished by the Horseman of Justice.

CHAPTER 32

VALE

We wake intertwined in front of the fire that burned low to embers sometime in the night. After a late brunch of chocolate cake and another soak in the ocean, this time with Z joining me, it's almost dusk again as we get ready to jump back to Dugal's, despite my hesitation.

I don't want to return to the real world yet.

I stand on the porch in a blue sundress Z gave to me and gaze out at the shimmery waters of the ocean, which twinkle like diamonds in the sun. I sense Z's approach before I hear him, and then his arms are around me, tucking me under his chin. Somehow, my senses are even more aware of him now. I didn't know it was possible to feel like this, like another person could be an extension of you. He leans down and presses a kiss to my neck, and gooseflesh rises on my skin in response.

"I sense your melancholy," he states. "What can I do?"

"Nothing, really, I just don't want to leave this place." I

turn in his arms until I face him. "If I could, I'd live here with you forever. But I know that's not possible."

His hand gently grasps my chin, and he presses the softest and most unhurried kiss imaginable to my lips. "It might not be possible now, but one day soon. This place will be our sanctuary from the world, if that's what you want."

I brighten at his words and dream of a future where darkness no longer hunts us, destroying everything beautiful and good in its path. Elohim created me with a purpose, and like the silver of the ring Z gave me, I was purified and forged in the fire so I could become this sword of Heaven I was meant to be.

I once questioned how Elohim could love me if He would allow such pain in my life. But now I can see that it would've been the opposite of love to allow me to remain as I was. The pain was the catalyst for growth, strength, and rebirth in my life. Elohim gave my pain a purpose. After all, the strength of a ship is not tested until it sails through a storm.

Fury snorts in the grass of the little cottage's front yard, drawing me from my reflections. I never knew an animal could be so impatient and demanding.

"At least someone is ready to leave," I huff, glancing at Fury. "He's so bossy. Kind of like someone else I know." I smirk at Z.

"I'm not the only one who's bossy." His husky voice and darkening gaze sends my temperature soaring as I remember last night with Z. He's not wrong, and my cheeks flush while I look anywhere but in his eyes.

He chuckles as a finger under my chin lifts my gaze to his. "You don't ever need to be embarrassed with me, Raindrop. I love every facet of you. I look forward to spending my life discovering all the pieces you keep hidden away."

I bring his hand to my face, pressing my cheek into his warm palm and closing my eyes. "I love you, Zion Cascus."

"And I you, my Raindrop."

∽

Arriving back at at Dugal's is like walking through a magic door and ending up in a bustling anthill. People scurry about everywhere. I glance at Z, and he looks like I feel. Furrowed brow, wide eyes, and a slight frown. He has a reputation for being intense, a bit scary, and definitely unapproachable, and right now, I can see why. Even though that's not how I see him at all.

"Is it just me or are there actually more people here now?"

"Yeah, I didn't know how this place could get busier, but it has." He gets that faraway look in his eyes that tells me he's chatting with his brothers.

Cai comes out of the cavern and heads toward us. "We didn't expect to see you both so soon."

"Trust me, I am questioning my sanity in returning as well," Z replies flatly.

I laugh and pat his chest. "He says that, but we both wanted to check on Elias and Roy, and see if we were needed for anything here."

"And how is it there are more people? We were at max capacity with the first round of refugees."

"Well, Nic went to check on the other groups of evacuees from The Refuge to make sure they had found good safe houses. The first group he found was too out in the open, so he brought them here. The other group was a little too close to The Refuge still, so he . . . uh . . . also brought them here." Cai winces.

"Okay, let's do this a different way," Z says. "Are there are any groups from The Refuge that are currently not here at Dugal's?"

"That would be a no," Cai says with a wry grin. "There were only three groups, and after two were brought here, we realized Seb and Isa were with the third and we definitely need their culinary skills if we're to feed this large of a group, so we just finished jumping them here an hour ago. They were sad to leave the kitchen of the safe house they were at, but we promised to jump them back anytime the urge to bake a chocolate cake comes over them again." Cai winks at us. He claps his hands together before holding them out, as if presenting the chaos to Z in pride. "The family's all back together!"

I can't help but laugh. There's just something about Cai that ensures you can't remain stoic for long. Z's head rests in his hand, and he let's out a sigh that has me thinking he might be the only person immune to Cai's charm.

"Look, I get your wariness, Z, but until we can break everyone into equal groups and find safe and secure locations to jump them to, this was the best option."

I feel Z's resignation come down the bond, and right behind it is his deep desire to see justice served in this situation. These people lost their homes and are now refugees running for their lives, and considering The Refuge is a safe house for those in need, this isn't the first time they've experienced that loss. He craves to see restoration brought to their lives.

I do the only thing I can think of and send my love, pride, and support down the bond to him as I grab his hand and lean my head against his bicep. He sighs before pressing a kiss to the top of my head.

"How's Elias?" Z asks Cai.

"Come and see for yourself."

My eyes adjust to the darkness of the cave. A crowd is gathered around one of the beds.

"Okay, you lot, time to disperse," Cai shouts from beside us. "Elias needs his beauty rest."

The group clears enough that I spy Lucia sitting on the bed with Elias, holding his hand. Sida sits on a chair next to him, holding a bowl and spooning something I pray is soup and not Dugal's brew down his throat. But I am relieved to see bright, lively eyes and a smile lighting his face.

Elias motions us closer, and we stand next to Nic at the foot of the bed. Elias lifts his hand to me, and I walk forward to grasp it. He glances at my new watery appendage as I approach.

"We're so glad you are okay," I tell him.

He drops my hand and begins signing. Sida puts down the bowl.

"He says of course you are water, the most persistent and steadfast of gifts for the Core of Perseverance," she interprets from her chair, giving me a wink as she does so.

My eyes widen at the sight of another talent I never knew she possessed. One day, I'll have to ask her what other skills she's hiding.

Elias's hands move rapidly in front of him, causing Sida to chuckle. "He's happy to see you finally wore down our obstinate Horseman of Iron-Will."

I laugh, looking back at a stoic Z, who smirks at the title. "Well, little did he know his stubbornness has nothing on mine."

Elias signs some more. "Was the resin effective?" Sida's soothing voice translates.

I wince, remembering the first pouch dissipating in the air, and the second being rendered useless in the water. "Not exactly. There were a few snags, but miraculously, I didn't need it."

One movement of Elias's hands. "He wants to know how," Sida says.

Z moves from the end of the bed to my back, and the heat from his presence soothes the frayed nerves that accompany any recollection of that time. I lean against him for support, steeling myself for the story I need to share.

"Seeing her manhandled and scared, reaching for me, was enough to pull me from the hold of darkness," Z's rough voice rumbles from deep in his chest, almost a growl, and everyone pauses. "And even if that hadn't been enough, watching her beaten and left bloodied by that savage coward would have done it. Yet, despite everything she suffered, she single-handedly fought him off, unshackled me, and saved my life after I was shot in the back. Most of which she did even before she got her gift of wielding water."

It's so quiet, you could hear a droplet of water splash against the dirt floor. Everyone has gone still at Z's revelation, and wide eyes all stare at me like they are seeing me for the first time. What I wouldn't give for a hole to open up in the ground and swallow me right about now. Instead, I grab Z's hand from beside me and bring it around my shoulders, holding his forearm to my chest as he holds my opposite shoulder with his hand, pulling me against his chest in a protective embrace.

Dugal approaches and quickly signs something to Elias.

Elias looks at Lucia for a moment, his brows knitted together, before he nods to Dugal.

"Lucia, someone who lives here wants to talk with you," Dugal says. "Everything is okay, and you are completely safe, but it might be startling for you."

"Oookaay," Lucia draws out the word, glancing from Dugal to Elias, who nods at her. Nic straightens at the sudden tension.

Lucia follows Dugal, and Nic begins to trail after them before he pauses, that far-off look in his eyes that says he's using his mental link. I scan the faces for the culprit and see a similar expression on Elias's face. Nic lets out a huff, crossing his arms across his chest, and leans against the cavern wall, his eyes intently tracking Lucia's every move. Something tells me Elias asked him to give her space for this encounter.

We all watch on in curiosity as Dugal guides Lucia in front of the makeshift hearth, where two chairs and a rug sit. He gestures to the chair but she stands firm. She wrings her hands and spares a glance back at Nic, who shifts on his feet. Dugal leaves the cavern, only to come right back in, trailed by a small figure. I recognize the short hair and mousey frame of Dee. Lucia gasps, and her hand flies to her mouth as they approach.

Nic takes a step forward, but stops himself. Dee begins to sign and Dugal appears to be translating. Lucia lifts a hand toward the large scar on Dee's face, but pauses midair. Dee suddenly drops to her knees on the rug, tears rolling down her face as she continues to sign animatedly. Then her hands stop and her head hangs. Lucia falls to her knees next to Dee and envelops the girl in a hug.

The emotions in this moment are thick, and I suddenly feel like an intruder. I don't know much about what happened between them, other than when we first arrived and Elias questioned Dee about her betrayal of Lucia. Elias is a pretty easygoing guy, so the intensity in his expression when he saw Dee took me by surprise. But I realize it just speaks to the deep level of betrayal that occurred.

Yet it's clear that Lucia forgives her. And what I just witnessed gives me hope. That even in the face of darkness, mistakes, and pain, there can be redemption if we choose it. And just maybe, one of the reasons we experience the instability of the human heart in this life is so that we can appreciate the strength and steadiness of Elohim's.

Nic sends Lucia a warm glance before heading out of the cavern, giving her time with Dee, I assume. Dugal chooses this moment to walk up to our group, now holding a sedate Roy in his arms. His spectacled gaze glances around, and the mood instantly lightens at the sight of the quirky apothecary holding a wild hawk.

I can't resist going to him and running a finger across her feathery head. "How is she?"

"Oh, just fine," he says, looking down at her fondly as he rubs a spot under her beak. "The broken bone in her wing seems to be healing nicely. I've given her a special concoction to ease her pain and made her a special bed to keep her comfortable, but she's a princess and prefers to be carried as such." He presses a kiss to her head, and I smile at the tenderness in his gaze.

"Thank you, Dugal."

"Yes, well." He coughs, as if to clear the emotion in his voice. "We all must play our part." Feigning nonchalance.

"Dugaaallll," a desperate voice from outside the cavern yells. Dugal's eyes grow wide, and he hurriedly places Roy on the bed next to Elias and Lucia before rushing off.

Elias gets that faraway look in his expression and Z

grabs my hand before turning to trail after Dugal. "Elias wants me to follow, just in case," Z explains, "and I can't bring myself to leave you." He squeezes my hand.

But nothing could prepare me for what I see outside the cavern and it's like I am thrust back in time.

In the middle of a small clearing, surrounded by people, is a face I worried I would never see again. My long-lost brother, Ash. He's dirty and disheveled, with blood trickling from a wound on his forehead. But what causes me to become rooted in place is the blade that is being held to his neck by Nic. I sense Z's gaze on me, though nothing can quench the power welling inside me.

"Ash," I speak his name aloud, making it all too real.

Like a geyser, I erupt.

CHAPTER 33

She's terrifying and mesmerizing at the same time. She saw her brother, and everything in her demeanor changed. Her eyes electrified, a mist gathered around her, and a dewy condensation built up on her skin. Anything I sent down the bond was blocked by a wall of water. It was like she had become her element right before my eyes.

I stare at her. There's a pause, like the one right before a scream, and then chaos breaks loose. Water erupts from the ground in streams all around us, blocking the crowd of people from view. Vale rises into the air, water cradling her legs. Her hair whips around her head in wild, pearlescent tendrils. She lifts a hand, and a jet stream of water hits Nic's arm from behind, sending the blade flying away from her brother's neck. Then another jet stream hits Nic in the chest and sends him into one of the geysers behind him, propelling him into the air.

Water lifts her brother off the ground, encasing him but not smothering him, simply cradling him above the ground, safe from any who might seek to harm him. She lifts her other hand and catches Nic with the water right as Lucia walks through the wall of water surrounding us, her body aflame.

Vale halts Nic's progression and, when he's about six feet off the ground, unceremoniously drops him. Lucia's flames flare brighter. Vale calls the water to bring her brother closer and lowers him to his feet in front of her. By the time the water releases him, he is bone-dry and washed clean of any remnants of dirt and blood from his ordeal.

The water dissipates around the crowd, and the wide eyes and dropped jaws that greet us mimic my reaction exactly. Vale stares at her brother, and all he can seem to do is stare back. Slowly, he lifts a hand toward her, but stops when it's halfway to her and begins to lower it again.

"Vale?" Ash's voice warbles. "Is it really you?"

She doesn't answer but walks straight to him, throwing her arms around his waist. He lifts a hand to her head, holding her to him as tears stream down his face. He squeezes his eyes shut while they cling to each other, and I can't help but feel like I am intruding on a private moment.

Lucia is helping up Nic, and it appears his ego is bruised more than anything. Finally, Ash pulls back from Vale, holding her by her upper arms as he looks her over.

"How is this possible? You have a leg of water!"

She smiles that radiant smile that changes her whole face and lights up her eyes. "It's a gift, and I'll tell you all about it. But what happened to you?" She glances over his shoulder at Nic. "And why were you holding a blade to my brother's throat?" Her eyes blaze a brighter blue.

Nic puts his hands up. "First, I didn't know he was your brother—I thought he was an intruder. He was sneaking into the camp, trying to go unnoticed. When I confronted him, he ran. Standard protocol is to secure any potential liability, which is what I did."

She pushes Ash behind her and glares at Nic. "Why was he bleeding from a head wound then?"

"Whoa, whoa," Ash says, walking around her. "It wasn't his fault, V, I arrived like that. And all I know is I saw a bunch of strangers had taken over my hermit of a mentor's home, and I thought maybe he was being held captive. So instead of drawing unnecessary attention to myself, I was going to sneak in and rescue him if he needed it. But there's no getting past this guy." He jabs a thumb at Nic.

"I wouldn't be a good Horseman if you could sneak past me." Nic rolls his eyes.

"Horseman? What does a horse have anything to do with this? Unless that is some kind of macho man club you're a part of? And why is no one the least bit concerned that that woman is on fire? What is going on here?" he barks, his frantic gaze darting around.

Lucia douses her flames, looking sheepish. Nic sweeps a hand around her, yanking her to his side so he can plant a kiss on her head. "Thanks for coming to my rescue, love." He winks at her.

Dugal takes the opportunity to approach Ash. "Ash, my boy," he says, slapping him on the back, "why did you return so early?"

Ash just stares at him, looking a bit flabbergasted by everything he just witnessed.

"Come, let's catch up, son," Dugal says calmly, leading him like one would a wild colt, into the quietness of the cavern.

～

Once inside the cavern, Dugal takes Ash to a table and chairs to sit, and I pull up a seat next to Vale, who clearly won't be leaving her brother's side anytime soon.

"One thing I've never understood," she starts, "why didn't you come with me? For years I thought you just wanted me gone—that maybe you blamed me for what happened."

"What? No!" Ash says. "Didn't the old woman tell you?" If only Sida could hear him refer to her as an old woman.

"She tried, but I didn't believe her. I thought she was sparing my feelings. I was the one that he was after—it only made sense for you to hate me for everything that happened."

"V, I could never hate you! Lyle's demented obsession with you was not your fault. The only person I have hated all these years was myself. If only I had listened to Mama's wish to leave Glennlyle, none of this would have happened. I didn't go with you because I believed you would be safer with a stranger than with me. Everything I love gets taken from me."

Ash lets out a sigh that seems to bear the weight of the world. Vale's face blanches, and she reaches across the table to grasp his hand. Ash returns her grasp with a white-knuckled grip of his own.

"So instead, I plotted how to get you away. And like a miracle, the old woman—"

"Sida, her name is Sida. She was with me that whole time, until recently, protecting me and helping me."

Tears well in his eyes, and he squeezes them shut against the onslaught, causing them to drip down his cheeks. He quickly wipes them away with his freehand.

"Sida," Ash says softly, "showed up like a miracle. She

came in a horse-drawn wagon. She came right up to the door, asking if I had need of some help. I don't know how she knew, but when she mentioned she worked with the Prophets of The Way, after everything Mama had said, I figured it was a sign. And there's just something about her. The whole encounter felt orchestrated by a higher power.

"When I showed her to you, she was adamant that we both go with you. I turned her down with the excuse that I would need to get rid of the wagon tracks or Lyle would find you, which wasn't a complete lie. I rode about ten miles with you and then followed the tracks home, erasing them as I went. Then I packed a bag and took off on foot in the opposite direction. That way, if Lyle was going to hunt someone, it would be me. Sida swore to me that she would keep you safe and hidden."

Vale's eyes connect with mine, and I sense the worry and concern come down our bond. Ash doesn't know about the tracker, and I sense she's hesitating about telling him. Maybe that's a conversation for another day. He already seems to have a lot to come to terms with right now.

"Ash, you were never responsible for what happened. Just because bad things have happened to you does not mean the blame lies with you." She pauses and takes a deep breath as her tears begin to fall. "It's like Rain used to say . . . It's not your job to bear the weight of everything—you are not superhuman.' He always admired you, not because you were perfect and held everything together, but because you had a big heart that wanted what was best for your family. If he were here now, I think he would tell you to stop letting the past chain you. Elohim has a purpose and path for your life, Ash, and even though the darkness tried to destroy you, Elohim will give that pain a purpose and find a way to pull blessings from it."

Tears stain his cheeks as his head drops to his hands.

Vale gets up from the table and drops to her knees by his side. "I love you, big brother. Thank you for saving me." His shoulders shake harder as her words presumably hit home. "Time to let it go. This isn't your burden to bear."

He pulls her into a hug, and they cling to each other in the aftermath of the emotional storm. When they finally pull apart from each other, Ash grasps her shoulders, a smile lighting up his face.

"Wow, V, you haven't changed. You're still a force of nature."

She pats her brother on the arm. "I'm telling you, Ash, I did change after everything—I was broken, too, and more than physically. But Elohim has been faithful to use every-thing that happened to shape me into the person you see standing before you. I had a choice, to trust Him and let go." She smiles at her brother and takes her seat again.

"Ash, my boy," says Dugal, "I didn't expect you for at least another couple weeks. What happened?"

"Honestly, I am not really sure. I was at our agreed-upon meeting place at the right time, but she didn't show. So I asked around, seeing if I could learn anything. Well, I overheard in one of the bars about a competition. Men from all over were traveling to compete for the hand of the daughter of the Lord Sovereign. It can't be coincidence. It has to be her."

"Her? Her who?" Vale says.

"Our client," Ash explains. "One of our prominent clients on the other side of The Wastes. She usually meets me just outside The Wastes at a market. She told me to call her Thia, but I have no idea if that's her real name or not. And she's always hooded, so I don't know what she looks like. But she compensates us richly for the product, and for traveling so far."

Ash looks contemplative, as if he's piecing together everything before our eyes. His gaze connects with Dugal's. "There's not many with access to those kinds of funds. She could be this daughter that is being married off, and that's why she was unable to meet me."

I am stuck on his casual comment of crossing The Wastes. "Wait, how can that be? No one gets through The Wastes."

"That's not exactly true," Dugal says. "There is one path only. It is far north, where The Wastes thin out. It is tricky to find and very few know of it, and it is treacherous to travel. Fewer still dare to risk the journey. But once you get to the other side, you'd find there is an entire society over there. Ruled by a man who calls himself the Lord Sovereign."

"How do you know about this?" I ask.

A shadow passes through Dugal's eyes, and he swallows, looking away. "From a past life, long ago," he mutters, making it clear the discussion is closed.

"What could she possibly want that she would be willing to have you travel so far and pay you enough for it to be worthwhile?" Vale asks.

"We never spoke of specific details," Ash says, "but I got the feeling someone she cares for deeply is sick, possibly even dying. Dugal uses a special blend of herbs, resins, and tinctures for a mix that eases pain and brings longevity. It is not true healing, but Thia is desperate.

"But, strangely, the gossips in the bar seemed most excited about the presence of a horseman in the contest. Of course, at the time, I thought it was just a man with a horse, but after hearing from Blue Eyes over there," Ash throws a thumb in the direction of Nic, now standing by Lucia next to Elias's bed, "I get the feeling it is more significant." He looks directly at me, obviously connecting the dots that I am one as well.

A pit opens up in my stomach. I think we just found out where Mav has been all this time. And something tells me this daughter of the Lord Sovereign is no normal woman.

Mav found his Core. And she's about to be sold like chattel.

EPILOGUE

Many waters cannot quench love;
Rivers cannot sweep it away.

Song of Songs 8:7a

ONE MONTH LATER

ZION

I squint, trying to keep my eyes trained on the blazing white inferno before me, but it's like staring into the sun. I can barely make out the figure of Lucia in the middle. Vale's electric-blue eyes glow in the mist surrounding her. She throws her hands out in front of her, sending a blast of water at Lucia, and it's like a bomb goes off. Steam explodes on the water's contact, forcing me to duck and sending Ash flying back into the dense foliage behind us.

"Ouch," comes his annoyed tone from the bushes. He stands, pulling leaves and twigs out of his hair and from his clothing.

"Do you need a hand?" I ask.

"No, no," he says, trudging back through the bushes. "I am perfectly capable of soothing my own wounded backside."

I smirk at his response. I've come to learn he has a similar sense of humor to his sister's.

Abruptly, the water dissipates, and Lucia's flames die down, replaced by the sound of laughter.

"You are incredible!" Lucia says. "I had to really focus to hold the flames."

"Me! You are a literal hottie!" Vale says, and they both start cracking up.

"Ahem," a disheveled Ash says from my side, drawing the girls' attention. "Warn me next time you decide to create your own personal bomb. I didn't expect to be blown off my feet just spectating."

Lucia looks sheepish, while Vale looks concerned as she hurries over to us.

"Oh, Ash, are you okay?" She takes in his mussed hair, dirty face, and the minor scratch across his cheek that's beaded with blood. But before he can even answer, she calls a ball of water to slam into him, picking him up and churning him about like a pile of laundry before depositing him next to me, clean and dry, albeit a bit dazed.

"There!" she says with pride. "All better!"

I stifle my grin. I feel like I am always smiling like a fool around her.

"Um, thanks, sis," Ash says, clearly trying not to rain on her parade, "but maybe a little warning next time you decide to send me through your washing machine." He wobbles over to her, giving her a pat on the shoulder before heading back toward Dugal's.

Her eyes turn from Ash's retreating form to find mine, and she winks. "Such a big baby."

I walk to her, taking her hand in my own as we trail Ash back. We come upon the clearing in time to see Dee rushing up to him. He bumps her with his shoulder, and she blushes as they head into the cavern together.

"I am happy for him, really," Vale says from beside me. "It's just hard to get used to, seeing my big brother . . . flirting. He never even dated growing up. It just shows how much has changed since Glennlyle."

"I am sure Ash feels the same," I say. "I mean, you're his baby sister and you can't keep your hands off me. You're like a wild animal. Must be so hard for him." I smirk at her. Teasing her has become my favorite way to pass the time.

She has that twinkle in her eye. "A wild animal, huh? Wow, I had no idea you felt so *attacked* around me. I will definitely curb my animalistic tendencies and have more control moving forward." She lets go of my hand and takes a step away.

"Whoa, whoa, whoa," I say with a mock pout, reaching for her and manhandling her into my arms until she is chest to chest with me. "Let's not get drastic here. I couldn't care less what your brother thinks, he's just going to have to deal!" I lean closer until my lips are by her ear. "And we both know I am more animal than you are."

A breathy noise comes out of her, and I laugh, pressing a quick kiss to her lips. But she fists a hand in my shirt, keeping me close so she can deepen the kiss before letting go.

"My needy Raindrop," I whisper into her lips.

A mischievous grin appears on her ethereal face. "I am needy, and you promised to give me anything I need."

"That I did," I say, getting the sense she's about to take this conversation in a totally different direction.

"And what I really need is help training."

My stomach sinks. "No, Raindrop, you can't ask me to do that."

"Please!" she begs. "You promised me help with anything, remember? Plus, I've been practicing. I am so much better, and if I screw up, you can heal me anyway."

Big, blue doe eyes look up at me, and I know it's futile to try to resist her.

"I hate this," I say, crossing my arms over my chest.

Her smile gets huge when she realizes she has won. "I know, but you love me."

I sigh. "Obviously, or I would never agree to this insanity."

She's practically beaming. "This is going to be so fun!"

She leads me to the highest point near Dugal's, a cliff that overlooks a valley, with not a single source of water around.

"I seriously don't understand why you can't be satisfied with practicing near the lake?"

"Z, honey, I explained this already," she says, as though she's calming a petulant child, which is not far off from how I am feeling. "That water is too available to do my bidding. I need the challenge of not being near a readily available source. I won't always have a lake or river right next to me."

"Okay, if you are going to make me do this, we will do this MY way."

She nods.

"We will start small to see how quick you can call it to you."

"That won't work, Z. If it's not a real danger, it won't be enough." She walks up to me and places her small hand on my chest, over my heart.

"I trust you. Don't you trust me?"

I sigh. I'm putty in her hands. "You know I do. But that doesn't change my nature. It's torture to think of you getting hurt and me being the cause."

"I know, but just be ready to kiss me back to health if I need it."

I inwardly curse Ansel for telling Vale about her capture by the Silent. Ever since learning how Ansel had to throw herself from the Amilign's helicopter, Vale's been insistent she learn this skill. Really, she's been single-minded in her obsession with training for every possible scenario. I think living among the people here has placed a burden on her heart to be ready to defend them. That, and she never wants to feel vulnerable again.

Apparently, she needs me to do this, because it needs to feel more like an attack would—something about it being less planned than if she did it herself.

"Close your eyes," I say.

She squeaks in excitement and smiles before closing them.

I pick her up in my arms, resigned to my predicament, and approach the edge of the cliff. I look down into the excited and determined face of the woman that anchors me to this world, and with all my strength, I throw her over the edge.

I watch her fall, breath stalled in my lungs. I don't think even my heart beats. She's just about to the trees when a bubble of water collects underneath her, catching her gently.

Phew. I take a ragged breath as I drop to my knees, chest heaving.

"I did it," she shouts, floating back to me.

"Always knew you could," I shout back, even though my heart rate and hyperventilating breaths say otherwise. Is this what a heart attack feels like?

"Yes, you are the picture of confidence, my love," she mocks as the water deposits her next to me. "What do you say, one more time?"

My eyes widen. I don't think I have it in me. But I get an idea. "Actually, I was thinking it's only fair if you help me, too. How about we go borrow Ansel's bow and you can shoot an arrow at my heart while I try to deflect it with a blade. I am pretty confident you wouldn't be able to hit me."

Her skin turns ashen as her eyes bulge, right before her expression changes to a glower. "Okay, okay, message received."

I chuckle and toss her over my shoulder to hightail it back to Dugal's.

"You heathen," she yells, and a ball of water hits me in the back of the head.

"Thanks, Raindrop, I was in need of some refreshing."

We finally reach a clearing, and I place her on her feet, her watery prosthesis instinctual now, as I whisper "Lavo Veshuv" to call our ride.

"Such a brute," she says playfully as Fury appears before us.

"Maybe, but I am your brute," I say, bending down to kiss her forehead.

I place her on Fury's back and hop up behind her as we head back to what's quickly feeling like home.

~

We jump back to the small clearing in front of Dugal's as the sun starts to fade from the sky. Seb stirs a big pot of something that smells like his incredible stew over a large fire, while Isa and Lucia appear to be chopping up items to be added to the pot. Arlo and his mother sit next to Sida and Elias, who is mostly healed now, sharing stories and basking in the glow of firelight. Now that there's just over a dozen people staying here, mealtime is a lot simpler.

It was too risky keeping everyone at Dugal's, so over the past month, Nic, Cai, and I scouted safe locations, then split the people into smaller groups and transported them. We check in with them weekly and make sure everyone is safe and well. It's not perfect, but it's the best option for now.

After Vale and I dismount, I pat Fury and send him off to graze with Adira and Ginger. I take Vale's hand in my own, and we're just about to join everyone when the sound of horse hooves breaks the silence, followed by the desperate scream of a horse.

Moon, Mav's dapple grey horse, comes slamming to a halt right before the group, who now stands frozen at the scene. Moon has an arrow protruding from his hindquarter, and Mav sits astride his back, possessively holding an unconscious, dark skinned, dark-haired woman in his arms.

"Take her," he groans, blood dribbling from his mouth, and Nic runs up to grab her from him.

Right as the woman is safe in Nic's arms, Mav topples from Moon's back, hitting the dirt face down, and revealing the four arrows that protrude from the Pale Horseman of Death's back.

AFTERWORD

Dear Reader,

Thank you for taking this journey into the Tales of the Four Horsemen. If you enjoyed this story like I hope you did, I would be ever so grateful if you would please leave a review. Reviews are the lifeblood of authors and mean the absolute world to us. Thank you for taking the time to do so!!

Additionally, if you loved this story, and can't wait for the next one, sign up for my newsletter at:

www.jesskchavez.com

Book 4 is in the works and will be released in 2026.

Until next time,
Jess

ACKNOWLEDGMENTS

First and foremost, I want to give thanks to my Heavenly Father, my Elohim Shomri, without whom I wouldn't be on this incredible journey in the first place. I can't believe I am three books into this series. It has been such a joy and also such a painstaking journey. It seems every book's theme I begin to write equates to an intense and revealing personal journey for me as well. Although this is a fiction fantasy tale, the threads of the love of Elohim woven throughout are completely inspired by my experiences with Jesus. His overwhelming and relentless love is foundational not just in this writing journey, but in my life overall. I wouldn't be who I am today without Him.

To the love of my life, my hubby and best friend, Josh, thanks for believing in me from the very beginning and giving me the push I needed to start. You are my greatest support, my safe place, my home—I know what real love is because God gave me you.

To my incredibly loving, loyal, and supportive teens, thank you for celebrating me and cheering me on, it's the greatest honor of my life being your mom. Being your favorite author is just an added perk.

To my mom and sister, thank you for being my biggest, most loyally devoted fans, and my very first readers. And to my sweet Daddy, who despite being a Marine who loves military action books, reads my books anyway.

To my incredible book-loving crew of beta readers;

Molly, Christine, and Stephanie. Your excitement, feedback, keen eyes, and encouragement were, as always, absolutely vital to me. I am ever so grateful for you guys!

To the amazing amputee queens and my incredible sensitivity readers, Alex and Lauren, your perspective and experiences were absolutely indispensable to the authenticity of this story and Vale's character. I will forever be indebted to you both for the painful walk down memory lane you took for me, and your vulnerability and honesty in your feedback.

To my amazing editor, J.J. Fischer, you are a real peach! Thank you for helping me grow as a writer and offering feedback in a way that only ever empowers me. I am so grateful the Lord led me to you.

And to my readers, who have supported me with lovely reviews, incredible messages of excitement and encouragement, sharing on social platforms, and spreading the word, I am beyond grateful for you! Thank you for choosing this series to begin with and for even reading this far. I set out to write the book I wanted to read and the journey has been made so much more fulfilling that I've found others who enjoy reading it too.

ABOUT THE AUTHOR

Jess K. Chavez is an author of the fantasy/romantasy genre. She has a B.A. in Journalism and a voracious love of reading. She's a wife to her best friend and high school sweetheart, a mom to three amazing and inspiring humans, a fur mom to two goldendoodles, and a lover and follower of Jesus. She lives with her crew in sunny Colorado, nestled in the landscape of the Rocky Mountains.

Sign up for her newsletter to stay up-to-date on new releases in the Tales of the Four Horsemen series, promotions, and all the exciting happenings:

www.jesskchavez.com

Follow her on social media here:

www.ingramcontent.com/pod-product-compliance
Lightning Source LLC
Chambersburg PA
CBHW032236310726
48973CB00008B/2157